5-

INTO
THIN AIR

INTO
THIN AIR

Thomas Zigal

For my mother and father

Published by
Delacorte Press
Bantam Doubleday Dell Publishing Group, Inc.
1540 Broadway
New York, New York 10036

This is a work of fiction. For the sake of the story I have taken occasional liberties with the geography and history of Aspen and the Roaring Fork Valley. All characters and incidents are a product of my imagination. Any resemblance to actual events, or to persons living or dead, is coincidental.
—TZ

ISBN: 0-385-31311-X

Manufactured in the United States of America

1

HIS DEPUTY WAS WAITING FOR HIM AT THE TOP OF THE trail. Muffin Brown was in her late twenties, the only daughter of a large Wyoming ranch family and the only female in uniform in the Pitkin County Sheriff's Department. She had waded into the river and her jeans and cowboy boots were soaking wet, her khaki shirt mud-stained to the third button. "Far as I can tell," she said, "there's one big hole just behind the left ear. Looks like an execution."

They trotted down the path to the water's edge, where the blanket-draped body lay on a clay embankment.

"Who found him?" Kurt asked, looking over at the small band of tourists, silent and tense, shading themselves under a canopy of narrowleaf poplars.

"The little boy spotted him first," Muffin said.

The child was sitting next to his mother on a fallen tree trunk. She held him close, her arm around his slender shoulders. He looked five or six, Lennon's age. Kurt wondered how he would explain something like this to his own son.

He knelt down and lifted the blanket. The body had been in the Roaring Fork overnight and the keen blades of river rock had carved up the man's softened flesh. Kurt winced. Ten years a sheriff, but he still hated this part.

"Looks Spanish to me," Muffin said.

She told him that the onlookers were architects in town for the annual Design Conference and that they'd hiked down to the river to check out a sound sculpture in the poplar grove. They were listening to the breeze whistle through the artist's hidden reeds when the boy noticed a jumble of limbs and loose clothing in the water. The body was still trapped in the boulders when Muffin arrived.

Kurt dropped the blanket over the dead man's face and stood up. *Jesus*, he thought, *the Tourist Bureau is going to love this.*

He looked over at the boy and his mother. "Radio Chip and tell him to bring a body bag," he said in a quiet voice to his deputy as he moved toward the gathering.

He greeted the architects with a friendly nod, then bent down to speak to the child. "I understand you've been a real hero today," Kurt said. He could see both terror and excitement in that small heat-flushed face. He didn't envy the mother—the nightmares she would have to soothe.

"Was that guy murdered?" the boy asked, his eyes wide with wonder.

Kurt smiled at him. "We don't know yet," he said, unpinning the sheriff's badge from his chest and fastening it to the boy's T-shirt. "Here ya go," he said. "You deserve to wear this today, my friend. You're the best cop around."

The boy pulled away from his mother and said, "Wowww, awesome, Mom," grabbing a wad of shirt to examine the badge.

"I've been wondering about Tommy, the Green Ranger," Kurt said, pointing to a Power Ranger on the T-shirt. He watched the program at suppertime every evening with Lennon. "Is he ever going to get his full powers back?"

"Next season," the boy assured him.

Kurt tousled his sweaty hair, stood up, and turned to the others. "If anybody knows anything about this, I want you to wait around till my deputies get back and give them your statement," he said. Pro forma. He could see that they were all still unnerved by the incident, having trouble meeting his eye. "Otherwise, we're done here. You can go have a drink."

He shook the boy's hand. "You take it easy now, champ," he said. He hadn't made up his mind yet if he would tell Lennon about the body in the river. He was always torn between telling him everything, so the child would be prepared for this world, or telling him nothing, so he could enjoy his innocence a few years longer.

Kurt waited for the last couple to straggle off, then walked back to sit on a stump by the broken body, marking time until his deputies returned to help him carry the corpse up the trail to the EMS van. There wasn't much he could do but watch the summer melt whirl around smooth limestone boulders. A few yards upstream a fat magpie danced in the wet sand, scratching for food. He closed his eyes and listened to the rush of water and tried not to think about this dead man beside him, who he was, what had happened to him. He tried not to remember the twisted spines of those two hikers caught in a Christmas avalanche near Pearl Pass. He tried not to see the lifeless, fractured face of his brother Bert, the way he had looked four summers ago after nine hundred feet of rock.

After delivering the body to the morgue in the basement of the county courthouse, Kurt went upstairs to the Pitkin County Sheriff's Office. His receptionist, Libbie McCullough, was eating blackberry yogurt and speaking on the radio mike to one of the deputies in the field. She pointed the spoon at an attractive Hispanic woman sitting in an armchair between a pair of tall, untended plants. "Zhish lady needs to shee you," she said with a full mouth. He could tell by Libbie's furrowed expression that matters were delicate here.

"Hello," said the woman, rising from the chair. "You must be Sheriff Muller." She extended her hand. "My name is Dr. Graciela Rojas," she said with a Latin accent.

"Please come in," Kurt said, opening the door to his private office, a small Victorian box with a window overlooking the prim courthouse lawn and the marble statue of a Civil War soldier no one had ever heard of. Above the tourist shops and cafés loomed the verdant north slope of Ajax, the mountain his father had helped groom into submission nearly forty years ago. This time of year you couldn't distinguish the wide green ski runs from a fairway out on the golf course.

"Forgive the mess," he said, unfolding a metal chair stenciled PROPERTY OF ST. MARY'S BINGO for her to sit on. "I'm working on a new filing system. Would you like some coffee?"

She glanced at the dark murky liquid settled at the bottom of a glass pot on the hot-plate burner and declined. "I have come about a friend," she said.

She was his age, mid-forties, the colorful Guatemalan dress just loose enough to conceal a body no longer taut and girlish. She was letting the gray have its way, a thick shock of hair choosing its own shape in the unfamiliar crackling air of this climate. He recognized the small inevitable signs of wear, deeper laugh lines and an unavoidable heft. The same things he noticed in the mirror every morning.

"My friend and I are attending the Global Unity conference at Star Meadow," Dr. Rojas said, placing her handwoven cloth bag in her lap. "He has not been at the seminars all day. It is not like him. I went to his room this afternoon but he was not there. No one has seen him since last evening."

Kurt sat on the edge of his desk and looked at her. "I was afraid you were going to tell me something like that," he said.

Her skin was the creamy brown of a *criolla*, a trace of the Europeans in her distant ancestry. He suspected she enjoyed the privileges of the ruling elite in her native country.

"His name is Omar Quiroga. He is a well-known journalist in Argentina," she said. "Tomorrow evening he is to speak on the Dirty War and *los desaparecidos*. The disappeared ones."

"Are you a physician, Dr. Rojas?"

She looked surprised. "Yes, I am," she said.

"Then I take it you've seen a dead body before."

Her eyes were bright, beautiful, almost golden, filled with concern. "Many," she said in a quiet voice.

"Would you come with me, please."

She examined the victim with cool, professional detachment. She probed the dark pulpy hole behind the ear, lifted the eyelids, checked the gold caps of his teeth. Then she combed back the man's wet black hair with her fingers and stared for a long time at the ruined bones of his face, her hands resting there in a tender caress.

"I am nearly certain," she said, her voice quavering.

"I'll send for his dental charts," Kurt said.

She nodded, then turned away. Her body began to shake.

"Come," he said, taking her arm. "Let's talk about this somewhere else."

They walked a block to the Hotel Jerome, where an assistant manager named Torben Rasmussen offered them the small, elegant tearoom for their private use. Torben was with the Mountain Rescue team that had secured Bert's body to a helicopter stretcher and hauled him up from Maroon Bells. Every Christmas Kurt sent each of the men a bottle of good Scotch.

"How well did you know him?" he asked the doctor when they were seated. A waitress brought them coffee from the hotel bar.

"For many years," she said, daubing her eyes with a tissue. "We studied at university together. I knew his wife since we were convent girls. She is one of the missing, you see. Seventeen years now. There are so many."

Kurt doled sugar into his cup with a tiny silver espresso spoon that felt ludicrous in his huge hand. "You said he was well known in his field."

"Yes," she nodded. "He has won many prizes. He wrote about the military junta and how they tortured him. Omar always said they should not have let him get away. Through his writing the world has come to know the horror of those years in our country."

Summer tourists strolled past the beveled window, a vastly different crowd than the skiers. Less beautiful, less pampered, less trouble.

"Are there other Argentines out at the Meadow? Somebody who might hold a grudge?" he asked.

She shook her head. The coffee lay untouched in front of her. "Only the two of us," she said. "But I cannot imagine it. Not someone in the conference. It is a gathering for world harmony, you see."

Kurt knew all about Star Meadow. His wife had taught yoga there, attended their every seminar in healing and massage. Star Meadow became her sanctuary from the tensions of a failing marriage.

"Is there someone we should call? Does he have family back in Argentina?"

"Yes," she said, staring somberly at the white tablecloth. "I will call his poor mother." She peered up at him. "He is not the first son she has lost."

2

STAR MEADOW LAY HIDDEN TWELVE MILES NORTHWEST OF Aspen in a peaceful grassland valley, an ancient alluvial outwash between eroded peaks of basalt lava and a range of gray-green shale pinnacles. The remote retreat had been founded by a wholesome Hollywood celebrity named Matt Heron and several white-bearded gurus who made use of the pastoral tranquility for their Conferences in Coexistence, as they called them.

"Have you met Heron?" Kurt asked, driving his dusty '63 Willys Jeep across a wooden bridge. In the distance they could see the multicolored roof of the conference center, a huge canvas tent shaped in oblique cones like the habit of some obscure order of nun.

"Yes," said Graciela Rojas. "He seems sincere."

Kurt hadn't been to the Meadow since those dismal days of the custody hearings, when he himself delivered the subpoena to the actor. Desperate to hold on to his little boy, Kurt had tried to prove in court that his wife was an unstable New Age zombie who had been seduced by Heron and his coven of Aquarian Svengalis. He felt a pang of regret even now, three years later, remembering his feeble accusations against a woman who deserved better.

"Is this the same river?" she asked, looking out the roofless Jeep at the water foaming below the bridge.

"Yes, it is," Kurt said. The same icy water that flowed from a source lake high up near the Continental Divide, wagged through Aspen, and emptied into the Colorado River forty miles downvalley. "We figure someone took your friend up the Pass, above town, to a place called the Grottos. It's rugged rock, and pretty isolated. The river cuts a gorge through it. If I was going to dispose of a body, that's where I'd do it."

"Then it wasn't done here at the Meadow," she said in a voice still husky with emotion.

Go easy, man, he told himself. *Slow down and go easy with her*.

"No, not the disposal, Doctor," he said. "This is downriver from where we found him."

If they dumped him here, he thought, *the body would be in the Colorado by now*.

The Jeep bumped along a weather-pitted dirt road through the cool cavern of shadows created by towering pines. Soon they emerged into stark sunlight and green rolling pastures, the road directing them toward the little village of solar-heated cottages and geodesic schoolrooms.

"I've got to let Heron know I'm here," Kurt said. "Then I would appreciate it if you'd show me the room where Quiroga was staying."

"Yes, of course," the doctor said.

A sign with woodburnt lettering pointed the way to the SENIOR FACILITATOR'S SPACE, a glaring white igloo-shaped dome with a pine-wood wraparound deck.

"You must be the facilitator's facilitator," Kurt said to Heron's receptionist, a pretty young Indian woman wearing a lightweight sari. She sat in a lotus position behind a floor-level lazy-Susan table scattered with used teacups. The office walls were papered with slogan posters—SAVE THE WHALES, SAVE THE BABY SEALS, SAVE THE SNAIL DARTER.

"Terribly sorry," the woman said in a British accent, "but Matt is in conference just now."

She was playing with a Rubik's Cube. Kurt had a strong hunch her job did not require dictation.

"Tell him Sheriff Kurt Muller is here on official business," he said.

The fact that he was in uniform, wearing a baseball cap embroidered with the county sheriff's insignia, made no difference to the woman. "He has left strict instructions," she said, her long brown fingers twisting and clicking the small plastic squares.

There was always an air of superiority about these Star Meadow people. "Don't bother to buzz," Kurt said, walking past her through the reception area to slide back a beaded curtain.

In the adjoining room, a spare meditation chamber bathed in white radiance from the skylight, four men sat on velvet cushions, conferring with knitted brows. Matt Heron looked up, startled by the intrusion, his mouth parting in surprise.

"Sorry to barge in like this, Heron," Kurt said, "but I need to talk to you right away. It's serious."

Tugging nervously at his blond mustache, the actor simply stared at Kurt, dumbfounded.

"It's about one of your guests," Kurt said.

"Yes," Heron said. The ever-present boyish cheer had disappeared from his tanned face. "You must mean Omar Quiroga."

Kurt studied the others, their eyes skittering about uncertainly, exchanging glances. He recognized them all. The Tibetan monk who was Heron's spiritual adviser, the martial arts instructor who kept the actor fit between movies, the button-down tax accountant who had rescued him from an Oklahoma land investment scandal. Captains of the Star Meadow board deep into crisis management. They already knew that the man was dead.

"This is a police investigation. I need a key to his room," Kurt said. "It's easier than kicking in the door."

The body had been IDed barely an hour ago, Kurt mentioned the man's name to no one except deputies Muffin Brown and Chip Bodine, and yet these people were already preparing a public statement.

"Sorry, Sheriff," Heron said, something defiant, almost victorious, in the glint of his Arctic-blue contact lenses. "Someone has beat you to it."

Graciela led the way to the dormitory, a long narrow log construction with solar paneling and a glass picture window facing the mountains. Stationed at the sliding door to Quiroga's room stood a tough grunt wearing a blue blazer, polished loafers, and menacing sunshades. His sandy hair had thinned prematurely, showing a pink scalp pimpled with sweat.

"Hold it," he said stiffly. "Nobody's permitted in here."

Kurt turned to the doctor. "It's one of those days when everybody's got an assignment," he said.

He stepped closer to the FBI agent and stared down into the sunglasses. "Go get your boss," he said. "I want to know why you boys are noodling around in my jurisdiction."

"Hello, Muller," said a voice behind the dark glass door. "It's funny how people keep getting blown away in your quaint little valley. Goes to show you, nobody's safe anywhere nowadays. Not even in Nirvana."

Kurt hadn't heard that voice in three years. Which wasn't long enough. "What are you doing here, Staggs?" he asked. "Who said somebody got blown away?"

A figure moved behind the glass. His white shirt shone in the darkness. "Let's not bullshit each other," the man said. "We know you've recovered the body."

Kurt breathed on the stocky agent standing guard. "It's amazing how word gets around."

Ever since the Erickson case Kurt had suspected that the Feds might be wiretapping him, monitoring radio dispatches, opening mail. Ever since Chad Erickson jogged out of the health club one crisp winter morning and sat down to start his Jaguar, and a crude projectile concealed under the seat reamed him from asshole to eyeballs and seared up through the ragtop roof without so much as a powder burn.

Federal Agent Neal Staggs slid open the door and stepped into the fading alpine light. He was well over six feet, a lanky man with short graying hair and a faint razor burn on his long neck. A semipro golfer, an upstanding member of his church, a former basketball star at some private college back East. He exuded the smug self-righteousness of an altar boy.

"You must be Dr. Rojas," he said, coming out to greet her. "It's a pleasure to meet you. I'm sorry it had to be under these circumstances."

Graciela shook his hand. "Everyone is being very kind," she said, regarding Kurt with a tired smile. "I am in good hands."

Staggs glanced at Kurt. "The sheriff does his best," he said.

Kurt's record with the Feds, and Neal Staggs in particular, was less than sterling. The first time the Bureau had sent Staggs out from Denver was when Ted Bundy jumped from the window of the county courthouse, while in Kurt's custody, and escaped into the mountains to kill again. And then there was the coke dealer Chad Erickson, with his five-million-dollar home in Starwood and his squadron of private planes. Erickson had promised federal prosecutors the names of his Colombian drug contacts, and the Feds were furious when his brains spewed through the roof. They accused Kurt and his department of everything from foot-dragging the investigation to harboring the identity of the killers to outright perpetration of the murder.

"Please come in and have a look around, Sheriff," Staggs said, extending his arm toward the door. "The Bureau is always happy to share its information with the locals." With a brisk nod Staggs dismissed the agent sticking his nose in Kurt's sternum. "We just wish the locals would occasionally return the favor."

Kurt knew what he would find in the room. Three Brooks Brothers suits, one dusting for fingerprints, one gingerly lifting objects with tongs and placing them neatly in labeled plastic bags. What he didn't expect was that the third man would be sitting at a typing desk reading through Omar Quiroga's personal notebook. Nor did Graciela Rojas.

"What are you doing?" she said, rushing to the agent. "This is not your property." She snatched the notebook from his hands and swept it against her chest. "I expect this from the thugs in my country, señor, but not from you. You are abusing someone's privacy."

The agent removed his reading glasses and stood up, a graying elderly man with shoulders rounded from decades stooped over small-print documents in bad lighting. He looked more like a librarian than a cop.

"It's okay, Bill," Staggs said, waving the man off.

Graciela Rojas clutched the notebook defiantly. She turned to Kurt, outraged.

"Dr. Rojas," Staggs said, "I'm sure I don't have to remind you how controversial your colleague's writing is. We'd like to know if he incriminates someone in this journal. Perhaps something he planned to say in an upcoming speech. Anything to go on," he said. "We all want the same thing here, ma'am. To apprehend the killer. But to do that we'll need your full cooperation."

Slick as owl shit, Kurt thought.

"Now, please," Staggs said, stepping toward the woman, "give us a chance to do our work."

Graciela sighed deeply, her upper body sagging on her hips. She looked again at Kurt.

"I'm afraid he has a right to confiscation," Kurt told her. "That is, of course, if this is the scene of the crime." He cocked his head at the agent. "You found blood here, I take it, Agent Staggs."

Staggs's forehead wrinkled in three long deep lines.

"Because if it didn't happen here," Kurt said to Graciela, "these gentlemen know they have to get a court order to monkey around with what's on the premises."

Staggs raised his chin slightly and studied Kurt through narrowed eyes. "Let's talk outside, Sheriff Muller," he said.

They walked toward a duck pond set back near a small stand of shedding cottonwoods. A pair of mallards, male and female, dibbled for food in the algae scum, their white tails high in the air as their heads bobbed underwater.

"What kind of shit are you pulling here, Muller?" Staggs fumed. "Sometimes I wonder whose side you're on."

"Tell me what you're doing here, Staggs. I like to be informed when somebody comes digging around in my backyard."

"I don't owe you any explanations, ace," Staggs said. "This guy is big. We're talking embarrassing international incident here. Bleeding hearts whining on every fucking network in the hemisphere. We can't afford to wait around for some Podunk hippie sheriff to pull his head out his ass and get the job done."

Staggs withdrew a handkerchief from his suit jacket and wiped his sticky lips. *The altitude*, Kurt thought. *The man is dehydrating. He and his boys wouldn't survive a good jog up here without a gallon of Gatorade.*

"No, Muller, not this time," he said. "You try to stonewall *this* investigation, I'm going to bury your butt in a federal pen."

Kurt listened to the ducks quacking in the quiet afternoon. Mates for life. Just last night he'd read the *Zoo Book* on ducks to his son. 'How come you and Mommy aren't for life?' Lennon had wondered aloud.

"I guess I'm just the curious kind, Staggs," Kurt said. "When the math doesn't add up, I get stubborn. You give me some clean numbers, I'll make sure the Rojas woman doesn't become a problem."

Staggs stopped dead in his tracks and dug his hands in his pants pockets, rattling change. "I'm listening," he said.

"Quiroga buy it in his room?"

Staggs shook his head.

"Any idea where?"

"I thought that was your department, Sheriff."

The sun had dipped low toward the peaks, and long jagged shadows stretched across the grassy meadow behind the geodesic domes. Kurt breathed in the cool thin air. Sometimes he wanted to quit this foolish job and take Lennon traveling. To the rain forests of the Northwest, the gentle beaches of the Caribbean, the great cities of Europe. Anywhere but this confining little valley.

"There's one thing that bothers me, Staggs," he said.

The agent reached into his shirt pocket for a cigarette. "What's that?" he said.

"You haven't asked to see the body."

Kurt turned and walked back to the dorm, where he found Graciela sitting on the carpet, legs folded underneath her dress, the notebook resting in her lap. The older agent crouched near her, waiting silently, patiently, for the woman to give it back. The two other agents went about their routines in a studious quiet.

"This man says that since I am not Omar's wife or next of kin, I cannot legally remove his papers," she said, peering down at the journal.

Kurt lifted his cap and scratched his matted hair. "These guys know the law," he said.

Bitterness darkened the corners of her mouth. "You must forgive me if I am not very trusting of their methods," she said.

Kurt knelt beside her, his old ski knees cracking. "I understand," he said. "But these gentlemen are right. Maybe there's something helpful in those pages."

It was clear that Graciela needed time to weigh everything carefully. She didn't move for several minutes, her gaze fixed on some vague patch of carpet. The older agent relaxed on his heels; Neal Staggs leaned against the oak paneling, arms folded, waiting.

Kurt watched the professionals at work, the fingerprint man dusting the chrome door-handle of the refrigerator, his colleague examining several blank postcards of snowy Aspen spread on a coffee table. He wondered why these men had shown up to turn over a man's room even before Kurt and Graciela Rojas knew he was dead.

Something underneath the refrigerator, behind the agent's polished wingtips, caught Kurt's eye. He could see it from his squatting position, a shard of glass lodged far back in the dark inch of space below the motor guard.

"Will you please see to it that this is given back to me?" she said to Kurt. The doctor had finally emerged from her shell of silence. "I want to make certain it is returned to his family."

"You got it," Kurt said.

He squinted at the object. It looked like the broken stem of a wineglass.

"You must promise me," she said. "I am putting the notebook in your hands."

Kurt nodded slowly. "I'll get it back for you," he said. "You can count on it."

He glanced over at Staggs. The man touched the tip of his index finger to his tongue and scratched a mark in the air. I owe you one.

You son of a bitch, Kurt thought. *What little you've told me is a lie.*

3

KURT RADIOED HER FROM HIS JEEP. "DEPUTY BROWN, please go to where I usually am this time of day and wait for my call. Give me twenty-five minutes. Do you copy?"

"What was that all about?" Muffin asked when he telephoned from the pay phone outside the Conoco station on Highway 82.

"It's no longer a paranoid joke that the Feds might be tapping our phones," he said. "When I got to the guy's room, the suits were all over it. Somebody had done a quick-and-dirty. Probably the Feds themselves."

She was sitting in the office at Lennon's day care center. "Why would they do that?"

"I'm not sure," he said. "They know a lot more than we do. They're not even interested in seeing the body. My guess is they already know what they'll find."

Muffin shook the snow scene in a glass paperweight on the director's desk. "Jesus, I don't want to guess what that could mean," she said. "Is the doctor with you?"

"They kept her for questioning."

"Think she'll be okay?"

"Nothing I could do about it," Kurt shrugged. "They are, after all, the highest authority in this great land of ours."

He asked if she had time to take Lennon home and stay with him till he got back. He needed to pay a visit to Miles Cunningham.

"Miles?" Muffin laughed. "I thought that crazy man checked into Betty Ford."

"When you get a chance, call Wing Taylor out at the hangar and ask him when he logged in a private plane full of suits. I want to know what time those guys came in today."

Miles Cunningham was a Pulitzer-winning photojournalist whose stark images of violence still haunted the American conscience. In Mississippi, a battered black boy hanging from a tree limb. In Vietnam, an acne-faced American teenager reaching his amputated arms to caress a dying buddy. In El Salvador, a hillside repository of bones. Miles had been beaten in Bogalusa, stabbed by an army bayonet in Manila, shot and left to die in the jungles of Angola. His body bore the scars of his relentless investigations. But now, at age fifty-five, fatigue and a gnawing despair had driven him to a shambled, reclusive life in a cabin on Castle Creek, near the rotted timber ruins of the old mining town of Ashcroft.

Kurt stopped at the metal gate and waited for a voice from the Jack in the Box drive-thru intercom attached to a fence post. Video cameras tracked the Jeep from three different locations—an aspen tree, a birdhouse high atop a leaning pole, the busted-out windshield of a rusted VW microbus up on cinder blocks.

"What do you want, you toad?" crackled the puppet head, its plastic smile leering malevolently.

"I've got to talk to you, Miles," Kurt spoke at the puppet.

"Where were you last night when I fucking needed you, law man?"

Miles phoned Kurt two or three times a week, usually around four A.M., to rave paranoid hallucinations brought on by recreational drugs.

"Miles, there are no Mormon gunboats on Castle Creek," Kurt said.

Last night the man had called screaming, 'Mormon gunboats at three o'clock! Dive, dive, dive!'

"The fuck you know," the puppet growled. "They're laying back there by the old sled-dog kennels, docked in the brush, biding their time. They know we've grown weak and decadent. No sense of vigilance anymore. Mark my word, law man. They'll take the town like Hitler took Paris. Three or four shells on a boutique and you'll present 'em with the keys."

"Miles—"

"They'll turn our women against coffee!"

"Miles, listen."

"They'll lay waste to our discos, searching for the tablets!"

"Miles, goddammit!" Kurt shouted. "Shut the fuck up and listen to me! I need your help. There's been a murder."

The Jack in the Box puppet stared back silently, fixed in a timeless sneer. Wind quivered the aspen leaves, an intricate dapple of green. Kurt could hear the creek shishing nearby. Moments passed, enough time for Miles to fill another drink.

"Would you like some fries with that?" the puppet finally spoke.

"Miles, open the fucking gate."

The electronic lock clicked and the gate swung back in a wide arc.

"Drive on through, please," the puppet said.

In the rocky plot of yard three surly Dobermans nosed around in a heaping landfill of Wild Turkey bottles, several of them lined in a row for target practice. Kurt cut the engine and honked his horn, but the dogs straightened like regal doormen and bared their teeth at him.

"I hope for your sake you're packing heat these days," said a voice through a crack in the cabin door. "It's the only way you're going to get past security."

"Miles," Kurt said, "come out and get your dogs."

"Are you insane?" Miles said. "I don't mess with those beasts. They'd like to rip my jugular and tinkle in the wound."

The three dogs lowered their ears and pranced toward the Jeep. The roof was down, the windows open.

"Miles, they're *your* dogs. Do something with them."

One of the animals strutted over to the passenger window and sprang up on hind legs, its muddy paws scratching at the metal finish. Another one circled around to Kurt's door, growling, its purple gums exposed, teeth as sharp as band-saw blades. Kurt's hands began to tingle. He reached slowly under his seat and unsnapped the holster.

Suddenly Miles appeared on the porch with an AK-47 and sprayed the air with bullets. The noise sent the dogs howling off toward the woods. Even after he stopped shooting, the roar still echoed through the hills. Smoke and the bitter smell of cordite wafted over the yard.

Kurt swallowed hard. "Wouldn't it be easier," he said, "to try a rolled newspaper?"

Miles dropped the weapon to his side. Shell casings were scattered across the wood porch like a child's messy jacks. "I thought about that once," he shrugged, "until they ate the paperboy."

The interior of Miles's cabin resembled an antiquarian bookstore kept by a doddering, piss-stained old Oxford man with food bits in his beard. Footpaths burrowed through shoulder-high mounds of yellow newspapers and tattered books, a maze of bewildering turns and random cul-de-sacs. The place stank of putrefying garbage. A filthy sofa draped with a filthy sheet occupied a small clearing near the stone fireplace, the floor around it cluttered with crushed Coke cans, potato-chip bags, nubby cigarette butts, and more empty Wild Turkey bottles.

"Want a drink?" Miles asked, collapsing onto the cushions. He reached into a champagne bucket, scooped out a handful of watery, rust-colored ice, and dumped it into a plastic souvenir cup from his fraternity days at Yale.

"You look like hell, Miles."

"Divorce will do that to a man," Miles said, pouring Wild

Turkey. "I expect a modicum of sympathy from a fellow traveler, Muller."

Kurt had lost count of how many years Miles had been divorced from his third wife. It was so long ago Kurt couldn't remember her name.

"You ought to move into town for a while," he said. "The solitude is not helping."

"The fuck you know." Miles picked up a remote-control device and changed channels on three TV screens suspended near the ceiling. New views of the front gate and his property line down near the creek. "I'm fast at work on my memoirs."

In the two months since Kurt had last seen Miles, the man's appearance had slipped another meter in the glacial decline that had steadily eroded his past twenty-five years. He had lost more hair on his oversized, baby-pale head; another tooth was notched with dark sugar-rot. The odd twisting of his mouth when he talked, the stiff angle of his neck, were all more exaggerated, more eccentric, the tics of unrepentant physical neglect. It was impossible to imagine how Miles Cunningham had looked in his twenties, when he was apparently quite the ladies' man, magna cum laude Ivy League, a streaking young comet in the galaxy of photojournalism.

"Have you ever heard of an Argentine writer named Omar Quiroga?" Kurt asked, noticing that Miles had removed the matted photographs and framed magazine covers, evidence of his old life, to free the cabin walls for gun cabinets and rifle racks. The place looked like the bachelor game room for an Afrikaner soldier of fortune.

Miles nodded, drinking. "Didn't realize you could read, Muller. His book somewhere." He pointed, sloshing liquid onto his wrist. "Met him in Buenos Aires during the junta trial. Good man, Quiroga."

"Somebody disagrees," Kurt said. "He was murdered. His body was dumped in the Roaring Fork."

Miles looked stunned.

"He was out at Star Meadow for one of their Save-the-Planet

do's," Kurt said. "The Feds have jumped on the case, but I don't trust the fuckers."

"The swine shall inherit the earth," Miles said. "I keep trying to tell you that, Muller. I wish you'd listen to your elders."

"I take it Quiroga liked to speak his mind."

"You got that right. He did some serious payback on the pock-faced degenerates who tortured and killed his countrymen for sport. There was even a TV documentary, if my memory serves. He didn't appreciate that they hooked his balls to a truck battery and lit him up like a Christmas tree. It's all in his book," he said, pointing somewhere, sloshing more whiskey on his worn checkered polyester pants.

Kurt studied the titles in one teetering column of books and gave up. "I need a crash course in Argentine politics, Miles," he said.

Miles spread his arms in exasperation. "How come a guy with a sixth-grade command of current events keeps getting elected to public office, Muller?"

"Ruthless party machine," Kurt said.

Ten years ago, angered by the rampant greed of real-estate developers and back-room chicanery in city government, a cabal of aging hippies and several flannel-capped old-timers whose lineage traced back to the mining era formed an opposition party. Miles ran for mayor, a stunt that brought national attention to the race. The election came down to the wire, but the Rabid Skunk party failed to pull off their upset. They lost every seat challenge except one: Kurt Muller became county sheriff by sixty-three votes. And for some unaccountable reason, possibly out of reverence for the Muller name, Kurt had held on to the post in two succeeding elections.

"So you want to know about Argentine politics." Miles made a croaking noise through his nose that sounded something like a scoff. He reached over and scooped more ice into his drink. "Well, my friend, there was a coup in seventy-six, as I recall. Isabel Perón wasn't killing enough subversives to satisfy the military's bloodlust, so they threw her out and took over the job themselves. What I read, about thirty thousand Argentine citizens ate it in the next three or four years." He shook his head sadly. "In those days, you wanted to see your friends, you didn't go to a café. You just stood on the banks of the Río de la Plata and waited for somebody you knew to float by."

Kurt thought about what the river had done to Omar Quiroga. He walked over and lifted the Wild Turkey from the sofa and drank straight from the bottle. The stuff burned like lye.

Miles raised a bushy eyebrow. "Jesus, I hate an undisciplined drinker," he said.

"I watch the news, Miles," Kurt said. "There have been elections in Argentina for a while now. How did that happen?"

Miles scratched at a large brown mole growing on his pasty forehead. "The Falklands," he said. "The colonels had worked themselves into a blood frenzy, feeding on unarmed philosophy majors and menopausal nuns, and thought they were ready to devour the Iron Maiden and her starch-and-brass navy. Unfortunate miscalculation. The cowards had never attacked somebody who could shoot back. When the smoke cleared, they'd blown their wad. Lots of obedient schoolboy recruits were hammered into dog meat, lots of tax money sank to the bottom of the sea. So much for lifting the national spirit," he said. "So much for the glories of yesteryear."

Kurt stepped over to the fireplace. Half-burnt rubbish smoldered in the brazier, where Miles had tried to kindle a fire. An awful acrid odor of eggshells, melon rinds, melted Styrofoam. It appeared as if the man had become distracted after the third match and wandered off.

"So the military appointed a commission to find out what went wrong," Miles concluded, "and the commission sent a handful of the more vicious piranhas to jail for their incompetence. The trial broke the scaly back of the junta."

Kurt spotted an old flintlock musket propped against the wall next to an ax and a shedding hearth broom.

"Doesn't make sense, the military punishing its own," he said.

Miles shrugged, placed his hands on his knees, and heaved.

With considerable effort he managed to hoist himself to his feet. "Grievous sin, vanity, hubris. Confession. The willing acceptance of punishment." He mumbled this litany, shuffling toward a pyre of books. "Sounds perfectly Catholic to me."

Kurt shouldered the smooth stock of the musket and sighted down the long, awkward barrel. The powder well smelled freshly capped.

"Here," Miles said, standing behind him with a hardcover book marked PITKIN COUNTY PUBLIC LIBRARY.

Kurt opened the cover and noticed the date stamp. Two years overdue.

"Omar Quiroga's account of the whole bloody debacle," Miles said. "He was a decent man. You might learn something about politics, Muller. Or human nature. Read it and weep."

Kurt headed off down a narrow passageway between mounds of brittle paper, trying to reconstruct how he'd gotten here.

"Thanks, Miles. After so much homey hospitality I hate to run."

He found the front porch and stuck his head out the door to look for the dogs. "Do us both a favor," he said. "Stop calling me in the middle of the night or I'm going to bill you for therapy."

He dashed to the Jeep. Miles stood behind the screen door and whistled for the Dobermans. "Yo, North! Yo, Secord!" he hollered. "Attack this toad, ye hounds of hell!"

By the time the Jeep reached the Jack in the Box head, the dogs were ripping at Kurt's back tires.

4

KURT LIVED IN THE HOUSE HE HAD GROWN UP IN, A SMALL hay barn the Bauhaus designer Herbert Bayer had converted into an Austrian chalet in the late forties for his good friends Otto and Hanne Muller. Settled on a stony plateau halfway up Red Mountain, the house held a spectacular view of Ajax and the tidy, red-brick town of Aspen.

When Kurt arrived home he went looking for Lennon in his bedroom and found a chaos of plastic creatures and decaled armored vehicles spread across the floor. This was the same simple room Kurt and his brother had slept in till they left for college. On the bunk-bed headboards, nearly forty years old now, Roy Rogers twirled a rope from a rearing Trigger.

"Somebody's going to clean up his room tonight," Kurt said.

"Hands up, you're under arrest!" a male voice commanded from the closet door. "Hands up, you're under arrest!"

Lennon stepped out and squeezed the trigger of his toy pistol and the recorded message repeated a third time. "Did I scare you, Dad?" he laughed.

"Absolutely," Kurt said, bending over to kiss him. Lennon's soft red hair smelled of sweat and summer dust and that unmistakable scent that was Lennon and no other child. Blindfolded, Kurt could find this boy, the meadowy smell of his hair, in a roomful of sleeping children.

"Did you lock anybody in jail today?" Lennon asked.

"No, buddy, not today," he said. He thought about the little boy who had discovered the body hurtling down the river. "But the day isn't over yet."

In the living room Muffin reclined in a window seat, scuffed Adidas kicked off onto the floor, an outdoorsman magazine resting in her lap. She had changed into khaki shorts and her tan, muscular hiker's legs were stretched out on the cushion. Her chestnut Dutch-boy hair was growing long and the bangs nearly covered her eye-brows. She was gazing through the open chalet window toward the deep blue twilight drifting over town.

"Thanks for getting Lennon," Kurt said.

"No problem."

"Muffie bought me a frozen yogurt on the way home," Lennon said, bounding over to hop in her lap.

"Lots of calls," she said, raking her fingers through the boy's hair. "The mayor wanted to know the grisly details. Nolan Riggs came by." The head of the Tourist Bureau. "Libbie put him off. And that kid from the *Daily News* was snooping around. I told him to wait for a statement from you."

"How about Wing Taylor?"

"He said the Feds flew in about one o'clock."

"Outstanding reaction time," Kurt said, hanging his cap on a peg with the jackets. "A full hour before you found the body."

"Did you talk to Matt Heron about it? He probably panicked and called them in."

"Why would he call the Feds? Why wouldn't he call his local sheriff to report a missing person? Like Dr. Rojas did."

Muffin smiled, a small tug at the corners of her mouth. "You can't exactly blame him if he doesn't appreciate the local sheriff," she said.

During the custody hearing Kurt's lawyer had grilled the actor for an hour, trying unsuccessfully to establish that he was Meg Muller's cultic lover. In the end the judge lost patience, dismissed the case, granted custody of Lennon to his mother. A month later she took the child and moved to Telluride.

"Libbie called to say that the Feds finally showed up at the courthouse," Muffin said. "They snapped a few Polaroids of the body. In and out in ten minutes."

"The bastards are just going through the paces," Kurt said.

Herbert Bayer's kitchen was a large friendly space enclosed on one side by an oakwood bar. Kurt went to the old Frigidaire to get a beer. "Boy, I'd like to wipe the smug smile off that guy Staggs's face," he said.

He watched Muffin snort into his son's neck, the boy wincing and giggling, fighting to wriggle free. She was a scrupulous young deputy, fiercely loyal, hardworking, her instincts uncanny. She'd grown up with five brothers and could do most things better than Kurt. Ride a horse, ski the frozen passes, rappel down sheer granite, fly-fish the Fryingpan, handle a gun.

"When are we getting back with Dr. Rojas?" she asked.

"Soon as the Feds are done," Kurt said, holding an icy Budweiser can against his forehead.

Muffin shook her head. "Maybe we should send a patrol car after her," she said.

They had slept together once, two years ago, the night of his last election. There was a victory celebration at the Jerome Bar and everyone drank too much. Muffin stayed till the thunderous breakup, sometime around three A.M., and then shyly asked him over. She lived alone in a trailer park then, at the foot of Smuggler Mountain. He was stumbling drunk and didn't know what to expect when he knocked on her door. It had never crossed his mind that she might be attracted to him. He'd been divorced for over a year but had no time for romance, not with his job, a tough reelection campaign, a little son newly deposited on his doorstep.

Somehow they ended up wrestling in their underwear on Muffin's cramped hideaway bed. She took great delight in trapping him in the high-school wrestling holds she'd learned from her brothers. There wasn't an ounce of fat on her hard, athletic body. He lifted weights with her at the Nordic Club and knew how strong she was, especially for a small woman, a hundred pounds lighter than Kurt but aggressive and agile, relentless.

'Is this why you asked me over?' he huffed, slipping through a half-Nelson and flinging her onto her back. He liked her heat, the glaze of sweat on her bare skin. 'To check out my moves on the mat?'

Dehydrated from too much liquor, he collapsed onto the rumpled quilt next to her, their breathing deep and labored in the frosty darkness of the trailer. When he was almost asleep she rolled over and rested her chin on his chest.

'Tell you the truth,' she said, 'I'm still trying to make up my mind about men.'

Kurt groaned, feeling nauseated from so much jostling around. Feeling, suddenly, the weight of three million years of male virility hanging between his legs. 'Do us both a favor, Muff, and pick on somebody else. I've got so much heavy baggage I need a trailer hitch.'

'Everybody has baggage, Kurt.'

'You don't understand. I've got a receding gumline, a hiatal hernia, and a messy past with the Columbia Record Club. I just bought my first reading glasses. My hair is falling out.'

She raised herself up with a curious squint. 'Where?' she said, brushing her fingers through the thick brown hair Libbie cut every couple of months. 'You're not going bald, Kurt. Where?'

'That little round circle. You know, the hurricane swirl. I'm losing shoreline there.'

She brought her face close to his and kissed him softly on the mouth. 'Okay,' she said. 'You've got your little secrets, I've got mine.'

'I don't know about this, Muffin,' he said, his eyes closed, fighting sleep. 'We work together. I hired you.'

She kissed him again. 'So why aren't you getting up to leave?'

Afterward, lying together under the quilt in the pale moonlight, she asked if it had felt the same as it did with other women. He laughed and pulled her onto his chest in an affectionate cradling hug, trying not to give away his apprehensions. Instead of the tough young cop who pumped iron with the jocks at the club she suddenly seemed to him an innocent and vulnerable ranch girl from Wyoming, skittish as a kid sister, and he knew then he had made another foolish mistake.

'I don't want you to think I didn't like it,' she said in a small unsure voice. 'But you were probably right. This was not a good idea.'

"Do you suppose they were lovers?" Muffin asked from the window seat.

"What?" Kurt said.

She was still gazing out the chalet window into the deepening twilight.

"Do you think Dr. Rojas and the writer were lovers?"

Kurt took his beer and went to sit on the floor beside Lennon. "No," he said. "No, I do not."

5

THAT EVENING KURT LEFT HIS SLEEPING SON WITH THE baby-sitter and drove into town to see Zack Crawford, a bartender who worked the late shift at Andre's. A landowner in Woody Creek was seeking a restraining order against Zack for skinny-dipping in the man's pond every morning in full view of teenage daughters. Though he'd warned Zack several times about trespassing, the bartender would not stay away.

"You off duty?" Zack said, holding up a tequila bottle with a silver spout.

"I'm never off duty," Kurt said. "But go ahead. This is a friendly visit."

Andre's was the toniest nightclub in Aspen. During the Christmas holidays, at the height of ski season, Hollywood celebrities packed the glass disco floor every night till the wee hours, rubbing shoulders in a glamorous scrum. Kurt had once lost his date in the fog of dry ice and discovered her an hour later snorting coke in a men's room stall with some hack actor from a canceled sitcom. Now he avoided the club during the season, especially at closing time. He happily let the city cops manage the arrogant drunks who insisted on driving their rented Porsches out in the snow. Last New Year's

Eve a rising starlet from *Melrose Place* was hospitalized when she threw a tantrum over a DUI and swallowed her boyfriend's ignition key.

"Come hell or high taxes, I've been swimming in that pond every summer since 1972," Zack complained to Kurt, who was sitting on a leather stool at the bar. Though it was June and business was at half tilt, disco music boomed from overhead speakers; colored lights flashed across the mirrored walls surrounding the dance floor.

"That fucker blew in from Texas six months ago and bought up the land. Who died and made him God? I ought to take his ass to court over homestead rights."

Zack was dressed in a starched white shirt with a black bow tie, his long graying hair gelled back behind his ears. His cheekbones had begun to protrude with age, and after so many years in this dry air there was now a papery texture to his tan.

"I can't do anything about the property laws, Zack," Kurt said, downing the shot of tequila. "Unless somebody changes them real quick, you'd better find another place to swim."

Zack exhaled a whistling breath and shook his head. A weariness dulled his eyes. "Hey, Kurt, remember me?" he said. "We used to smoke dope together and ski bare-assed down Ajax in the middle of the night. I was there at Crater Lake when you met Meg. I don't recall you talking property rights back in seventy-six when me and you and Bert cut down all those billboards on the highway." He wiped the sheeny black surface of the bar. "Tell me something, man. If Bert was still alive, would you bust *him* for taking a quick dip every morning in his birthday suit? 'Cause your brother was the one who showed me the pond. We used to swim there after we came home from Nam."

Kurt rested his elbows on the bar and stared down at his reflection in dark glass. A carnival face peered back at him, a warp of distortion, the image pushed out of shape and mired in wavy tar.

"What am I supposed to do, Zack?" he said. "You wanted me

to be sheriff, just like everybody else. So what the hell am I supposed to do?"

Zack poured him another shot of tequila. "Go pop the people
that are hurting somebody," he shrugged, "and leave the rest of us
poor bastards to our pathetic little pleasures."

Zack noticed a couple at the far end of the bar and left to greet
them, clasping hands with the man in a cordial power shake. Kurt
turned to see who it was.

Jake Pfeil had arrived for the evening with a beautiful young
woman on his arm. He gave Kurt a nod of recognition, their least
unpleasant exchange in several years.

Their fathers had created this resort, put it on the map. Kurt
and Jake had grown up together. But there was too much history
between them now and they made no effort to hide their animosity,
especially since the Erickson investigation. Jake and Chad Erickson
had shared real estate interests in Acapulco and Hawaii, and Kurt
brought Jake in for interrogation. During their meetings Jake was
hostile and elusive, antagonistic. He kept calling Kurt 'little
brother.'

Tonight Jake was wearing an eggshell-white linen suit with a
wildly floral tie. His salted hair was razor-cut to neat perfection, a
style better suited to a younger man. He was a good twenty years
older than his date.

Kurt ignored the couple and leaned back against the leather
bumper, finishing off his drink. The Design Conference accounted
for most of the clientele, a small but enthusiastic gathering. The
dance floor writhed with snaky limbs, the music all bass and messy
synthesizer, a painful, pounding throb. He watched the matches
taking shape, the awkward flirtations, strangers meeting, dancing
together, a momentary abandon in a far-off place. He couldn't remember what his pathetic little pleasures were, or the last time he'd
had any fun.

A loud whoop went up at one of the tables, a gang of British
rugby players in town for the regionals.

"I hate those assholes," Zack said, sauntering back to his seltzer hose. "They come in here and grope my waitresses and leave lousy tips. Look at those two over there," he said, "hitting on that lady. I wish you'd let me carry a cattle prod, Kurt."

Beer steins in hand, two burly ruggers hovered over a booth near the stairs, speaking to the lone figure sipping a glass of wine. There was an alluring presence about the woman, her arm poised on the tabletop, smoke curling from her fingertips. A cluster of tiny plastic fruit dangled as ornament from each ear. She seemed to be staring at Kurt, imploring with lovely dark eyes. It took him several seconds to realize that the woman was Graciela Rojas.

He walked over to the booth. "Hello, Doctor," he said.

"Hello, Sheriff," she said, a sadness in her smile. The day had taken its toll on her.

The two men weren't happy about Kurt's intrusion, but they heard who he was. "A bit unfair, in'it, mate," one of them remarked, grinning, "you poaching all the local game?"

Kurt was the only man in the club larger than these Piltdown knuckle-draggers. "Run along, boys," he said. He wasn't in uniform, but in his pants pocket he carried a container of pepper spray the size of a breath freshener. Enough to ruin their evening.

"S'all right, Buff." The second man clamped a hand on his friend's shoulder. "She's too soddy old to fuck, anyway."

Kurt gave him a nasty shove. "Hit the street, jerk," he said. "I don't want to see your ugly face around here again."

The rugger didn't like the stiff jab to his solar plexus. He was thinking about doing something stupid, like throwing a forearm. Kurt gripped the container in his pocket.

"C'mon," the other rugger said, screening his friend away from Kurt. "We're wasting good time here. Let's go find us some real quim."

Kurt watched them leave the club. "Sorry about that," he said.

"Boys will be boys," Graciela smiled.

"I left a message for you at the Meadow."

"I went for a drive," she said. "I couldn't stop thinking of Omar."

She invited him to sit down.

"They wanted to know his sexual preference," she said, describing the interview with the FBI, her face sinking into the long grim countenance of grief. "They asked if he sometimes purchased drugs. I find it horrible that no matter the country, the secret police has the same obsessions."

Kurt told her he had picked up Omar Quiroga's book and intended to read it.

"Ahh," she said, her face sparkling for an instant. "Omar's book. It must be difficult for someone who lives in this country to understand the cruelty in that book. The official policy of torture and murder. I don't think I understand it myself."

She told Kurt what had happened to her the first year of the junta. How thugs in plain clothes came to arrest her in the clinic where she worked, the slums of Buenos Aires. "My husband ran a bookstore," she said. "That same day they closed his shop and took him away. Our daughters were four and two years old then. Someone phoned my husband's parents to tell them to watch the children, we would not be coming home again."

Kurt thought about Lennon, safely asleep in his Roy Rogers bed. He remembered the agony without him, those months the boy lived with his mother in Telluride.

"The soldiers kept us blindfolded, myself and many others, in a small compound that was once a primary school," she said. "When they found out I was a doctor, they put me to work reviving those they had tortured nearly to death. The ones unconscious from electroshock, or bleeding in the kidneys. Once I delivered a baby," she said, her mouth beginning to tremble. "It was to that school, maybe the third month, I cannot say for sure, that they brought Omar."

He had been beaten mercilessly, his teeth broken, his hair yanked out in patches. They strapped him to a chair, hooked his testicles to an electric generator, and questioned him about his associations, demanding that he name names.

"He didn't, of course," she said. "And in the end they commanded me to administer a lethal dose of anesthetic."

Graciela lit another cigarette, her hands unsteady.

"I gave him only enough to make him sleep. There was a small chance, you see, that somehow he might survive the Plata," she said. "And he did. He woke when his body hit the cold water. God smiled on him and he lived."

She tapped a matchbook absently against the tabletop. "But not this time," she said. "Not this river."

Kurt rubbed his beard, a nervous habit. He needed another drink. "How about you?" he said. "How did you get out?"

She sipped wine and gazed off across the club. "They let me go," she said. "After five months and ten days they let me go home. I don't know why. No one will ever know why some lived and some disappeared."

"And your husband?"

"My husband is another story," she said. "The dear man was an incurable romantic. He believed that democracy would eventually prevail in our sad country. I am told he cried for our children night and day. They lied to him, you see, telling him the girls were given to another family to raise. In the end he broke down." Her eyes roamed toward the bar. "I did not find out for a year—when one of his cellmates came to our house. My husband hanged himself with his belt in the prison toilet."

They sat together for quite some time without speaking. Kurt ordered another shot of tequila. Dancers paraded back and forth to the mirrored ballroom, drinking and laughing merrily. The music boomed louder and louder. He and Graciela made a curious picture, the only two people in Andre's not having a good time.

"Do you know that young woman?" Graciela said after several minutes of ruminating silence. She was staring at Jake Pfeil's date, a stunning Mediterranean beauty dolled up in one of those coquettish off-the-shoulder party dresses. Her liquid brown skin was generously exposed—legs, shoulders, back—the way Jake liked it. "I've been trying to place her, but I cannot."

"I've never seen her before," Kurt said. She was just another pretty appendage to Jake's tailored sleeve. He collected them like cuff links.

"Excuse me, please," Graciela said. "I must speak to her."

She slid from the booth and walked to the bar. Kurt watched the languid movement of her body and realized how attracted he was to this woman. She introduced herself to Jake's date and the young beauty smiled, shook her head, black curls brushing her bare shoulders. Jake looked amused. He stroked one end of his mustache, an old cocaine tic, and studied Graciela with lascivious interest. Calculating, Kurt guessed, how he could get them both in bed.

"She is Italian," Graciela said, returning to the table. "My mistake."

Kurt tossed down his drink. "I ought to be going," he said. "I have a five-year-old at home with a baby-sitter."

Graciela smiled warmly. "You are married, Sheriff Muller?" she asked.

"Divorced," he said. "Lennon's mother left him at my office one day, a couple of years ago, and went off to an ashram in Oregon."

He could see the confusion in Graciela's face.

"Yoga, curry, meditation," he explained. "It's an Eastern thing. She's on the path to personal fulfillment. She calls every now and then, when the spirit moves her."

Something troubled her. "So many loves vanish from our lives," she said, looking into Kurt's eyes. "Yet we go on."

Lately he had been thinking a lot about Bert. How much he missed him. The numbness had finally worn off and he was beginning to feel the loss.

"Sheriff Muller," she said, "do you think you will find out who murdered my friend?"

"Yes, I do."

She was sitting close to him now, her knee resting against his.

"I bought a map," she said suddenly, digging into the woven

handbag on the cushion beside her. "I located those Grottos you were speaking about. Where Omar might have—"

Unfolding the large, awkward trail map she knocked over her wineglass, spilling a trace of dark liquid across the table. "I want to see this place for myself," she said.

Kurt set the glass upright. She had had more to drink than he realized.

"My deputies and I are going out there at daybreak," he said. "I don't usually invite civilians along, but in your case I'll make an exception."

Graciela unfolded more squares, turning the map from side to side, trying to tell north from south. "Thank you, Sheriff," she said, distracted by her effort, "but my flight back to Argentina is scheduled for tomorrow morning. My daughter is graduating from university at the end of the week. I'm afraid I do not have the luxury of time."

Kurt wasn't sure of her intentions.

"I have a rental car," she said. "You're welcome to come along."

"When?" he asked incredulously. "Now?"

"Yes. Now."

He laughed. "You're joking, right?" he said. She was in no state to go anywhere except directly back to Star Meadow for a good night's sleep. "The Grottos are not a place to wander around in the dark. Especially if you've never been there before."

"I am not joking," she said, raising her chin defiantly, her eyes meeting his. "I cannot possibly return to my room and wait there all night, wondering if anything will be done for Omar after I am gone."

Kurt sighed. He was feeling the tequila buzz himself. "Dr. Rojas," he said, "we can't accomplish anything out there this time of night. Besides, the whole idea that he was . . . disposed of in those rocks is a long shot at best."

"Thank you, Sheriff," she said, dropping her eyes to study the map. "I appreciate your caution. I will be careful."

"You've had too much to drink," he said.

"*Claro,*" she said, rattling the paper folds. "It is late and I am a bit out of sorts. But I will find these Grottos myself."

He was not happy that she seemed to be questioning his competence. "Let me do my job, Dr. Rojas," he said. "I'll get whoever killed Omar Quiroga."

A thick wave of hair veiled one eye. "You will not be terribly offended, I hope, Sheriff," she said, "if I tell you that for many years now I have had little reason to trust men in uniforms."

He glanced down at his hands cupped around the empty shot glass. "You're determined to do this, aren't you?" he said.

"I must know what happened to him," she said. "His family will want to know."

He drove her southeast of town along the winding two-lane highway toward Independence Pass. The night was dark and moonless, the forest blacker than the sky itself. The Jeep's headlights ranged into deep, cavernous gorges chiseled in the bedrock. They passed no other vehicles, an eerie sensation that they were alone and isolated on top of the world. Graciela slouched silently in her seat while Kurt considered the two dozen reasons he should turn the Jeep around and take her back to Star Meadow.

"Look, is there any way I can talk you out of this?"

They were pulling over onto an access road near the Grottos. Graciela sat up and took notice of the wooded darkness.

"I see now," she said, "why they brought him here."

Kurt parked the Jeep at the trailhead, his high beam illuminating the fractured cliffs above a rushing stream. Glacial meltwater had grooved the rock, leaving striations and a honeycomb of shallow caves.

"I really don't expect to find a smoking gun, Doctor," he said. "Even in daylight it'll take hours to cover that ground."

"Come," she said, hopping from the Jeep. "Show me the way."

"Hold on a minute," he yelled after her, opening the glove compartment to look for his flashlight.

She ignored his warning and roamed out into the darkness. "It's not so difficult," she said, ascending a smooth whaleback ridge, Kurt's flashlight beam chasing after her.

At the crest they stood together, Graciela breathing hard in the crisp night air. She wasn't used to the altitude. Kurt pointed the light through fir trees toward a rocky flume. Water hurled down the long ragged split of granite.

"Is that where they pushed his body?" Graciela asked.

"It's possible," he said.

She took the flashlight from his hand and made small quick steps down the ridge and across a deposit of chunky scree, her arms aloft, swaying for balance like someone treading over broken glass, the beam dancing wildly in the trees. Kurt trailed her to a scattering of boulders near the ledge. Graciela stepped up onto a mound of sandy shale and aimed the shaft of light into the deep shadows below, where darkness prevailed, ghostly stone silhouettes looming in the bottomless void. The summer runoff was so loud Kurt could scarcely hear his own voice.

"Nasty drop!" he called out. "You don't want to get any closer!"

Graciela turned to look at him, loose stones underfoot skittering off into the abyss. She lowered the flashlight, resting it against her pants leg. Now all he could see was the strange glowing outline of her body.

"Come on, Dr. Rojas," Kurt said, holding out his hand. "Let's go back to the Jeep."

"I couldn't save him," she said finally, her voice choked and distant. "I couldn't save him this time."

He took a step closer, reaching out for her. "Here," he said. "Let's go talk about this someplace warm."

Graciela hesitated, then placed her icy hand in his and leaned forward, collapsing deadweight against him. "I'm sorry," she said, her warm breath in his ear. "I have had too much to drink. Please let me sit down."

Her legs were unsteady and she stumbled, seizing his arm, sinking down awkwardly in front of him. "You were right, of course," she said, hunching against the cold. "There is nothing to be done for Omar out here."

He draped his brown leather jacket around her shoulders. "Catch your breath," he said, squatting down beside her, "and then I'm taking you back."

She clicked off the flashlight and they sat for several moments in silence. At ten thousand feet in the Rockies, the dead of night without enough clothing, he was beginning to shiver. A fine mist drifted from the waterfall, settling on his thick hair and beard.

"He was my best friend," she said softly. "I shall miss him."

"Your best friend," Kurt said. "Was he also your lover?"

Her body began to shake with deep laboring breaths and he realized she was fighting emotion.

"It makes a difference, Graciela," he said. "It makes a difference in the investigation. I need to know where you were, what you talked about, what you did, the last time the two of you were together."

He knew the questions were inappropriate now, at this moment, in this place, but he couldn't restrain himself. He had to know.

"I am wondering if I was right about you, Sheriff Muller," she said in a husky voice. "If you are a good man who can be trusted."

Though they were only inches away, the darkness came between them like a sheet of black ice.

"Is there something you're not telling me, Graciela? Something about Quiroga?"

She brought her knees to her chest and drew the jacket around her. "Many years ago," she said, "yes, Omar and I were lovers. For a brief time before the junta. My husband was away in Paris." She hugged her knees, rocking for warmth. "That was another lifetime. After the loss of our loved ones we talked about marriage, but—but our hearts were not in it. Something could not be recovered between us," she said. "For fifteen years Omar and I have been the dearest of friends. Political allies. And nothing more."

Her admission struck close to home. He still felt guilty about his own marital deceptions.

"Have I been wrong about you, my friend?" she said to him. "I thought I could trust you. I have seen the loss in your eyes as well. A child without a mother. Loved ones gone. But now you are beginning to ask questions like all the others."

He thought he heard a crunch of rock, a footstep. The runoff spumed in a haze of steady white noise and he strained to listen. He thought he heard it again. Graciela took hold of his shirt and pulled him close. He could smell the sweet wine on her breath, the coconut fragrance of her hair brushing his face.

"Someone is watching us," she whispered in his ear.

Suddenly a disk of light torched the blackness, blinding them both. Graciela gasped and clutched at Kurt, her long nails digging into his arm. He spun to his knees and raised a hand, shielding his eyes from the glare.

"Turn that off!" he said, reaching for the pepper spray in his pocket.

The blow caught him above the eye. The only thing he would remember later, in the many long nights of regret, was the shrill sound of Graciela screaming.

6

THE COLD BROUGHT HIM TO. HIS HEAD THROBBED, HIS neck was stiff as a plank. Something sticky covered his face. Dizziness overtook him when he tried to sit up. He crawled on his hands and knees, searching for Graciela, calling out her name, his voice muffled by the waterfall. Pulling himself to his feet, he fought back nausea and waited for the liquid night to stop lapping at his ankles.

He made his way back to the Jeep in the dark to find three of his tires punctured by bullets and the CB radio wires ripped loose. He flipped on the high beams and scanned the Grottos, calling her name again and again, desperate for some sign of her. There was no movement but the wind in the invisible spruce trees.

He retrieved the pistol underneath the seat and headed out, the wound in his forehead bleeding down his face, a hot gash of pain. Two miles down the highway, a moving van hauling furniture from Santa Fe crept around a curve. Kurt stepped into its headlights and raised his badge.

Muffin showed up at the hospital in time to watch the doctor administer the last of four stitches. The deputy's face appeared drawn from sleep and her hair looked as though she'd walked in through a fierce gale.

"Your sitter called the night dispatcher," she said. "She thought something was wrong when you didn't check in."

"Lennon okay?"

"Sleeping like a hound dog."

She bent over to look at the wound. "What'd he use?"

"Butt end of a pistol, I imagine," Kurt said.

"That would be my guess," the doctor confirmed. He was applying a gauze patch over the stitches.

Muffin smiled. "My guess is a sap was involved," she said.

"Ha ha," Kurt said. He closed his eyes again and laced his fingers across his chest.

"What the hell were you doing at the Grottos in the middle of the night?" she asked.

"It's complicated," he sighed. He didn't want to think about how stupid they'd been. "Find Chip," he said. "He's probably still at Shooter's practicing his two-step. And round up a half dozen of the others."

Muffin turned to the doctor. "Shouldn't he be in bed?" she asked.

"Of course," the doctor said. "This is quite a nasty blow."

"I'll be all right," Kurt said, raising himself up on his elbows. "We've got to get back out there."

"You need some rest," the doctor said.

"Later," he said.

For two hours the search party roamed through the shallow caves and deep jagged clefts of the Grottos. They used lamps with the voltage of klieg lights, and the rock formations glistened like veins of silver. They found nothing, not even Kurt's flashlight or his leather jacket.

"How was it that the guy could just walk up and crack you?" Muffin asked.

"It was dark," Kurt said.

"My god, Kurt, it's never *that* dark. Were you and the doctor a little distracted?"

They were climbing down a ravine toward the waterfall. Kurt suddenly felt very weak. The anesthetic was wearing off and his head weighed a thousand pounds. He sat down on a smooth ledge of granite, his hiking boots dangling into darkness.

"I still don't understand why you two came out here," she said.

Kurt leaned back against a boulder. The doctor was right—he needed to sleep. He could close his eyes right now and happily drift off till morning.

"I think she was testing me," he said. "She knows more about Quiroga's death than she's letting on, but she doesn't know who to trust. She has a problem with cops."

Muffin slid down beside him and turned off her lamp. "Has it occurred to you that this might have been a setup?"

It had occurred to him, yes. But he wouldn't let himself believe it. "Setup for what?" he said.

"Maybe she needed to disappear," Muffin said. "Maybe she's dirty in the Quiroga murder."

Kurt didn't want to hear this. He reached into his down vest and found the plastic container of painkillers.

"This afternoon I got in touch with Quiroga's newspaper publisher in Buenos Aires," she said. "Fernando Lugones. Nice guy, speaks the Queen's English. Omar was his friend and he took the news pretty hard. Lugones had his personnel department fax me some information. Omar Quiroga has a nice fat life-insurance policy, Kurt. Guess who his beneficiary is?"

He swallowed two pills, his mouth dry as cardboard. "She didn't have to disappear to collect the money," he said. "In fact, it would be better for her if she didn't."

Wind whistled through the gorge. Muffin hunkered down in her parka, silent, thinking.

"So who hit me, then?" he challenged. "Who'd she get to do that?"

"How about her husband?" she said, unsure now.

"Her husband is dead," Kurt said.

Muffin made a scoffing sound. "Where did you get that?"

"She told me."

The deputy stood up and bounced on her toes, trying to stay warm. "I imagine she told you a lot of things tonight, didn't she, Kurt?"

"Her husband is alive?"

"Lugones knows Dr. Rojas too and gave me the name of the hospital where she's on senior staff," she said. "I finally located an administrator who speaks English, and she told me that Dr. Rojas and her husband are on a business trip to the States. 'Isn't it nice,' the woman said, 'that the two of them could arrange holidays in North America at the same time.' Imagine the fun vacation they're going to have now, Kurt. Vegas, Tahoe. Looks like they're coming into some money."

Kurt waited for the drugs to kick in, but it wasn't happening fast enough. He felt like resting his head on a rock until all of this was over.

"You know, Kurt, my brothers used to say, 'Never let the little head do the thinking for the big.' " She casually kicked at a stack of rocks and they skittered into the gully, bouncing and clattering into the dark chasm below. "Is that what you've done tonight, Sheriff? Let the little head do your thinking for you?"

He was too exhausted to feel humiliation. He wanted to go home. "Help me up, Muffin," he grumbled.

He held out a limp arm and she regarded it without moving. "Have you compromised yourself in this investigation, Kurt?"

"Fuck off," he said.

The wind was getting colder now, almost two miles above the ancient seabed in the black hole of night. With his last ounce of strength he rolled to his knees.

"Always the martyr," she said, looping his arm around her neck. Cheek to cheek, her skin smelled like the brown nut fragrance of soap that hangs from a string.

At home under warm sheets he dreamed of women. He dreamed about the time he'd made love to Meg in the Grottos, and about Graciela Rojas, that he had found her many years later, living in a small tropical hotel by a lagoon.

When the telephone rang he woke in a fog of narcosis, disoriented from pills, believing he had dreamed this call. "Graciela," he said, certain he would hear her voice on the other end. Certain she was calling to tell him she was all right. Waiting for him, somewhere. "Graciela," he muttered, "where did you go?"

"Wake up and shake a leg, law man!" a drunken voice howled into the line. "Red alert! Oooga, oooga! Mormon gunboats on Castle Creek! Dive, dive, dive!"

7

MUFFIN SPENT A COUPLE OF HOURS DOZING ON THE living-room couch and came upstairs around seven to check Kurt's stitches. For a moment, in his drowsy confusion, he thought she might have slept with him. She replaced the gauze, then went down to the kitchen to make breakfast for Lennon and a sick tray for Kurt. Lennon kissed his father and wrestled with him on the bed, asking to see the stitches.

"Does it hurt, Daddy?"

"A little," Kurt said.

"I'll give you a magic touch," Lennon said, placing his spidery fingers over the swollen ridge. This was a ritual Kurt had invented when the child was having trouble adjusting to day care: a magic touch on Lennon's head every morning to make the day a perfect one.

"This means you'll find the bank robbers today," Lennon said, his fingers lingering a second longer. Lennon thought every criminal was a bank robber.

At eight o'clock Muffin helped the boy gather up his Key Force vehicles and ushered him out the door for the day-care center. Kurt slept another hour, then forced himself to rouse and shower. He set the Pitkin County Sheriff cap low on his forehead, trying to conceal the wound, and drove down dusty Red Mountain Road into town, thinking all the way about Graciela Rojas. In the brisk morning air his head began to clear and he slowly came to acknowledge how bothered he was by Muffin's suspicions. He wanted to believe that whoever had killed Omar Quiroga was also stalking Graciela and had followed them out to the Grottos. But why had she lied about her husband? How much of her story was true?

Tired and numb, Kurt pulled into his space at the courthouse and sat staring at the sign that said *For Sheriff Only*, dreading the morning ahead. He knew that only one thing was irrefutable: he was with Graciela Rojas when she disappeared. Any way you sliced it, he had to be the worst excuse for a cop in the entire state of Colorado.

In the office Chip Bodine was leaning back in a swivel chair, reading the *Aspen Daily News*, his Birkenstock sandals propped up on the receptionist's desk. Omar Quiroga occupied the lead story.

"The phone's been ringing off the hook," Chip said. "They're starting to hear about this Quiroga thing in the real world."

"For Chrissake, Bodine," Kurt mumbled, "you're an officer of the law. Get yourself some regulation shoes."

Chip lowered his long knobby hands, crumpling the newspaper in his lap, and studied Kurt's forehead. "One season I had a gash like that," he said. "Wiped out on a freaking barrel marker."

Kurt pressed the flesh between his eyes. "Did the APB go out on Graciela Rojas?"

"Statewide," Chip nodded. "So far, *nada*."

Chip Bodine had once been a world-class skier, in the late sixties, early seventies, and had raced on the American team in the '72 Winter Olympics. His best showing was forty-third in the downhill, placing him behind gaunt, graceless tribesmen from equatorial Africa. He blamed late-night parties, hashish, and a bum knee. The knee required several operations, and he finally gave up the sport to service the escort needs of a succession of aging widows in the Roaring Fork Valley. These days he was keeping company with

Miss Norway 1959 in her gingerbread chalet near Buttermilk Mountain. Kurt would have fired him years ago, but Chip was the best snowmobile driver in the Valley and knew every obscure trail within a hundred miles. There was also Wednesday-night poker, which went back twenty years.

The phone rang. "I'm not here," Kurt said to Libbie McCullough.

"At eleven the mayor's coming by with Nolan Riggs from the Tourist Bureau," she said, chewing on a carrot stick. "Pitkin County Sheriff's Office," she spoke into the receiver.

"Isn't there something you could be doing?" Kurt glared at Chip.

"Like what, *Jefe*?"

"Like checking on the prisoners or something."

Chip shrugged lazily. "Nobody in lockup except two Brit ruggers the city cops caught pissing in the fountain." He twined his fingers, stretched, and cracked knuckles. He was the only man Kurt knew who still wore his hair in a shoulder-length braid. "Helluva duke-out getting those shitheads in the tank."

When Kurt opened the door to his office, a man was waiting for him in a stenciled folding chair. A frail man with skin so translucent he might've been hiding for several summers in a root cellar. He sat patiently with his fingers resting on the kneecap of his crossed leg. There was something fussy and formal and fastidious about his carriage.

Kurt turned back to Chip.

"Oh, yeah," the deputy said. "There's somebody waiting for you."

Kurt gave Chip a chilling smile. "Remind me to replace you, Bodine, when things settle down."

He stepped into his office and removed his cap.

"Sheriff Muller," the old man stood, offering his damp hand, a specimen of delicate bones. "My name is Hans Gitter and I have come about Omar Quiroga."

Another visitor with a foreign accent. Not exactly German. Kurt's parents had a German accent. This was something close.

"I am with the conference at Star Meadow," Hans Gitter said. "Quiroga and I have made friends, yes? We have spent much time together walking the grounds and discussing *philosophie*. I deeply regret the news of his death."

The man had to be pushing eighty. His hair was long and plumelike and white as an egret, with the kind of haphazard, brushed-through care of a tidy old professor who doesn't see well. His lively blue eyes held moisture, not from emotion but from some physical condition of age. There was a slight tremble about his head and hands. Omar Quiroga's death had cast a sleepless sorrow across his shrunken face.

"I have been thinking about it all night, trying to remember if anything he said would be helpful to the authorities."

Hans Gitter wore a goatee that matched the faintly yellowing whiteness of his hair, and he stroked it while he spoke. "Then I remembered our sojourn into town," he said.

He explained that last Tuesday afternoon the two of them had driven into Aspen to look around the resort village. They strolled along the pedestrian malls, browsed through shops, rode the gondola to the top of Ajax and had lunch in the restaurant, "a most expensive, and most terrible, wurst," he said. At the end of the day, when they stopped for coffee in the Victorian parlor of a Main Street bookstore, Omar Quiroga noticed a beautiful young woman perusing the magazines.

"'Twas as if he'd seen a spirit," Hans Gitter said. His face glowed with the memory of her. "A tall creature with the skin of a Moorish princess. I at first thought Omar was struck by her beauty. But no. He seemed to know her."

Hans Gitter explained that Omar rose to speak with the young woman and that there followed what appeared to be an awkward misunderstanding. "They spoke in Spanish, so I did not understand," he said. "The young woman left the bookstore soon after.

When I asked Quiroga what it was all about, he shrugged and simply said he had taken her for someone else."

Kurt examined the coffee mug on his desk. It hadn't been washed in a week. "Long black hair?" he said, pouring coffee from the pot on the hot plate. "A string of dark freckles across her nose?"

Hans Gitter looked surprised. "Why, yes," he said. "Do you know her?"

"Were they speaking Spanish," Kurt said, "or could it have been Italian?"

The professor looked insulted. "Spanish, I assure you," he said.

"Is that the only time you saw them together?"

"Yes," he nodded slowly. "We were virtually inseparable, Quiroga and I. I never saw her again." His eyes gleamed. "It is the only thing out of the ordinary I can remember from our four days together, Sheriff Muller. Nothing of importance, I'm quite sure. But I thought the authorities ought to know."

Kurt thanked him for coming in and offered coffee, but the old man declined with a trembly wave of the hand.

"Now that you're here, Professor Gitter, do you mind if I ask you a few questions?"

"Not attall," Gitter smiled weakly. He shifted his thin legs and sat a little straighter in the chair.

Kurt leaned against a corner of his desk. "What is your impression of Dr. Graciela Rojas?"

Hans Gitter wagged his head, a gesture of indifference. "An intelligent woman," he said, pursing his lips. "Very dedicated. I'm sure she's taking it hard, poor dear. They were very close, you know."

Kurt blew on his coffee. "How close?"

The old man blushed, the first sign of color in his ancient face. "Sheriff Muller," he said, "discretion prevents me—"

"This is very important, Professor Gitter," Kurt said. "A man is dead and I need to know the personal details of his last days here." He was not going to mention Graciela's disappearance. Not yet.

"I assume," Hans Gitter said, embarrassed by such talk, "that they were lovers, Sheriff."

Had she been lying all along? Kurt wondered. "Did Quiroga tell you that?"

"No."

"Then why do you assume it? Did you see anything to confirm this?"

"No, I do not have empirical evidence," Hans Gitter said. "I—" He caught himself, crimson with confusion, his eyes drifting toward the slack hands trembling in his lap. "I—I am not sure why I think it so. Please forgive me, sir. It is the idle assumption of a silly old academic."

"Are you aware she's married?"

He was beginning to probe with the persistence of a jealous suitor.

"I have only just met the woman," Hans Gitter said.

The intercom buzzed and both men started. Kurt leaned over and barked into the box. "Libbie, I told you I'm not here!"

"Sorry, boss," Libbie's voice hummed. "Neal Staggs on line one. He says it's an emergency."

Kurt yanked up the receiver.

"We've got a situation out here in Emma," Staggs said. "I don't want to cross wires on this one, Muller. Let's make nice and play it by the book. Townies and Feds on the same team for once."

"What's the deal, Staggs?"

"One of my agents has been shot," he said. "We've got Quiroga's killers holed up in a farmhouse. You want in on it?"

Kurt and Chip Bodine took the cutoff near Old Snowmass and sped down a country road that rose and fell like a dragon's backbone through tranquil hayfields and the horse-grazing pastures of gentlemen farmers. In the distance they heard staccato volleys of automatic gunfire, the echoes of a small war in a far-off country.

"Sounds like they started the fun without us," Chip drawled.

On a hill overlooking the besieged farmhouse Kurt hit the brakes and the county squad car skidded to a halt in loose gravel. He had never seen anything like it. A helicopter swerved low over the roof, guns blazing, wood shingles dancing like dominoes. Sharpshooters dressed in camouflage took aim from a weathered barn. Round after round exploded against the stone masonry in puffs of white smoke. Windows shattered, the gutter dropped from the roof, the screen door split off its hinges. Kurt couldn't imagine what had provoked such a vicious attack. He saw no signs that anyone inside was returning fire.

He knew this farmhouse. He had been here once, years ago, to pick apples in the small grove behind the house. Now the trees struggled to survive, their limbs scrawny and bare and starved for attention. The ranch fence had collapsed from neglect, and except for the beat-up Buick parked next to a dilapidated tack shed, it was hard to imagine that anyone had set foot on the property in months.

Chip raised his binoculars. "Down, down to the valley of the shadow of death rode the brave five hundred," he intoned.

The shooting had stopped abruptly and the commandos were rushing the house. Kurt steered the squad car down the slope toward a monstrous armored Winnebago positioned on the road near the mailbox. Neal Staggs was emerging from the coach door with the serene indifference of a summer camper stepping out for a swim. He had ditched his blazer and tie; his white dress sleeves were rolled back neatly.

"What the hell's going on?" Kurt said, jumping from the car with his .30-30 rifle.

"We had the place boxed up and one of those crazy wetbacks inside started shooting at the chopper," Staggs said, pulling a Smith & Wesson .40 from a hand-tooled leather holster that hugged his ribs. He peered around a corner of the Winnebago. "We had no choice but to respond," he said.

Kurt chucked back the bill of his cap. "Who are we talking about here?"

"Dope dealers," Staggs said. "House full of illegals. Jesus, Muller, don't you know what's going on in your own county? Maybe you ought to give some thought to enforcing the drug laws."

A photo ID was clipped to Staggs's shirt pocket. Even in a firefight his graying hair remained in place like the aging preppie's in the picture.

"My man Jenkins found something in Quiroga's journal," he said. "The guy was working on a magazine assignment about illegals, tracing their squirrely little routes through Central America into the U.S. He was planning to make a trip out here to meet these people. They all do grub jobs in Aspen—dishwashers, janitors, most of them without papers."

Commandos crouched under jagged windows, huddled near the screen door. The helicopter still hovered overhead, a deafening whir.

"We came out to talk to them about it," Staggs said, raising his voice. "They opened up on us before we reached that gate over there. Jenkins is a year from his pension. He's lucky to be alive. Most of his shoulder's blown away."

"Where'd you get all this backup?" Kurt asked.

"Grand Junction," Staggs said. He seemed to notice Chip Bodine for the first time. "Had 'em on the ground in less than an hour."

One of the commandos kicked in the front door and a half-dozen men swarmed through the opening; others rose up and pointed their weapons into broken windows. There was a short burst of gunfire from inside.

"I'm going to go sit in the car," Chip said. "Wake me up when they start bagging the charred bodies."

Staggs looked annoyed. "Where'd you scare up this freak, Muller?" he said, eyeing Chip's braid. "Rummage sale in the Haight?"

Kurt used Chip's binoculars to survey the outbuildings. The place had once belonged to a ruddy-faced organic farmer everyone called Adam Appleseed. For the better part of one afternoon, sometime in the late seventies, Kurt and Meg and Bert and Maya Dahl had made apple juice out here in Adam's ancient New England wood-press. Kurt wondered whatever happened to Adam Appleseed. It had been years since he'd thought about this farm.

"Any chance they might have a hostage?" he asked.

Staggs lit a cigarette. His top button was unfastened and Kurt could see the gray pad of a bulletproof vest. "Now who would that be, Sheriff?" Staggs said.

The bastard knows about Graciela, Kurt thought. *He's picked up the APB.*

An agent wearing a headset stepped from the Winnebago door. "Lead unit says all clear, sir," he reported to Staggs. "Okay to proceed ahead."

"You coming?" Staggs asked Kurt. He tossed his cigarette and jogged off toward the house.

"Let's go, Bodine!" Kurt shouted at the county car. "And bring your rifle!"

"Aw, Kurt," Chip grumbled, "you know how much I hate to lug that thing around."

By the time Kurt arrived, three shirtless Hispanic males were bound facedown in the living room, their wrists and ankles secured by nylon tie-wrap. One of them, a teenager, was bleeding badly from the neck and choking with boyish sobs. The interior of the farmhouse lay in ruin, Goodwill odds and ends scattered about in pieces, army cots upended. Splinters of glass covered everything like a jeweled frost.

A commando paced the hallway holding a brown-skinned infant, trying to hush the baby's screams.

Kurt propped his rifle by the door. "Jesus H Christ." He rubbed his beard. "This is way over the top, Staggs."

"Spare me the violins, Muller." The agent knelt down in the living room to examine a pile of weapons. A .30-06 hunting rifle, a twelve-gauge shotgun with a wired-together stock, several cheap makes of handgun. "You shoot one of my men, you pay for it. These pricks aren't choirboys. Look at this shit."

A commando with charcoal streaked under his eyes walked into the room with a freezer bag of uncleaned marijuana. "More of this in the back, sir," he said.

Staggs turned to Kurt. "You're a joke, Muller," he said. "Any punk greaseball in the fucking Western Hemisphere can run dope out of your county."

Kurt could see a blood-spattered body lying on the dining-room floor. "These people didn't kill Omar Quiroga," he said.

"Yeah? Well, the way I read it, the guy came snooping around out here for a story and stumbled on their plant shop," Staggs said, "so they iced him." He weighed the bag of dope in his hand, then unsealed it and crumbled a bud. "But what really bothers me about this, Muller, is who these assholes clock for. My sources tell me they're in real sweet with an old friend of yours."

Kurt looked at him. "What the fuck are you talking about?"

"Agent Staggs!" Another commando trotted into the room. "There's a door leading down into a cellar, sir. Looks like one of them was trying to get down there. A woman, sir. Her body's in the kitchen."

"Seal off that door!" Staggs shouted.

Kurt walked slowly into the kitchen. The body lay a few feet from the stairway down to the cellar. A quarter of her skull was bared to the brain, and her thick dark hair oozed with blood. The commandos were tracking through the red pool spreading from her head, leaving sticky bootprints across the checkered tile. One of them stooped to drag her into the next room.

"Hold it," Kurt said. "Get out of the way."

He knelt to lift her, his knees wetting in her warm blood. When he turned her over he saw that she was not someone he had ever known.

"Toss in a teargas canister," Staggs ordered the men assembled in the kitchen. "Anybody's down there, he won't be for long."

Kurt could hear the baby screaming in the hallway. He hoisted the dead woman into his arms and carried her to the back of the house, where he placed her on a cot and draped her body with a quilt. He didn't want the child to see her mother this way.

Chip Bodine couldn't bring himself to enter the house. He circled around to the backyard and wandered over to examine a long, low-lying coop wedged into the side of a grassy knoll. A ramshackle structure held together with chicken wire, railroad ties, and splintering wood slats. Chip guessed it had been some sort of potato storage bin. He cupped his eyes and peeked inside but could make out nothing in the musty darkness. Bracing his rifle against a post, he sat down and sagged back against the rusty wire. The farmhouse was quiet now. He kicked off his sandals and closed his eyes. He knew Kurt would eventually find him. He always did.

Suddenly something hard and blunt and metallic pressed into the back of his skull. "Don' talk," came the voice behind him. "Don' say nothing or I blow you fucking head."

"Hey, amigo, *¿qué pasa?*" Chip said.

"Don' turn around," the voice said in broken English. He was kneeling behind Chip in the soft dirt of the coop. "Don' make a quick move."

"I'm not with the guys who did all the shooting," Chip said in passable Spanish. The blunt thing jammed against his skull was the barrel of a sawed-off shotgun. *"Mira,"* he said, gesturing at his clothes. "I'm just an old vaquero."

"If you move to the rifle, vaquero," the voice said, "I will kill you."

Chip fixed his gaze on the windows of the farmhouse, praying someone inside would notice his raised hands. "I don't like guns," he shrugged. "It's going to stay right where I put it."

He felt a strong hand on his shoulder. "Okay, vaquero," the voice said. "We go now to the car."

Kurt looked around the bedroom. The walls were bare except for a Mexican crucifix of bloody Jesus hanging at an angle like a license plate with a missing screw. Someone had constructed a child's mobile out of string, drinking straws, and a deck of cards. There were rumpled sleeping bags, a couple of cots, loose clothing stashed in corners. He stepped over a drugstore baby-rattle to the shattered window and peered into the sunlight. A pleasant breeze ruffled the few leaves left on the apple trees. He felt angry and sick to his stomach. *This is not why I wanted the job,* he thought. In the beginning he had believed he could keep the peace without destroying people's lives.

Chip Bodine was lounging back against an old coop, his rifle propped up beside him. *You've got the right idea, my friend,* Kurt thought. *Leave the wet work to the professionals.*

Chip slowly raised his hands. He was talking to himself. A little strange, even for Chip. There was something troubled and urgent in his eyes. He stood up in the awkward, stiff-legged manner of a man with bad ski knees and began to edge sideways along the coop. He cleared the structure before Kurt realized there was someone behind him, a much smaller man with a grip on the back of Chip's khaki shirt and a shotgun slanted upward against his skull.

Kurt pulled the .45 from his holster and crawled through the window.

"Sorry about this, man," Chip said without moving his head. Long ashen lines creased his face. "I guess I fucked up again."

"Everything's okay, Chip," Kurt said, marching toward them. "Just stay loose."

"Stop there," the gunman said to Kurt. "Don' walk no closer or I pull the trigger."

Kurt recognized the man. He had seen him in town with the group of Hispanic service workers who hung out in the pool hall below the pharmacy. No taller than five feet five, long shaggy hair, Indian features, a tank top that showed off his muscled shoulders. Kurt remembered the cougar tattoo prowling the man's forearm.

"Now listen to me, son," Kurt said to the gunman. "Listen very carefully. You don't stand a chance here. There are men inside the house who are crazy. They don't care about you or this fella here. If you don't put down that shotgun real quick and give yourself up, they'll blow you into small pieces and scatter your bones in the wind. Do you understand what I'm saying?"

"Throw the pistol," the man said, guiding Chip to the dented old Buick parked next to a tack shed. "Throw the gun behind you and stand still. I shoot this *cabrón.*"

Kurt stopped and holstered the weapon. He had seen the riflemen in the windows, their scopes trained on Chip Bodine's chest. Several others were fanning out across the yard, running at a crouch, semiautomatics wagging in their hands.

"Look around you, son," Kurt said. "You don't have a prayer. Now drop your gun and kneel down nice and slow, and place your hands on top of your head. Do it while you still have time. These guys are fixing to blow your shit away."

Chip looked scared. "Stay with us, Kurt," he said. "Don't let the cowboys handle this one."

"It's okay, Chip," Kurt said. "I think your friend is a reasonable man. If he does like I say, nobody's going to get hurt."

By the time the two men reached the passenger door of the Buick a dozen barrels were sighted, focused, ready for the word. From the kitchen window came the tinny sound of a human voice filtered through a bullhorn.

"We have you surrounded," the voice said. "Put down your weapon and come forward with your hands above your head. I repeat . . ."

"Give it a rest, Staggs," Kurt said to the agent standing at the window. "The man's got my deputy as a hostage."

There was a moment of uneasy silence. The car door creaked open. The gunman shoved Chip inside and crouched down next to him, the shotgun barrel visible against Chip's throat.

"You will not be allowed to leave the premises," Staggs announced through the bullhorn. "I repeat, if you try to leave the premises you will be terminated."

"For Chrissake, Staggs," Kurt said, "knock that shit off. The guy barely speaks English."

Chip sat behind the wheel. The engine cranked, a gassy roar;

the muffler popped and clattered. There was resignation in the deputy's eyes, a sad smile wrinkling his mouth. He had been with Kurt since the beginning, ten years in the department. Poker buddies. At Bert's funeral Chip had pinned a beautiful red poppy to Kurt's lapel.

"This is your last warning," Staggs barked through the horn.

"No, goddammit!" Kurt shouted at him. "No shooting!"

The Buick's worn tires began to spin in place and the car lurched forward, peeling gravel, Chip steering the clumsy beast in a 180-degree turn. Gunfire erupted and bullets riddled the trunk, springing it open, the raised lid acting as a shield. All around the car, clods of farmland blew high in the air, a rain of loose dirt. Taillights spewed into a thousand scattered rubies. Yet the Buick bulled ahead, unslowed, cutting awkward *S* figurines across the field, plowing up dust, the tires miraculously intact. When the car reached the Emma road, it was out of firing range.

Kurt expelled the breath that burned his lungs. "Good for you, you lazy old ski bum," he said aloud.

Then he turned to Staggs. The agent stared back at him through the kitchen window, his jaw set, visibly angered that this was not going down by the book. Kurt thought about shooting him with his .45. Instead he ran for the squad car.

He caught up with them on a stretch of Highway 82 that curled alongside the tree-shrouded stream of the Roaring Fork River. The Buick's trunk lid bounced up and down with the contours of the road. Kurt kept his distance, not wanting to panic the gunman. He could see Chip's nervous eyes darting back at him from the side mirror. If the deputy handled this Buick the way he handled a snowmobile, nothing was going to stop them from reaching Aspen in twenty minutes.

"Deputy Brown, Deputy Muffin Brown," Kurt spoke into his mike. "Do you copy? We've got a code three in progress. Please come in."

Muffin was at a trailer park in Woody Creek, talking to a woman whose estranged husband had threatened to kill her and her new boyfriend with a hunting knife. She was on the highway in less than five minutes.

"Get some backup quick," Kurt said into the mike. "See if our boys can set up a roadblock somewhere around the airport. I don't want this guy anywhere near a plane."

"Where are the cowboys?" Muffin asked.

"Back at the ranch," Kurt said. "They don't have anything much faster than a Winnebago. I haven't seen them yet."

The highway lifted onto a narrow, winding terrace, a passage hewn into the dark shale wall of the valley. On the left the land fell away, an abrupt drop-off hundreds of feet to the river. The Buick's tailpipe was belching black smoke. Only a four-inch fringe of tiny aqua-blue squares clung to the rear window frame. When the trunk lid dropped with a sudden bump, Kurt could see the gunman grinning back at him, a wild expression on his face. He rested the barrel of his shotgun on top of the seat, leveling it at the sheriff's car.

"Holding course north northwest on Eighty-two," came Muffin's voice over the radio. "Triangle Peak now visible."

The trunk lid dropped again and the shotgun roared, peppering Kurt's windshield with bird shot. He jerked the wheel and swerved onto the dirt shoulder, but lost little time guiding the car back on course. This guy was beginning to piss him off. Didn't he realize Kurt was his only friend in the whole goddamned world?

As Kurt pulled closer he could see the guy laughing at him, laughing and aiming the shotgun again. If he was this insane now, just for sport, what was he going to do when they hit the roadblock?

Chip's worried eyes stared at Kurt from the side mirror. *Steady, man,* Kurt thought. *Keep your cool. You could always drive better than you could ski.*

"Damn!" crackled Muffin's voice. "Kurt, we've got company."

A huge motor thuttered somewhere over the ridge. The gunman heard it, too, and stuck his head out the window to search the sky. The rackety cadence now echoed across the hills, but Kurt couldn't locate the source. Until the Buick rounded the curve ahead.

The helicopter swooped down like a giant predatory bird, hovering eight feet above the highway, a fuming whirlwind of dust and scrub brush. Chip hit the brakes and the monster Buick locked into a slide, the chassis swinging sideways, burning rubber, a long high screech of resistance. The chopper rose effortlessly out of his way and the car disappeared beneath the skids like a stone hurled into a smoking cave. Kurt saw the vehicle emerge from the dust, dangerously close to the cliffs, and knew then that Chip couldn't pull out of the spin. The Buick crashed through the railing and sailed out over the valley. The next few seconds were suspended in an eerie windblown silence while the car traced a perfect rainbow arch into morning sunlight. It landed on its roof with a frightening boom, tires springing free, the body tumbling, tumbling, pitched high by the bouldery moraine. Kurt slammed to a stop near the drop-off and watched what was left of the Buick explode into a ball of fire.

He got out of his car and stood looking down at the burning wreckage. He thought about the poppy again. Chip had found it growing wild on the mountain. Ashes and sleep.

The chopper touched down in the middle of the highway and cut its whistling engine. Neal Staggs hopped from the cockpit with two other agents and trotted to the broken railing. Kurt was vaguely aware that someone was running toward him, calling his name. It didn't matter who. Nothing mattered anymore.

"Hey, motherfucker," he said, striding after the three agents gathered at the ledge. "Hey, Staggs, you done the wrong thing here, hoss. You fucked up my friend. Now I'm going to shoot your ass."

Staggs turned to him and glared. His cold eyes dared Kurt to come ahead. Kurt withdrew the .45 from his holster and paused to steady the grip with both hands, the way they had taught him in the army.

"Kurt!"

He was hit full force by a flying tackle that knocked him to the ground. When he got to his feet again, stunned and gasping for breath, he saw that Muffin had taken hold of the pistol's long Western nose and was pitching it over the cliff.

"Go back to your unit," she said to him, her lip bleeding from the tackle. "Go back to your unit and pull yourself together, man. It's over, okay? This one is over. There's nothing we can do."

8

AT SIX O'CLOCK THE EVENING NEWS FROM DENVER SHOWED footage of the riddled farmhouse in Emma and FBI agents examining marijuana plants growing under track lights in the cellar. Neal Staggs told a young reporter, "We're looking into the strong possibility of a tie-in between these people and at least one murder in the Aspen area." No specific mention of Omar Quiroga. The reporter signed off the story from a roadside turnout overlooking the charred wreckage of the Buick.

Kurt clicked off the television and popped another beer. He could hear Lennon playing Nintendo in his bedroom and wished to hell there was something he could do to forget his phone call to Chip's parents in Vermont. When he glanced up, Muffin was leaning against the door in the mud porch where the skis were racked, her arms folded, a look of weariness and disappointment on her face.

"Time to get out of the business," Kurt said, "when you don't hear somebody walk into your own house."

"I can't believe you're going to give the commissioners what they want," she said. "After all the grief you've taken from them for so long."

Kurt moved his foot, toppling a small construction of beer cans he'd been building for two hours. "I pulled a gun on a federal agent," he said. "I would've shot the man."

"You were stressed out of your head. Jesus, watching what happened to Chip—"

"That's the nature of the job," he said. "Grace under pressure. Get used to it. I recommended you as my replacement."

Muffin shook her head. "Libbie showed me your letter," she said. "I don't think I'm ready for it, Kurt."

He knew there would be some resentment from the other deputies in the department, all of them men, but Muffin was the best cop for the job, hands down. No one else had her discipline or training.

"You need more time to think about what you're doing," she said.

"I've had ten years to think about this fucking job and I'm sick of it," he said. "I'm sick of busting old friends for rinky-dink bullshit. I'm sick of defending the assholes with all the clout. And I'm sick of having to buddy up with psychotic bullies like Neal Staggs. Christ, lady, I don't like who I've become."

Muffin walked over, twisted a beer from its plastic ring, and took a long drink. She bent down and studied the bandage over Kurt's eye. "You probably haven't even changed the dressing today, have you?" she said.

He shrugged. It was the least of his worries.

"I hope this hurts like hell," she said, ripping off a piece of tape.

It hurt like hell. Kurt winced as she poked around the stitches. Her warm hands smelled like dispenser soap.

"Daddy's got a girlfriend, Daddy's got a girlfriend."

They both turned to see Lennon coming out of his bedroom.

"What are you two guys doing?" He grinned devilishly. "Making sex or something?"

Muffin looked at Kurt. "Cable," he explained.

She raised an eyebrow. "Go get some gauze for your father, you little delinquent."

They waited for Lennon to return from the bathroom with the box of medical supplies.

"What about Graciela Rojas?" Muffin said. "She's the one who's still missing from the FBI sound bite."

"That's your worry now, Sheriff."

"You're starting to piss me off, Muller."

Lennon raced into the room with a messy shoe box full of small stained bottles, half-opened packages, cotton balls, rolls of unidentifiable cloth. "Let me do it!" he cried. "I want to do it!"

"Why don't you tell Staggs your theory about the insurance money?" Kurt said. "It has a nasty little ring to it. But then again, it might cause some problems with his wetback conspiracy."

She dribbled hydrogen peroxide onto a cotton ball and helped Lennon wipe his father's brow. "You telling me you're not going to lift a finger to help find Dr. Rojas?" Muffin said.

Kurt winced again. The wound was stinging. "You read my letter," he said. " 'Resignation effective immediately.' "

"Dad, do you feel any better now?" Lennon asked.

Muffin dabbed away the white foam bubbling around the stitches. "All right, if that's the way you want it," she said, "I'll find the woman myself. But let me offer you some advice, Muller." She stood up and hummed the wet cotton ball at an ashtray. "Next time you're out in the middle of the night trying to impress a date, consider a cheap motel."

After supper Kurt drove to the West End to drop Lennon at the home of an old family friend. Mildred O'Carroll was a widow now and lived alone in a modest fifties bungalow that had become almost invisible in this hodgepodge neighborhood of remodeled baby Victorians and industrial-sized winter residences. She and her late husband had been the first professional filmmakers to prop cameras on their shoulders and follow pioneer hot-doggers down the rugged new snow trails of Western America. When he was a boy, Mildred

O'Carroll had a flair for riding pants and tight pullover sweaters, cut her hair like a man, and sported a silver cigarette holder. She introduced his parents to Gary Cooper. Now she could have been anybody's grandmother.

"How's my beautiful boy tonight?" Mrs. O'Carroll greeted them at the door. She gave Lennon a hug, then released him to inspect the awkward tripods and archaic movie cameras arranged about her paneled den.

"What do you hear from your mother?" she asked cheerfully.

"It's too hot in Scottsdale this time of year," Kurt said. "I wish she could come and stay awhile."

For nearly forty years Mildred O'Carroll and Hanne Muller had been best friends. They drank coffee together late in the afternoon, when shadow spilled down the mountain and the skiing was over. But now Kurt's mother lived in an artificial green suburb manufactured out of desert. 'This is your old gal, *der Ewige Jude*,' she would announce over the phone, 'the wandering Jew, calling from the Dead Sea.' Her doctors insisted that the Aspen altitude was bad for her heart, the winters too long.

"I ought to give her a call," said Mrs. O'Carroll. "I've been thinking about her. Maybe I'll go visit her after the leaves turn."

Kurt smiled. "I'm sure she'd love that," he said.

She hunted down her glasses for a better look at the bandage on Kurt's forehead. "My, my," she said, her eyes enlarged through the lenses. "Is everything okay, Kurt?"

"Of course it is." He patted her wrinkled hand, then turned to leave. "I shouldn't be out more than an hour or so."

He drove into the business district and parked his Jeep in the alley adjacent to Silvia's Diner. He noticed a tow truck slowly cruising the lantern-lit streets and stepped out to speak to the driver.

"I think you know my Jeep, Dwight," he said. "I come back and it's gone, I'm going to be very upset."

The driver gave him a Skoal-lipped, leering grin. "S'matter, Muller," he said, "have a bad day at the office?"

Tow-truck drivers circled silently through the small business district like vultures preying on fresh kill. They demanded big cash to remove a boot, threatened tourists with tire tools, shortchanged the city its cut.

"Dwight, I'm going to be honest with you. I hate tow-truck companies," Kurt said, resting his hands on the window frame. "I hate tow-truck drivers. If I had my way, you'd all be run out of town."

"What I seen on the news," Dwight said, "you'll prob'ly git run out of town 'fore I do."

Kurt gazed down the street, watching tourists huddle in front of Elvis's sports car on display at Boogie's, considering whether to cuff Dwight upside the head. He reached through the window and grabbed the man's collar. "You tow my Jeep, Dwight," he said, knotting the shirt tighter, "I'll come looking for your sleazy ass."

Silvia's Diner was located in a hideaway corner below a warren of trendy, overpriced dress shops. Hers was the only place in Aspen where county road crews ate alongside millionaire film producers. Three wooden picnic tables with counter service, unless Silvia liked you and brought out the food herself. Customers chose their drinks from an ice chest and paid by the honor system at the end of the meal.

Silvia was a tall, gregarious Chicana from southern New Mexico. She did everything—cooked, ran the register, scrubbed pans. When Kurt walked in, she was standing at the grill in the rear, speaking Spanish to the two Salvadoran girls who helped with the cooking. Her long black hair was tied back in a ponytail.

"Hello, Kurt," she said, brushing past him with two steaming plates of her incredible chile rellenos.

"I need to talk to you, Silvia."

"It's a busy night," she said, hurrying to place the plates in front of a middle-aged couple wearing a conspicuous amount of turquoise jewelry.

Kurt noticed three young Hispanic men hunched over a table next to the ice machine, eating in silence. Service workers, either cooks at another Mexican restaurant in town or condo maintenance men. They had noticed him, too, and began whispering to one another.

"Silvia," he said when she rushed past him again, "this is real important."

"I'm swamped, Kurt," she said, returning to the grill without meeting his eyes. "Maybe you should come back some other time."

He went behind the counter and took her arm. "It's important, Silvia," he said, leading her toward the back door.

One of the Salvadoran girls saw what was happening and began protesting in excited Spanish.

"Tell her it's okay," Kurt said.

Silvia said something to the girl and then allowed Kurt to lead her through the rear door to the dark disposal area out back, a nest of foul-smelling garbage cans.

"What the fuck are you doing, Kurt Muller, coming into my place like that and pushing me around?"

Silvia was wearing a soiled apron over a magenta tunic that reached her knees.

"Is there something you wanted to tell me about some friends of yours living out in Emma?"

She sighed and folded her arms across the apron. "Those people weren't hurting anybody, man," she said. Her anger was palpable. "So they were growing a little dope in their cellar. So fucking what? You had to blow them away for that?"

"We had a deal," Kurt said, pressing toward her, "and I've kept my end of the bargain. I don't hassle your people for green cards, I don't let Immigration tromp around my county looking for illegals. Otherwise half the help in this town would've disappeared a long time ago. All you had to do was let me know if they started acting like bad citizens."

"I told you I wasn't going to narc for you, man."

"I don't pop people for lids of grass. I never have, goddammit. You know that. But the Feds say those people killed that writer, Silvia. Now I want somebody to tell me what's going on."

She looked at him and laughed dryly. "You're making them

sound like Colombian drug lords," she said, "instead of dipshit *mojados* with holes in their shoes. Jesus Christ, Kurt. I've known those people three, maybe four years now and they wouldn't do something like that."

"One of them took Chip Bodine hostage and he ended up dead," he said. "He tried to blow me off the road."

"That was Guzmán," she said. "Guzmán was a little crazy. The others aren't like him. They work hard and send their money back home to mama and the *niños*. They go to Mass on Sundays. So they smoke a little dope sometimes. You ever scrub pots for a living, Kurt?"

He could see into the open kitchen door of the German restaurant across the alley. Waitresses with blond pigtails darted about dressed in dirndls.

"A federal agent was hit, Silvia. A chopper was fired on. Are you telling me Guzmán was the only one with a gun?"

Silvia sighed. "I don't know. Figure it out yourself, Kurt," she said. "Their house was surrounded by cops, a helicopter was scaring the shit out of them, and they knew if they got busted their kids would be taken away someplace and they'd all be deported. What would you do if you thought you might never see your little boy again?"

He had known Silvia for years, since she first opened her restaurant. She'd catered most of the parties in his reelection campaigns. He wondered if Silvia was the 'dear old friend' Staggs had linked to the *mojados* and their dope.

"In Mexico," she said, "if somebody pounds on your door, cops or not, you don't come out with your hands up. It's not *machismo*, man, it's survival sense. The guys outside are going to waste your ass one way or another, so you may as well go down fighting."

He could still see the woman lying facedown in the kitchen, commandos tracking through her blood. The child crying in the hallway.

"The Feds are going to pin a murder on them," he said. "Is

there anyone who'd know if that writer went out to Emma? Anyone still alive."

She thought for a long time before speaking, her tall lean silhouette facing him in the dark.

"Angel Montoya," she said finally.

"Angel Montoya?"

"He lives out there," she said in a quiet voice. "But he was here washing dishes when the shootout went down."

"Where is he now?"

"He won't talk to you, Kurt."

"Why not?"

"You killed his brother."

He felt as though the wind had been knocked out of him. "You know me better than that," he said.

He looked up at the sky. Low cloud cover, not a star in view. Last night in the Grottos the stars appeared close, stark, the Milky Way like crushed glass.

"Get him to talk to me, Silvia," he said.

"You're wasting your time."

"Tell him I'm not one of the Rambos."

Silvia untied the apron and looped it over her head. She stood there in silence, carefully folding the white cloth. "I hope to god, Kurt, you didn't have anything to do with shooting those people," she said, struggling to control her rage.

With the edge of his boot Kurt scooted a flattened aluminum can toward a barrel. "We've known each other a long time, Silvia," he said. "I don't know why you think I could do something like that."

She looked away. Everything about this conversation was slowing down, taking on added weight. "Nobody knows what to expect from you," she said. "When you first started, it was all a joke. Hippie sheriff of Aspen. Everybody had a good laugh."

Kurt rubbed his beard, remembering that first chaotic week in office. The national publicity. The cameras following him everywhere. She was right. Even *The Village Voice* had taken potshots at him.

"People talk about how the job has changed you," she said. "I guess it had to. Everything else has changed. The world's so fucking hard now. I just don't know who Kurt Muller is anymore."

He didn't know who he was now either. A man without a job. A little boy's daddy. A witness to a senseless slaughter.

He stepped toward her and tugged the sleeve of her tunic. "Tell Angel Montoya I want to talk to him," he said.

She would find out soon enough that he'd resigned. He turned and walked off down the alley. "And tell him I didn't shoot his brother."

He needed to sort things out. He needed to find a nice quiet corner to nurse a beer and brood over the pieces that wouldn't fall in place. But after tonight's news coverage he knew he couldn't walk into one of his favorite bars, Little Annie's or Shooter's or the Jerome. Too many solicitous bartenders, too many opinionated regulars. Too much cheap advice from the bottom of a bottle.

Around the corner from the pedestrian mall a pair of California developers had opened a posh restaurant, nouvelle cuisine with razor-edge decor from the L.A. art world, heartless and cold as stainless steel. Another resort investment destined to go belly up in six months. No one Kurt knew could afford to eat there.

He ordered a drink in the smoky bar and sat at a table far in the rear. These turnover places stored layers of history like ancient cities, one civilization on top of another. He could remember other names, other lives within these walls. He came here with Meg and Bert and Maya in the days when folksingers used capos and sat on stools.

The waitress didn't recognize him. Only one party was waiting for dinner, three glamorous young couples straight out of a Michelob commercial. They were occupied with appearances and the sound of their own sparkling laughter. Kurt drank his designer beer slowly and thought about Quiroga and Graciela Rojas. He had to find out what had happened to them. He figured he had another twenty hours of grace before the commissioners accepted his resignation and people stopped giving him the time of day.

At a pay phone outside the men's room he dialed Jake Pfeil's number. He couldn't recall the last time he'd spoken to Jake without a lawyer present. Now Jake was the only person in town who could help him.

"This is Gordon, darling," Kurt said when the answering service picked up. Jake was always meeting with guys named Gordon. "I'm supposed to have dinner with Jake tonight but I've forgotten which restaurant. Was it Abetone's?"

He knew Jake dined out every night, a rotation of Aspen's finest restaurants.

"I'm sorry, sir, I can't give out that information."

"Be a dear and tell me, hon. He's going to hate me if I'm late again."

"I'm sorry, sir. If you leave your number, I can have him call you when he checks in."

"Was it Primavera?"

"I can beep him if it's an emergency."

"Yes, of course it's an emergency, darling. I'm late for dinner."

"Please give me your number and I'll let him know you're trying to reach him."

Kurt found another quarter in his jeans and rang Mrs. O'Carroll to tell her he might be later than he thought.

"No bother. Take your time. Everything's fine here," she said. "We're making fudge brownies."

"Oh, lord," Kurt said. "Please don't let him have more than one. He'll start climbing your walls."

He ordered coffee and waited at a table near the telephone. Twenty minutes, thirty. The call never came. He decided to go find Jake Pfeil the hard way.

Among his many real estate holdings Jake owned the Blake Building, an entire block of downtown Aspen he had purchased a decade ago and converted into bars and boutiques. The penthouse suites on the upper floor rented for four thousand dollars a night during ski season. Kurt walked two blocks to the Blake's apartment entrance and pushed the button marked *Pfeil*. No one answered the intercom. He crossed the street and leaned against the brass railing in front of the Hard Rock Cafe, determined to wait him out. After a few moments a teenage girl wearing a tie-dyed T-shirt banged out of the café, looked around, then hurried over to Kurt. "Are you Dweezer's dad?" she asked, her teeth a sprocket of silver braces. "He said to tell you he's still not finished with his milkshake but he can find his way back to the condo by himself."

"I think you want one of those guys over there," Kurt said, nodding at a couple of fathers waiting impatiently against a brick wall.

He had never imagined he would end up this way, a middle-aged man mistaken for someone's cranky dad. He could envision himself in ten years, killing time out here with the other frustrated parents: 'Lennon said to tell you to stop acting like a fat cop on a half-ass stakeout and go home. You're embarrassing him.'

He listened to Hendrix sing "All Along the Watchtower" on the café speakers and remembered when this place was the Elks Lodge, a spare, dim-lit hall where old codgers played dominoes at long cafeteria tables. The Blake Building across the street had been abandoned for years, a beehive of squalid rooms before some wealthy patron fashioned them into artist's studios for a handful of New York renegades in the late sixties. Kurt had crashed one of their parties the night before he went off to boot camp. A painter named Rosenquist was spraying antiwar graffiti on the Sheetrock walls while a strange, messy-haired Yugoslav wrapped the old wood banisters with cellophane. Kurt's friends found him sleeping in the Hyman Street fountain the next morning and dragged him to the army bus.

A turnstile of parents came outside to smoke, bitched about the music, returned to argue with their kids. One guy began to reveal the painful details of his custody battle back in Atlanta. Kurt left his post and moved closer to the Esprit shop to get away from these people. After an hour of this he was ready to give up his son for adoption.

Around ten o'clock Jake appeared on Galena Street with his entourage. Kurt watched them saunter toward the Blake, a boisterous band of revelers walking arm in arm. One of the laughing women draped herself around Jake as he applied his magnetic card to the double doors. This was obviously not a good time to question Jake. But then, it was never a good time to question Jake Pfeil.

After the group had disappeared into the suites, Kurt went around to the alley and found the fire escape up the side of the building. At the top landing he looked off across the flat roofs of the original town, that miner settlement called Ute City, and watched an ATV's single light bounce along the dark slope of Ajax, a crewman for the Mountain Association making his rounds. Kurt knew those ruts and ridges and shadowy formations the way someone might know the body of an old and familiar lover in the night. The surface was as immutable now as the face of the moon.

He preferred to believe that the mountain itself had brought his father and Rudi Pfeil together, but in reality it was the industrialist Jacob Rumpf who had bought up this obscure little ghost town as a getaway diversion after the war and convinced his two friends to come out from Chicago and help him transform the place into a classical European notion of Utopia. In Austria, and later at the University of Chicago, Kurt's father had been a professor of music and an aspiring composer, and with Rumpf's financial backing he created the Aspen symphony, the artist retreats, the literary festivals. Rudi Pfeil was an experienced ski instructor who knew how to groom a slope, where to run cable for a lift, what kind of gear to stock in the shops. For a dozen years the three men and their families were dearest friends. But when Jacob Rumpf died in 1962 there was a fierce and unexpected struggle for control of their corporation, and the family friendship quickly disintegrated into a rubble of backstabbing, rash accusations, and costly lawsuits.

Kurt crossed the crunchy gravel toward a rooftop patio, an umbrella table with garden chairs, and stood before a sliding glass door that looked in on a horseshoe-shaped sitting area with more cushions than a sultan's palace. There was a murmur of conversation somewhere inside, sudden laughter. He recognized the theatrical trilling of the woman draped around Jake's neck. When he tried the latch, the door slid open. Foolish man, he thought. Still living in the Aspen of yesteryear, when no one locked their doors.

He passed through the sitting area and down carpeted steps to a bedroom where purses and handbags had been left on an immense circular bed. The suite had that unmistakable smell of newness: strong wood polish, synthetic fabric, drapes fresh from a box. Jake lived here only four months a year.

Light wedged into the dark room from a door ajar and Kurt was drawn to the opening with a reckless curiosity, his movement quiet and swift. In the next room Jake knelt over a silver coffee tray, cutting rails of cocaine with a razor blade. His friends were lounging around him on the floor, exchanging witty remarks and tittering at one another's observations.

"So much better for the cholesterol than cheesecake," said a balding man with a Florida tan.

Kurt stepped back into the shadows, trying to remember when he'd first realized that the kid next door had become a drug dealer.

Back in the mid-sixties Jake had gone to UCLA on a football scholarship but tore up his shoulder the first season and dropped out of school. No one knew where he was for two years, until he started sending postcards from Morocco. When Kurt returned home from the army in 1970, he learned that Jake had set down stakes somewhere in Mexico and was living off the harvest of the land. Then one day, a few months after Kurt took a job managing an outfitter store, Jake wandered in looking for camping gear.

'Well, well,' Jake said. 'The hero is home from the war.'

Kurt didn't recognize him at first. Jake was wearing a soiled poncho and worn-out huaraches, and his hair was long and stringy, his sunburned face disguised by a Fu Manchu mustache.

'I was in Germany,' Kurt told him. 'Bert was the one in Nam.'

'Mighty white of Uncle Sam not to send you both,' Jake said.

They talked for a while about the war, about music. They avoided any mention of their fathers.

'How's my favorite receiver?' Jake asked. 'He back in one piece?'

Jake and Bert had been the best pass-and-catch combination in the history of Aspen High football, and Jake still owned the passing stats in the Valley.

'You ought to go say hello,' Kurt said. 'He's working at the electroplate shop on Hunter.'

That evening the two brothers had a good laugh about Jake's change in appearance. 'He's dealing, you know,' Bert said.

'Come on. Jake?'

'He's tied in to some kind of Michoacán pipeline. He asked if I wanted to be his connection in the Valley. He promised it would be a more liquid career than making leaf necklaces.' Bert laughed. 'In two years I'll have my own penthouse with a private pool.'

'What did you tell him?' Kurt asked.

'Does it come with a lava lamp?'

And now, two decades later, Kurt was fairly certain that their old chum had been involved in a murder. The Chad Erickson hit. Kurt wasn't able to prove it, of course, but Jake was where all the arrows pointed. His longtime business associate had decided to roll over for the Feds.

Kurt noticed something on a dresser and went over to examine it. He lofted a small gold football trophy inscribed DISTRICT CHAMPIONS, 1964. His own had disappeared years ago, probably in one of those charity sales his mother was so fond of. He touched the jagged place where the player's stiff-arm had broken off.

No Aspen team in thirty years had equaled their 11–1 record. Kurt had played defensive end that season, the only sophomore starter. Jake led them all the way to the regional 2A playoffs, where they lost a close one to the farmboys in Delta.

The door opened and a young woman wobbled into the bedroom, her arms outstretched in front of her, warding off the darkness. "Oh," she said, startled by Kurt's presence. She was wearing a black spaghetti-strap dress as flimsy as a slip. "I'm looking for the little girls' room."

"That must be it there," Kurt pointed to a door near the bed.

The woman took several uncertain steps on stiletto heels, then paused. "You a friend of Jake's?" she asked.

"Yeah," Kurt said. "We've known each other since we were kids."

"Oh, reeeally," she cooed, as though he'd just told her a heart-warming story about a found puppy. "I love that," she said, leaving the door open while she peed.

He watched her at the mirror. She was a stunning young woman, blond hair snarled in a fashionable mess, skin like ice cream. With a small wand she applied a rich red gloss across her top lip and then worked her mouth.

"Were you at dinner?" she asked, catching Kurt's eyes in the mirror.

"No," he said.

"I didn't think so," she said. Her teeth were grinding from the cocaine. "I would have noticed."

She turned and walked toward him, her pretty green eyes jittering wildly, showing a dark curiosity about the bandage on his brow. She grasped his beard with both hands and pulled his face down to hers. Her mouth tasted like pâté and lipstick and something sour. The spaghetti straps fell off her shoulders and the dress loosened in front, revealing small girlish nipples, pink as evening primroses and erect. She kissed him with a thinly veiled hostility, biting at his lip, chewing him. He wasn't enjoying this and took hold of her wrists.

"A little too rough for you, baby?" she asked. Hairs from his beard curled in her open palms.

"Do me a favor, darling," he said, leading her to the door. "Go tell Jake his old friend wants to speak with him in private."

He sat down in a reading chair in a corner of the bedroom. On the lampstand Jake kept a framed photograph of Jacob Rumpf with his faithful lieutenants, Rudi Pfeil and Otto Muller. The three friends were standing halfway up Ajax on skis as long as rails, their arms around one another, smiling triumphantly. Somewhere in a trunk Kurt still had that silly knit hat his father always wore when he skied. He looked so damned young and happy back then. It was hard to believe that all three men were dead.

"Well, little brother, you just about got yourself shot."

Jake Pfeil stepped into the room and tossed a small pistol onto the bed next to the purses.

"I'm going to have my lawyer here in five minutes, Muller," he said, lifting a portable phone to his ear. "You got some kind of search warrant or court order, friend, you talk it over with him."

"Relax, Jake," Kurt said. "Put down the phone. I'm not here to bust you. I'm not even a cop anymore."

Jake looked at him, the receiver still in his hand. "I guess I should have shot you, then."

A large square-shouldered profile appeared in the doorway, blocking out most of the light. "Everything okay, boss?" the man asked.

"Sure, Rusty. Tell my guests I'll only be a minute."

After the man left, Kurt held up the photograph. "I don't think I've ever seen this one before," he said.

"You like it, I'll have one framed for you," Jake said.

He was wearing a summer-weight dinner jacket, Italian cut, with a tieless black silk shirt buttoned at the neck. Long vanished were the days of the Mexican poncho and patched jeans.

"What happened to the badge?" Jake asked.

"A misunderstanding with some old friends of yours, the Feds. But it doesn't matter, I never was worth a damn as a cop, anyway. If I had been," Kurt said, "your ass would be in jail right now."

Jake shoved aside a woman's shawl and sat on the edge of the bed. "You know, someday, little brother, we're gonna have to get over all this shit between us," he said.

For a man blown on coke he seemed amazingly relaxed, reflective.

"Not real soon," Kurt said. "I'm just starting to enjoy it."

"Anger's a waste of time, man. Don't let it own you."

"I'm not angry anymore, Jake."

"Sure you are. You're so angry and bitter you won't even acknowledge what's eating you alive."

"I'm only human," Kurt said. "I don't like it when somebody gets away with murder."

Jake shook his head slowly. "I'm talking about Bert," he said.

They hadn't exchanged a word about Bert's death in the four years since the fall. Real estate investments, yes. Business arrangements, property holdings, Jake's whereabouts on the day Erickson was killed. But never Bert. Not one word. Kurt didn't even send Jake a thank-you card for the wreath.

"I didn't come here to talk about Bert," he said.

"I'm sure you have a good reason for breaking into my apartment, little brother."

Kurt stood up and went to the window. Down below, at the tables of a sidewalk café, a quintet of summer music students played for passersby. Cello, violin, woodwinds. Teenage prodigies, two of them Asian girls with faces as delicate as paper masks. Kurt's father had started all of this forty summers ago.

"Last night you were at Andre's with a young woman," he said, peering down at the busy foot traffic. "Italian girl, I think. Who was she?"

"I thought you were giving up the cop business."

"This is personal," Kurt said.

Jake was silent for a few moments. "She's not your type," he said. "You'd have to spend a lot more time on your wardrobe."

"I don't want to share her fluids, Jake. I just want to talk to her."

Jake smiled, deliberating with himself. Kurt knew he was on delicate ground. Everything depended on whether Jake was in a generous mood.

"I don't know much about her. I met her at the Nordic Club," Jake said. "She's just another spoiled college girl. Her family has a place here somewhere." He snorted and cleared his throat. "But she's a kinky little bitch, I'll say that for her. Likes to tie up her date and slap."

Kurt watched a father walking hand in hand with his son. They stopped to look in the window of a camping-gear store. Kurt glanced at his watch and realized it was long past Lennon's bedtime. "She hangs out at the club?" he asked.

"Try the weight room," Jake said. "That's where I met her. She breaks a nice sweat at the Cybex machines."

A loud chorus of laughter erupted in the living room. Someone was telling a humorous story.

"I've got to get back to my party. I'm sure you can find your own way out."

"Jake . . ."

Jake picked up the pistol on the bed and slid it into his jacket pocket.

"He broke the first commandment of climbing," Kurt said. "He went up there alone."

He hadn't said these words aloud before. Not to anyone.

"You've got to put it behind you, little brother."

Kurt had no idea why he was saying these things to Jake Pfeil. "He was the best fucking climber in the Valley," he said. "He never made mistakes."

Jake looked at him. "It only took one."

They regarded each other, a long calibration of the years. Kurt had known him forever. He couldn't remember a time before Jake. There was so much between them, some of it good, most of it very bad.

"Jake, darling, what's keeping you so long?" a woman said from the door. "We're starting a game of charades."

9

A S HE MADE HIS WAY DOWN THE ALLEY TOWARD HIS JEEP, Kurt looked up at the dark mountain and thought again that he'd like to take Lennon away from this narrow valley and the rock walls that hemmed their lives into a remote and claustrophobic corner of earth. There was no reason to stay here anymore. His wife had left him. His family was gone. The handful of friends with the same shared history had drifted somewhere into America. Only the job had kept him here, a stretch of years past common sense, and now that was over and done with too.

When he grabbed the door handle a gun went off near the Dumpster and the bullet struck the Jeep, a jolt like an electric shock up his arm. He dropped to his belly and rolled, and another bullet tore out a chunk of ground, splattering dirt in his hair. He scrambled to the far side of the Jeep and reached under the seat for the .45, then remembered Muffin had flung it over a cliff. In an instant he saw Lennon sitting on his bed in somebody else's home, looking at old photographs of his father and trying to recall the sound of his voice, the feel of his beard.

He raised up slowly and saw a dark figure dashing across a parking lot toward the center of town. *Who the hell is after* me? he wondered.

Promenading tourists scattered from the sidewalk when they saw Kurt's 220 pounds lumbering toward them. The only one who didn't stop to stare was the running man, the dark-haired shooter racing past the art galleries and bars, a youthful build on short swift legs.

"Everybody down!" Kurt commanded. "Out of the way, goddammit! Get down!"

What are you doing, you dumb son of a bitch? he thought. *Still acting like somebody with a badge? You don't even have a weapon.*

When he rounded the corner at the Esprit shop he knocked down an elderly man videotaping his wife as she passed by in a horse-drawn stagecoach. Kurt picked him up, brushed off his backside, and apologized. The old gentleman showed more concern for his camera.

"Hey, Fagan!" Kurt called out to the coach driver, a weathered local wearing leather chaps and a sweat-stained Stetson. "You see somebody running?"

"Mexican?" Fagan mumbled through his drooping mustache. Kurt shrugged.

"Pool hall," Fagan nodded.

Kurt jogged across the street and stopped at the door that led downstairs into the pool hall. He took a deep breath and tried to compose himself. He was very angry and very scared and his legs were shaking. He gave a second thought to finding a phone and calling the city police, but that would take too much time.

The place was crowded with young Hispanic men, as it had been every night these past few years, since the flood of migrant workers. Kurt had always liked the old cellar. When he came home from the army this was where he hung out, drinking hard, shooting pool all afternoon with Bert and Zack, a peculiar restful silence between them, not another soul at the tables.

He walked casually to the bar, where Thurman Fisher was arguing with two stool customers about a baseball game on the overhead TV set. A tall, potbellied man with wire-rim glasses and a salt-and-pepper beard, Thurman had owned this pool hall for almost thirty years, this and a small corner grocery store he'd sold off when the new supermarket stole all of his business. Kurt had gone to school with his daughter and was there when she'd drowned in a kayak accident on the Colorado.

Thurman lifted a glass from a long gleaming row and set it on the bar near Kurt's sleeve. "Braves are ahead seven–three," he said. "Draft all right?"

Kurt rested against the walnut casing and eyed the pool shooters, more than a dozen of them. "A Mexican just ran in here," he said. The place had grown quiet the moment he'd stepped down the stairs. "Which one was it?"

"Been following the game," Thurman said.

Every face had turned to study Kurt. Short, dark, tattooed men wearing sleeveless shirts, their arms thick from fieldwork.

"The guy's carrying a gun, Thurman," Kurt said. "He tried to kill me."

Thurman placed both hands on the bartop and looked out at the players. "Lord," he said calmly. "You sure he came in here?"

"Somebody saw him."

Thurman was good to these people. He let them shoot for free before the paying customers arrived for the evening.

Kurt leaned over. "I don't have a weapon, Thurman," he said in a quiet voice.

"You want me to call for some backup?"

"No," Kurt said, "there's no time. You're going to be my backup."

He pushed off from the bar and walked directly toward the tables. At the first one a surly young *vato* with a scrawny mustache and goatee pulled away from the cue ball and straightened himself, waiting. His partners stared at Kurt, their eyes narrowed in hatred. He knew what they were thinking. *This* pendejo *blew away our friends.* Kurt passed each one slowly, cautiously, looking them over to see who was breathing hard from a run. An older, barrel-chested man with his shirttail hanging free, sleeves rolled back, the shirt unbuttoned and open wide, stood powdering his stick, the up-and-down motion of his hand an obscene gesture of contempt. Kurt stopped in front of him to read the words *Más Mota* on his T-shirt.

"Did somebody here want to say something to me?" Kurt asked loudly.

He could hear the rustle of shoes behind him and turned to face down three youths who'd moved in close, their pool cues gripped like sabers.

"Well?" Kurt said. "One of you boys want another shot at me?"

He was surrounded now, a dozen bodies edging toward him. He glanced over at Thurman. He knew the old fellow kept a .38 Special under the bar right where he was standing.

"What you want from us?" said the older man powdering his stick. His face was pitted from an ancient bout with acne. "We don' make no trouble."

"I want the guy who just tried to kill me," Kurt said. "You got any idea who that might be?"

The man shrugged. "Some crazy Colombian," he said.

His companions laughed.

Kurt waited. He could see this was going to take more persuasion. "I'm looking for Angel Montoya," he said.

The man shrugged again. "Never heard this name," he said.

His companions mumbled. No one here had ever heard of Angel Montoya.

"His brother was killed in Emma today. And two of his friends. I want to know why."

One of the players said something in Spanish. The young *vato* with the goatee spat on the floor.

Kurt took a step toward him. "How 'bout you, hotshot?" he said. "There something you want to tell me?"

The young man didn't flinch. His butt was braced against the table's cushion, his hands wrapped around the slender neck of the cue.

"I'm listening," Kurt said.

Bodies shifted again, moved in tight. He was beginning to feel crowded. Out of the corner of his eye he saw Thurman slip the .38 onto the bar.

"Your name Montoya?" he asked the young man.

Footsteps rumbled down the stairwell and two uniformed Aspen policemen hurried into the bar, their hands secured over their holsters. Kurt knew them both, a rookie from Durango and a guy named Magnuson who sometimes joined the poker group.

"Any trouble in here?" Magnuson asked Thurman Fisher. "We got a report some guy's running around the streets with a gun."

Then he noticed Kurt. "Muller!" he said. "What's going on?"

The pool shooters had backed off as soon as they saw the uniforms. But not the guy with the goatee. He held his ground, the long slender cue locked in his hand.

"Just shooting a little stick with the boys," Kurt said.

He snatched the cue from the young man and bent over the table. "What's going on with you, Mike?"

"Some fucker's out scaring the tourists tonight. Knocked down an old man in the street."

"If I see him," Kurt said, popping the five ball in a corner pocket, "I'll tell him to turn himself in."

Magnuson laughed. "What a fucking town!" he said. "It's still like Dodge City around here sometimes."

He and the rookie sat down at the bar and ordered Cokes. Soon they were arguing with Thurman Fisher about the pennant standings.

Kurt dropped another ball with a nice soft touch and handed the stick back to the *vato*. "Tell Angel Montoya I want to talk to him," he said in a quiet voice. "Tell him I know who killed his brother."

10

THE NEXT MORNING, AFTER TAKING LENNON TO DAY CARE, Kurt drove to the Hickory House for breakfast. In his youth the log café had been a locals' favorite because of its mom-and-pop friendliness and truck-stop menu. Those were the years when men rose early to cut wood and a handful of miners still worked the old shafts. But now the café catered to budget skiers lodging in this low-rent side of town, and to a dwindling number of old-timers who still preferred their toast white, their yolks running into the hash browns.

Kurt picked up a copy of the *Aspen Daily News* outside the door and requested the darkest corner of the smoking section. The Hickory House was the only restaurant in town that still tolerated smokers, but he knew the section would be empty.

The newspaper skewered him. A self-righteous intern reporter from some Ivy League school had been critical of the sheriff's office for an entire year now, and he really went after Kurt on this one. 'Uncooperative with FBI agents, who eventually broke the murder case on their own.' 'Apparently unaware of a major drug-trafficking operation in Pitkin County.' By the time Kurt came to 'a question of bad judgment in the handling of the escape attempt, which resulted in the death of Deputy Chip Bodine' and 'possible impropri-ety with regard to a missing witness in the homicide investigation,' he was ready to shove the little bastard's nose in his omelette.

"You don't look too happy this morning."

Muffin sat down at his table. He hated the idea that she knew where to find him.

"It puts me in a nasty humor," Kurt said, "to learn from a newspaper that my professional conduct is in question."

Muffin looked as though she hadn't slept all night. Dark rings surrounded her eyes—a glimpse of her in five years, when the job would finally rob her tomboy charm.

"I don't know where that little prick got his information," she said. "When he talked to me I told him you've always been squeaky clean, and that I know you did your best."

Kurt folded the newspaper and dropped it in an empty chair. "You make me feel so appreciated," he said.

He knew that Muffin's flashpoint lay just below the skin. This morning she seemed capable of biting through her lip.

"They want an internal investigation," she said, removing her sheriff's department cap and shaking out her thick brown hair. "I'm getting a lot of pressure, Kurt. It isn't my idea."

"The commissioners?"

"The commissioners, the mayor, the Tourist Bureau." She let out a deep breath, picked up his cup, sipped coffee. "And Neal Staggs."

Kurt pushed aside the plate. "What does Staggs want?" he asked, hearing the resentment in his voice.

"It's hard to say. I know he's glad you're out," she said. "He's making noises he might be mounting his own criminal investigation of your terms in office."

Kurt laughed darkly. "Let the bastard dig through my sock drawer. I don't have anything to hide."

Muffin rocked back on the chair's hind legs and cocked a cow-boy boot over her knee. "I've been doing some more calling around on the Rojas case," she said, her eyes avoiding Kurt's. "I found out her husband is an attorney, and that he's been in San Francisco for some kind of political conference."

Kurt could see that she was uneasy about what she was going to say. But determined nonetheless.

"Last night I finally got in touch with one of his associates at the conference," she said. "He told me that Rojas checked out early, without saying good-bye."

She raised her eyes and looked at Kurt. "He thought the man might be joining his wife in Colorado."

Kurt made a steeple of his fingers and brought them slowly to his lips.

"Kurt," Muffin said, "there are some things here you're gonna have to face."

"You know, Brown," he said calmly, "I'm curious how you and your new friend Neal Staggs are working this one out together. He thinks Omar Quiroga was killed by Mexican drug traffickers, and you think he was killed by Graciela—and her husband. So tell me, dear. Who is it *I'm* working for? A bunch of fry cooks from Chihuahua, or a doctor-and-lawyer assassin squad from Argentina?"

Muffin's face colored. "I don't believe that crap about the wetbacks any more than you do."

Kurt chewed at a piece of brittle toast. "Somebody tried to kill me last night," he said. "My guess is it was some pissed-off young fool who heard that men wearing badges shot up his brother. And now he figures it's payback time. Better watch your backside today, Officer."

"Telephone!" Doris the cashier, a middle-aged woman with bad teeth and the rough features of a ranch wife, signaled from the register. "It's your dispatcher."

Kurt and Muffin both slid back their chairs. They looked at each other, and Kurt almost smiled. "Sorry," he said. "Go ahead."

In a few moments Muffin returned to the table. "Come take a ride with me," she said. "They've found something up near Weller Lake."

* * *

A mile downstream from the Grottos, two mountain bikers had stopped to soak their feet and saw the twist of clothing on the sandy embankment under a footbridge. They probed at the bundle with a stick, and when they discovered the blood, one of them bicycled into town to inform the sheriff's department.

Kurt recognized the Guatemalan sweater. Mud-dried, ripped at the shoulder seam, a long smear of dark blood down the front.

"It's hers," he said.

Muffin refused to look at him. She left the sweater where it lay and crouched down, searching the shadows beneath the bridge.

Kurt knew now that there was no hope of finding her alive. And no one was to blame but himself.

"You ought to get some men up here to cover the area," he said.

"The sweater's dry," Muffin said. "It hasn't been in the water since yesterday afternoon."

Kurt began to wander downstream, his eyes fixed on the gushing snowmelt waters of the Roaring Fork River. He was willing to walk fifty miles over broken stone to find her body.

"Look where it is, Kurt!" Muffin called after him. "The river didn't wash it up. Somebody wanted us to find this thing."

He turned and shouted back at her. "Do your job, Brown!" he said. "Get some people up here to help comb the area."

"Where are you going?" she yelled.

He followed the river, the white rushing stream so loud no human voice could distract now. Water crashed around sand-colored boulders, eddied quickly, and flowed on. There was an occasional branch to watch, its swift projectile movement the only true measure of the current, how everything was displaced moment after moment and then gone. When he finally realized how far he'd walked, and how much time had lapsed, he sat down on a smooth flat shelf of rock near the riverbank and tried to collect his thoughts. He felt tired. He hadn't slept much these past few nights, and now, in the aftershock of the bloody sweater, his body ached for rest.

He found himself thinking about Meg, about a particular

black Mexican shawl she had worn over her bare shoulders one summer evening when they'd first met, nearly twenty years ago. He had a photograph of them sitting together in a booth at the Red Onion, her long wavy auburn hair falling across the dark shawl.

Graciela was right, he thought. It was tragic how old loves vanished from your life. You always believed you would see them again, in some distant city, on the street perhaps, a chance encounter, and forgive one another, embrace, and move on.

When Meg left Lennon at Kurt's office that morning and then disappeared, it was not cruelty, he knew, but an act of desperation. He knew, without a word exchanged, that something awful had happened in her life to make her give up the little boy she loved so much. He had lost her years ago, in the slow erosion of their love, and now Lennon had lost her too. The world was fast becoming a vague and troublesome place adrift with missing souls.

Kurt had no idea how long he'd been sitting there, mesmerized by the water. He stood up and dusted off the seat of his pants. There was little chance of stumbling upon her body in this vast wilderness; the search was more than one man could undertake. If the river had her, it would give her up in its own sweet time.

Defeated, he made his way back upriver, following a trail through the tall firs. As he reached sight of the footbridge he noticed a huddle of cops off in the brush, about thirty yards from the water. Three uniformed deputies were circled around something on the ground. Muffin was talking to a man in a gray suit. When Kurt drew closer he realized that the man was Neal Staggs.

"Kurt!" Muffin said, breaking from the group. She looked worried. "Where the hell have you been? We found your jacket."

Wearing surgical gloves, a deputy named Dave Stuber knelt over a dark bulky mass, trying to scoot it into a large garbage bag. It was Kurt's brown leather jacket, crusty and stiff as a run-over dog on a country road.

"My my," Kurt said. "Somebody must be planting an entire wardrobe out here."

Staggs was regarding him with that familiar sneer, the same

one Kurt had seen through a swirl of helicopter dust out on Highway 82. He clenched his fists so hard his thumbnails throbbed.

"Come over here," Muffin said, taking his arm. "I need to talk to you."

"What the hell is he doing here?"

"Come on," she ordered, maneuvering him away from the cops.

When they were near the bridge she said, "Keep walking, Kurt. Go on home. I'll call you in a couple of hours."

"Did you radio that son of a bitch?"

"He's got a stake in this thing, Kurt. What's happened to the Argentines is turning into a major diplomacy problem."

Kurt looked over her head at Staggs. "Don't trust that reptile," he said. "He's got his own agenda."

"Staggs wants you pulled in for questioning on the Rojas disappearance," Muffin said. "He's not buying your story about what happened at the Grottos."

"Tell him to go fuck himself," he said loud enough for the agent to hear.

"He wants me to bring you in for a peaceful low-intensity interrogation. You know the line," she said with a cynical lift to the eyebrow. " 'In the spirit of cooperation between law-enforcement colleagues.' "

"They're getting desperate."

"He wants it to happen today," she said.

Kurt thought about walking over and popping Staggs in the face. "What if I say no?"

"Don't do that to me, Kurt."

Staggs was watching them, hands in his pants pockets, a spiteful, vindictive man whose career depended on a personal affinity for quick judgment and condemnation. The kind of man Kurt had come to know and despise in the army.

"Just tell me one thing, Muffin." He paused to study her vexed face. "What do *you* believe? That Graciela's sitting in a hot tub somewhere, sipping a nice umbrella drink with her husband?"

Her face revealed nothing. "Go on home and wait for my call," she said. A hint of the intimacy that had once passed between them surfaced in her voice. "This thing here may take a while, and I don't want you two anywhere near each other."

"You don't have to become one of the suits, Muffin."

"Go on," she said, giving him a push. "I'll call."

Kurt knew he was running out of time. If he was going to find out what had happened to Graciela Rojas, he had to do it now. He had to talk to the girl.

He drove to the Nordic Club, a massive fitness facility that hosted a nationally televised tennis tournament every spring and served as the local celebrity set's off-season playground. Kurt parked his Jeep a few spaces from where Chad Erickson had spit out his brains. Any other car bomb, there would have been a permanent scorch mark on the concrete. Whoever had rigged the Jaguar had shown an admirable appreciation for ecology.

Kurt couldn't afford a club pass, not on his salary, but he was on friendly terms with all the silky tan, blond young goddesses who worked the front desk and they looked the other way when he dropped in to use the weights or play a little racquetball. This morning, though, a Finnish girl named Marta seemed troubled by his arrival and he wondered if the newspaper article had anything to do with her hesitation to let him through. He decided to ignore her dark looks and press on. He was halfway down the corridor to the juice bar when he heard her call his name, but he kept walking.

The long hike to the weight rooms was a passage through the oily, camphor-thick circles of athletic hell. Along the way Kurt liked to stop and observe the hard bodies undergoing their grim and torturous regimen and guess which ones would outlive their strokes. But today he was in a hurry.

He found the young woman exactly where Jake had said she'd be, straining through a series of pectoral exercises at a Cybex machine. She looked sexy as hell in her gray sleeveless cotton T-shirt and metallic blue spandex tights. There was a small enticing crescent of perspiration on the T-shirt just below her lovely damp neck. Sweat beaded her face and the dark freckles on her shoulders.

If she knew who he was, if someone had pointed him out as the sheriff or she recognized him from a newspaper photo, this was not going to work. He carried his gym bag into the men's dressing room and slipped into his sweats. He asked the Hispanic attendant for shaving cream and a razor. He had wanted to do this for a long time, two or three years, but there had never been the right moment, or an adequate explanation to Lennon, to make such a drastic change in his appearance.

"Many years?" asked the bemused attendant, making a stroking gesture at his chin. Kurt thought he recognized the young man from the pool hall last night.

"Since before you were born."

The attendant watched him shave off twenty-two years of personal biology. When Kurt was finished he apologized for the mess in the sink.

"S'okay," shrugged the attendant. "I will bring the fire hose."

Kurt splashed on burning after-shave and stared at the face in the mirror. There was a strange man peering back at him, partly his father, partly the lad he'd been in the army. What surprised him most was how closely he resembled Bert, the strong jawline and diminished upper lip. He'd forgotten that when they were kids, people used to mistake them for twins.

"All riiight," he said aloud, turning his head from side to side. He looked ten years younger. Something that might count with a woman half his age.

When he came out of the dressing room the young woman was lying on her back, knees locked down, struggling through bench presses in the free weight area. A half-dozen musclebound college boys with short retro hair had positioned themselves near her to watch and be noticed. Kurt walked over and looked down at her beautiful wet face.

"If you don't mind me saying so, miss, I think you'd get a lot more tone—and probably do less harm to your muscle tissue—if you'd drop down about ten pounds on those weights," he said. "It's not about how much, but how steady. . . . Rhythm is everything."

He gave the kid at the next bench a get-lost nod, and the boy moved on without complaint. Kurt removed his shirt and began to add twenty-pound weights to the bar. He had to attract her attention somehow and suspected she wouldn't be particularly interested in his brains.

Out of the corner of his eye he saw that she had stopped to watch him. A couple of the college boys were watching him too. Nobody had walked into the room this summer and stacked that much weight on a bar, but Kurt had been a weightlifter since the days of the Charles Atlas ads in comic books. There were years at a time when he'd let his body go, but when Meg took Lennon and walked out on him he had felt so angry and depressed he found his way back to the gym as a pressure release.

After he'd performed enough bench presses to stun an Olympic coach, he took a break to wipe himself down. The young woman was sitting up now, daubing her neck with a towel, smiling at him, intrigued. Vanity attracted her. She was perfect for Jake Pfeil.

"You look very familiar," Kurt said to her, his throat parched from the workout. "Didn't we meet the other night at Andre's?"

"I don't recall," she said with a slight accent.

"Weren't you there with Jake?"

Her pretty face toyed with memory. "I'm afraid I don't recall speaking to you," she said. "Were you with someone?"

Kurt stood up, the towel over his bare shoulder. "I was alone," he said.

The sweat stain on her T-shirt was larger now, dipping closer to her breasts. "Are you an instructor here?" she asked.

"I do private consultation."

"Ahh," she said, a tiny smile at the corner of her mouth. "I thought as much. What you said is no doubt true. Rhythm is everything. I'm looking for someone who can coach me."

Her eyes were all over him, a bicep, a thigh.

"Do you live here?" he asked.

The question seemed to surprise her. "My father has a home here," she said. "I am here for the summer."

"That's enough time."

She smiled and pushed a strand of dark hair from her eyes. "Are you expensive?" she asked.

"Depends on what you want."

She looped the towel around her neck and rose, her eyes still dancing over his body. "I want the most advanced course," she said.

"That can be arranged."

He could see that she enjoyed this kind of play. "Come with me," she said, patting perspiration from her cheek. "I am late to meet my father at the courts. On the way we can discuss the terms of"—she paused—"our arrangement."

"I don't think I want to meet your father," Kurt said.

She smiled and bent over to get her things. "Don't worry," she said. "It's not a wedding I have in mind."

As they walked along the observation deck high above the tennis courts, she told him her name was Cecilia Rostagno and that she was a college student in Miami.

"Rostagno," he said. "Are you Italian?"

"Yes," she said. "My father is a diplomat. We have lived all over the world."

They stopped to watch her father's match on the court below. He was a slender, silver-haired man around sixty, with a devastating tan. His legs were muscular and youthful, and he had an impressive serve. He was playing Bob Graeber, the club's owner.

"There is a party tonight at our home in Starwood," she said, her forearms resting on the railing. Her face was still radiantly flushed from the workout, and Kurt saw why Jake found her so appealing. "Will you come?" she asked.

"Parties make me nervous," he said. "I usually work one on one."

She inclined her head to smile at him, dark hair falling across an eye. Something in that look reminded him of Graciela.

"There's an old storeroom I want to remodel into a weight room. I would like a professional to look at it—in private consultation. To advise me what is best for a body like mine."

Kurt watched the tennis players, his elbow touching hers. "As long as I don't have to mix and mingle," he said.

She peered up at him through long black lashes. "We'll find something more stimulating to do," she said.

Down on the court Cecilia's father was pointing his racket at a mark two inches out of the service area and loudly arguing with Bob Graeber. Her father seemed to be quite a competitor too.

Kurt walked down to the juice bar, ordered an extra-protein Smoothie, and sat thinking about the crescent of sweat on Cecilia Rostagno's shirt and the tawny glow of her skin. This girl was somehow connected to the events of the past two days—Graciela's reaction at the bar, Gitter's story about the bookstore. Not much, but what else did he have?

In the lobby he made a phone call to Bert's old girlfriend, Maya Dahl. He hadn't seen Maya in a year and was unexpectedly nervous about hearing her voice.

"Kurt!" she said. "My god, I can't believe it."

He had known her since the early seventies, even longer than he'd known Meg. One spring break Maya left her dorm at Mills College and hitchhiked to Aspen, like a pilgrim to a shrine, vowing to ski until the snow was gone. She never went back. To pay her rent she took a scut job cleaning rooms in a lodge where Bert was working maintenance. They made love in the cozy quilted beds of wealthy tourists out on the slopes.

"How about lunch?" Kurt said. In recent years Maya had been a successful caterer and always knew the gossip around town. Who was who, who was doing what. "My treat at Szechuan Garden."

"Why don't you come out here? It's such a nice morning."

"Is Don Juan at home these days?"

Maya's husband was Cuban. When Castro came to power,

Juan Romo was studying business at Wharton and decided to stay in America. Now he was a millionaire stockbroker named John Romer.

"He's in New York. Come on out and we'll ride the ponies."

When he hung up, the receptionist was waiting to speak with him. "Sheriff Muller?" she smiled shyly. "I wasn't certain it was you."

"What do you think?" he asked, patting the tender skin of his face.

"Sheriff Muller," Marta said, her fair cheeks glowing red, "I have been instructed to ask all of our patrons to show their cards before using the facilities."

Kurt looked down into her ice-blue Finnish eyes and grinned dumbly. "Marta," he said, "you know I don't have a card."

She averted her eyes. "I'm sorry, Sheriff Muller," she said. "I have been instructed."

Kurt smiled at her quaint European formality. "Who's doing all this instructing?" he asked.

She was a sweet girl, and he could see this wasn't easy for her. "Graeber?" he helped her.

She hesitated, then nodded.

"I bet Graeber read the paper this morning," Kurt said.

Marta remained in front of him, embarrassed but polite, observing some unwritten law of Scandinavian decorum and waiting to be dismissed.

"It's okay, kid," he said, touching her shoulder. "It was only a matter of time."

He first noticed the truck idling about in the parking lot of the health club. It caught his attention because there weren't many old Ford pickups in town these days, not since the Range Rovers had taken over. But his mind was preoccupied with a dozen puzzling details and he didn't think about the truck again until he'd passed through town and crossed Castle Creek Bridge and happened to glance in his rearview mirror. It was the kind of truck that made perfect sense downvalley, and because the driver kept his distance along the dusty summer haze of Highway 82, in no special hurry, Kurt figured he was on his way home. Five miles later, when Kurt turned off for Woody Creek and trailed down through the cotton-woods toward the old iron river-bridge, the truck followed, its worn gears grinding. In the mirror Kurt could see a driver with black hair, his T-shirt bright as a sheet below a dark neck and face. Maybe one of the Mexicans from the pool hall, he thought. Maybe the gunman. He felt under the seat to make sure his father's old Luger was within reach, the replacement he'd hidden there this morning. Now that he wasn't going in to the department anymore, he had to resort to what was in his attic.

Maya's husband owned fifty acres of ranchland along the east ridge, overlooking the deep, tree-choked trench of the river. She had met him at the dessert table at John Denver's Christmas party a couple of years ago. 'I'm getting married,' she called to tell Kurt not many weeks afterward. 'I'm tired of being noble and hardworking and poor.'

He saw the archway for the ranch up ahead and glanced in the mirror again. The pickup was slowly closing the distance between them. Kurt maintained his speed, patient, calculating the moment, and then swerved off abruptly toward the Romer gate, his tires screeching, the back end of the Jeep juking away from him. He fought the wheel and gunned the vehicle out of a bar ditch and onto the white pea gravel of the driveway, his front tires skidding to rest atop a cattle guard. The pickup honked angrily but kept going. When Kurt turned, all he could see was a rattling tailgate receding in the distance. It had all happened too fast to get a good look at the driver.

In the back of his head he could feel the creeping, irreversible onset of paranoia. Maybe the guy really lived around here, he told himself. Maybe he was heading home. Kurt wondered if he was going to start suspecting every Hispanic kid in the Valley of coming after him.

He reached under his seat to make sure the Luger hadn't come loose in the skid and something on the floorboard caught his eye. A blue fabric strap protruding from under the passenger seat. He took hold of the strap and pulled, and a lady's handbag slid out. Graciela's handwoven bag. He realized instantly that she must have stashed it there when they went walking into the Grottos.

Kurt sat rigidly for several moments, staring at the handbag in his lap. He thought about their meeting in his office, the bag resting like this on her knees, how the colors had suited her. He remembered everything about her—the graying shock of hair, her intelligent eyes, the way her hands had caressed the battered face of her old friend.

A handbag was so intimate, he thought, like a diary or a bundle of love letters. But ten years as a cop got the best of him and he drew open the pull-strings. There was a fair amount of clutter. Lipstick and hairbrush, a key to her room at Star Meadow. Postcards of Aspen and that damn unwieldy trail map. Travel pack of Kleenex with Spanish wording, bottle of aspirin, small Minolta camera still set for the first picture, ballpoint pen. A coin purse with weighty Argentine coins and quarters and pennies and folded bills from both countries.

He flipped through her passport. The photograph showed a slightly younger woman, her face leaner, the jaw more handsomely defined. She had a beautiful smile. He pulled dark strands of hair from her brush and rolled them between his fingers. He remembered the coconut fragrance, her face close enough to whisper in the dark.

At the bottom of the bag there were two small square boxes wrapped in tissue paper. One contained a tiny gold stickpin, a skier in motion, the other a silver-plated aspen leaf attached to a necklace chain. Gifts for her two daughters.

He found a well-worn red notebook in the jumble and thumbed through the ruled pages, trying to decipher the Spanish, the lists and dates and scribbles. Impatient with his ignorance of the language, he skipped to the end to see what she had recorded last. In the middle of a clean page she had printed her final entry, a single word followed by a question mark:

PANZECA?

Kurt had no idea what the word meant. Was it someone's name? A place?

He returned the items to the bag, slid it back under the passenger seat, then drove onto the Romer property.

The gravel road leveled out through an open pasture where polo ponies grazed. At the end of the long drive, beyond the prim white stables, Maya Dahl stood at a corral fence with one fist cocked on her hip, watching her trainer lead a beautiful new colt around in circles. The sight of Kurt's Jeep brought a smile to her face and she turned to wave at him, a hand shading her eyes from the sun.

"Is that really you, Kurt?" she said, striding toward the Jeep in riding boots. "For a minute there I almost thought you were—"

She stopped and folded her arms and looked at him. The smile slipped away and then returned as something dreamier, more melancholy. "Well," she said quietly, "I guess you probably know what I thought."

"Hello, Maya," Kurt said, stepping out of the Jeep. "How have you been?"

"Well kept," she said. Her cool blue-green eyes studied his face. "What happened there?" she asked, staring at the stitches.

"Ran into a door."

She squinted at him. "Why do I even ask?"

Taking his arm she escorted him toward the main house, an imposing flagstone fortress she now called home.

"I heard about Chip on the news," she said. "I should've called you. I don't know what's happening to me out here. I'm getting awful about keeping in touch with my old friends. I guess I was too embarrassed to pick up the phone. I was afraid you'd say, 'Maya who?'"

She had put on a little weight and the dry climate had finally begun to mistreat her face, giving her wrinkles where she'd never had them before. Her golden hair was shorter now, darker, though still satiny and fine. But her eyes were showing her age, Kurt thought. Their eyes were giving them all away.

"I don't suppose you've seen today's paper," he said.

"One of the nice things about living out this far."

"I've been taking some vicious slams," he said. "It's not worth it anymore. I handed in my resignation to the county commissioners."

She didn't slow her stride. "Good for you," she said. "I don't know why you ever wanted that job in the first place. Whose idea was it, anyway?"

Kurt grinned. "As I recall, you were a charter member of the Rabid Skunk party. Maybe I should hold you personally responsible."

Maya smiled sadly. "I miss it," she sighed. "I miss the madness."

"What do you expect?" he said, nodding toward the house. "You're living like Barbara Stanwyck in the Big Valley."

She laughed that sexy, throaty laugh he remembered so well. "Luxury is a bitch," she said.

They entered the house and passed the stone fountain trickling in the foyer, then descended steps into the sunken living room, plush couches arranged in seating squares. The only time Kurt had been here was for Maya's wedding reception, which had been quite a feast. But today, without the many guests burbling about the rooms, there was a cathedral air of space and quiet.

"When was the last time you had a tequila sunrise?" Maya asked, a knowing sparkle in her eyes.

One year in the seventies, he couldn't remember which, that was their drink, the four of them. There was a designated rest spot along every hiking trail in the Valley where they stopped to pour themselves tequila sunrises from an icy canteen.

"It's been a while," he said.

"I'll ask Consuelo to bring us a pitcher."

On the sun deck they sat on canvas chairs with a grand view of the clover green pasture where her husband had once raised buffalo, before he'd sold them and reinvested in polo ponies. Beyond their property line rose another ridge, the uplift softer, more feminine, than the craggy peaks in these parts, its forest of spruce as violet as Kurt imagined the landscape of Wales. On the evening of Maya's wedding everyone came out to watch a full moon float above that ridge like a luminous silver hot-air balloon.

Kurt tasted the sickeningly sweet tequila sunrise and remembered why he'd stopped drinking them. He leaned back in the chair, propped his boots on the deck railing, and told Maya about the shootout in Emma, at the farmhouse where they'd eaten peyote and made apple juice in a wood press. He had trouble getting through the part about Chip going over the cliff.

Maya sighed and reached out to hold his hand. "Poor Chip," she said. "I remember when he came back from the Olympics. His ego was crushed. We spent quite a few afternoons together, back then, smoking hash and watching the clouds roll by."

Kurt turned to her. "You and Chip?" he grinned.

"Me and Chip," she nodded. "In those days there was something darkly tragic about him, like Hamlet. I guess I found that appealing."

Her hand was dry and hard and no longer the delicate instrument that created culinary artworks for the rich. It was obvious she had taken up horse-grooming.

"Why in God's name did all that have to happen?" she asked.

"The Feds needed a quick fix for the Quiroga murder," he said, an accusation he wasn't ready to share with anyone else just yet. "They were in a hurry to book it and wash their hands, so everybody could get home for the weekend. It made me look like I couldn't handle my job."

Suddenly his eye caught a flash of mirror across the pasture, sunlight on glass. A vehicle was slowly weaving through the grove of trees near the fence line.

"What do you know about the Rostagno family?" he asked, sipping his drink. "They have a home in Starwood."

Maya shrugged. "Claudio Rostagno is some kind of Italian diplomat, I think," she said, slipping off a riding boot. "His wife is Patricia Graham, one of the society ladies in Les Dames. I did some catering for her back in marriage number two, when she lived in Mountain Valley with her husband the oilman from Texas. The asshole who once dragged her out of a party by her hair."

"She must have a thing for men with bad tempers," Kurt said.

Maya pulled off the other boot and settled her stocking feet on the railing next to Kurt's. "John thinks there's something phony about Rostagno," she said. "We all sat at the same table at a Les Dames gala, and after a few drinks Rostagno and John started speaking Spanish to each other. They both got a big kick out of it. Rostagno said he'd picked up his Spanish on a post assignment in Madrid. I'm not sure he realized John is Cuban."

"Well, I guess Don Juan ought to know a phony."

Maya kicked his boot with her stocking toes. "Touché," she said.

"What about Rostagno's daughter?"

Maya gave him a sidelong glance. "So," she said, "we finally get down to the subject of this innocent little inquiry."

"I have a date with her tonight," he said. "Anything I ought to know?"

Maya sipped her sunrise and made a false smile at him. "I hear she collects scrotum. Wears them on a leather strap around her neck," she said. "Better hang on to yours."

Kurt dropped his feet to the deck, stood up slowly, and gazed out beyond the pasture toward the county road. He thought he could see a dark vehicle parked beneath the trees near the turnoff.

"I went to visit Jake last night," he said.

Maya said nothing for a while. Then finally, "And how is Mr. Jake Pfeil? Flourishing, I expect."

"He thinks I'm still angry about Bert's death."

Maya was silent. Kurt drank and watched the tree line.

"Are you?" she asked.

"I was going to ask you the same thing."

She was standing now, facing the soft purple ridge. "All of that happened centuries ago," she said. "I'm too busy to be angry."

He turned a slow circle, his eyes taking in the pasture, the house, the stables up the road. "This place must be good therapy," he said. "Where do I sign up?"

She smiled at him. "How about Jake?" Her voice was quiet now. "He miss his old buddy?"

He shook his head. "They hadn't been friends for a long time."

She looked surprised. "Oh really?" she said. "Then why were they hanging out together that last year?"

She was probably confusing the years, Kurt thought. Time and tequila could do that to a memory.

"I gave Bert a hard time about it," she said. "He said they were just two old Aspen boys shooting the shit about how it had been."

"Bert thought Jake was a joke."

Maya's voice shrank even more, to a small sad note. "I suppose there are things about Bert we'll never understand," she said.

He watched her feathery hair ruffle in the breeze.

"Maya," he said, "there's something else we haven't talked about in a long time."

"We're covering a lot of ground this afternoon, aren't we?" she said. "Maybe we ought to save some of this for next year."

She was probably right, Kurt thought. But he wasn't ready to let go yet. "I still wonder if he knew," he said.

She studied the ice in her glass. "Oh, Kurt," she said. "It's not as if we were serious."

He knew what she meant. Isolated occasions. A half-dozen times over the seventeen years they'd all spent together. The evenings when Bert went camping with the Mountain Rescue team and Meg was on retreat in some holy place like Chaco Canyon or Taos.

"What about Meg?" she asked.

"No," he said. "I never told her. There was no point."

"Do you ever hear from her?"

Kurt tried to remember the last time he'd spoken with his ex-wife. "She calls every couple of weeks," he said.

"How is Lennon dealing with it?"

"He thinks his mother is not well," he said. "He thinks she'll come back and see him when she gets better."

"God," she said, the sound choking in her throat. She wiped away sudden, unexpected tears. "What the hell happened to us all?"

Kurt didn't know. He really didn't know. He figured everything in life fell apart sooner or later. It was only a matter of when.

He put his arm around her, and she laid her head on his chest and cried a little. After a few minutes she pulled away and rubbed his arm. "Need another drink, cowboy?" she sniffed.

"What I need," he said, "is a pair of binoculars."

Moments later Maya returned with binoculars and a fresh pitcher of tequila sunrise. Kurt stood at the railing and searched the tree line by the fence. There it was, black as asphalt, hidden in a gully beneath the cottonwoods. The old Ford pickup.

"Have you taken up birding, Kurt?"

When their visit was over, Maya walked him to the Jeep. "What are you going to do now that you're unemployed?" she asked.

"I'm thinking about traveling," he said. "It's time for Lennon to see the real world."

He drove off, watching Maya in the rearview mirror as she waved and then disappeared into the stone fortress. A hundred yards from the house he pulled over to the edge of the woods and got out of the Jeep. He tucked the German Luger in his belt and hiked into the trees, following the natural trails that split off through the dappled noonday shade of blue spruce and poplars. He crawled through John Romer's barbed-wire fence like a farmboy and jogged down into the gully by the county road. Thick cedar bushes and a nightmare of bramble vines slowed his footing, but before long he could see the rear of the pickup truck and crouched in the brush to watch and wait.

In a short while he began to creep closer, a few yards at a time, listening, the Luger tight in his hand. The day was warm and he was sweating through his denim shirt. Finally he drew close enough to see the back of the driver's head through the rear glass, his bare arm resting along the top of the seat like a relaxed young stud watching a drive-in movie with his girl.

Kurt stayed low, crab-crawling through the loose soil to the truck's tailgate. He braced his back against the dented Colorado license plate and took deep breaths, trying to talk himself into his next move. He sucked in one last breath, let it out slowly, and spun around the side of the truck, keeping low until he reached the window.

"Don't move," he said, rising quietly and pressing the Luger to the driver's temple.

The boy was young, not a day over twenty. He reached for the pistol lying beside him on the seat and Kurt adjusted his aim six inches and fired, blowing out the back window. The boy grabbed his ears and cried out in pain.

"I told you not to move," Kurt said, flinging open the door, seizing him by the T-shirt and yanking him to the ground.

He was a skinny kid, all elbows and knees, light as a sack of cotton balls. Kurt pinned the boy's left arm behind his back and drilled a knee into his tailbone, then pressed the gun against the back of his skull.

"That was a very stupid thing to do," he said.

The boy was Hispanic, all right. But Kurt had never seen him before. He didn't recognize him from the pool hall.

"You the guy that took a shot at me last night?" he said, twisting the arm until the boy moaned. "I don't hear you, *carnal*. You the asshole that wanted to kill me?"

When the boy began to whimper, Kurt eased up a bit.

"What's your name, son?" he said, releasing the arm and squatting back on the boy's legs. "Come on, I'm not going to hurt you. What's your name?"

The boy fought tears. "Angel," he said. "Angel Montoya."

"Why'd you want to kill me, Angel?"

Angel lifted his head a little, then let it drop slackly, resigned to a life spent facedown with a gun at his neck. "I make a mistake," he said in broken English.

"And you were tailing me just to say how sorry you are."

"Somebody tell me you no shoot," he said. "You no shoot my brother. They tell me you know who."

Kurt stood up. "I'm going to put away the gun," he said, sliding the Luger under his belt, "but if you try something stupid again, I'll hurt you bad. You understand?"

"I understand."

For some time Angel lay immobile on the ground. Then he rolled over slowly and curled into a sitting position, his knees pulled to his chest.

"The cops say your buddies killed a man," Kurt said. "A writer from Argentina."

Angel looked up at him, puzzled. With a lazy swipe of his shoulder he brushed yellow grass blades from the side of his face. "We don't kill nobody," he said. "The gringos start the shooting."

"The cops say the writer came out to your house to look around and you put a bullet in his head and dumped him in the river."

Angel's dark eyes flared with a wild intensity. He shook his head. "*No*," he said emphatically. "Nobody come to our house. We don't know this *escritor*. We don't hurt nobody."

The boy rose slowly to his feet and Kurt took a step backward, giving him room.

"So why they come and shoot?" Angel asked, his face reignited with anger. "Who is these men that kill my brother?"

Kurt walked over to the truck and reached in the open door for the gun on the seat. It was an old .45 with a taped grip, the same vintage as the one he'd owned until Muffin hurled it into the void. He checked the clip and saw it was half empty.

"Listen to me, Angel," he said. "I ought to drag your butt to the jailhouse in Aspen and have them lock you up. You can't go around shooting at people. Do you understand? You make a play for the men who killed your brother, they'll kill you. It's that simple. They won't think twice about wasting your skinny ass. You're just one more nameless wetback with no goddamn papers and nobody to take up for you. People around here don't care if you live or die, son. There's nothing to stop those men from blowing your brains out and winning a medal for it."

Angel seemed to be listening. He seemed to understand.

"I'm very sorry about your brother," Kurt said. "I'm sorry about everything that happened at the farmhouse. But my best advice to you, son, is to fill up this old pickup and head out of the Valley." He took out his sweat-stained wallet and found a twenty, a ten, and four ones. "Here," he said, stuffing the bills in Angel's jeans pocket. "This'll get you down the road. You have friends someplace?"

Angel Montoya stood there, stubbornly toeing the dirt.

"Do yourself a favor and go look for work where you've got other compadres," Kurt said. "Maybe you should think about going back home for a while, I don't know. But you stick around here, you're going to get in trouble. Sooner or later you'll get mad again and then you'll do something stupid, like taking another shot at somebody. There's nothing here for you anymore, my friend, but a lot of serious grief."

He was a good-looking kid with a square jaw more Indian than Spanish, and short black hair that had the dry, downy shape of a feather duster. There was a sweetness about him, and a clear impression of diligence and loyalty to people who were good to him. Kurt didn't want to see him get hurt.

"I must know who is these men that killed my brother," Angel said in a calm, determined voice.

Kurt stuck the old taped-up .45 in his belt next to the Luger. "Come on," he said, gripping Angel's arm and shoving him toward the truck. "You're getting out of here. I don't want to catch your ass around here again."

Angel tried to work free of Kurt's grip but saw it was impossible. He stumbled into the cab, and Kurt slammed the door behind him.

"If I ever see you again in this goddamn valley, I'm going to have you thrown in jail. Do you understand me, Angel?" He stared hard at the boy sitting behind the wheel. "You go to jail, son, you're not going to come out of it the same. Unless you want that to happen, you better go find yourself another location to work in. New Mexico, Utah, California. Anywhere. Just stay out of my sight."

Angel sat in silence, his expression frozen and remote. "You saw them kill my brother," he said finally. "He don't do nothing and they kill him anyway. What will you do?"

If I had any sense, Kurt thought, *I would take my own advice, pick up Lennon, and go on a long trip somewhere, maybe a permanent one. Before I do any more serious thinking about what happened at Emma.*

"Get going," he said, slapping the pickup's roof, a hollow rumble like a kettledrum. A loose chunk of spiderwebbed glass fell into the truck bed. "Go on and get out of here, kid, before I change my mind."

11

WHEN HE GOT HOME THERE WAS A MESSAGE FROM MUFFIN on the answering machine. They'd searched the area for two hours but had found no body. She requested that Kurt come to the office at three o'clock "to get these FBI charges out of the way."

There was also a message from Miles Cunningham: "What transpires, law man? Some kind of palace coup? I have weapons, I have bawling hounds! We'll by god barricade the courthouse and make the bastards come to us! You have a sacred obligation, citizen. Ye have taken the oath. Have you no pride, man? Don't let the fish-belly bureaucrats take your badge. We'll fight this thing together. The Rabid Skunks shall rise redolent from the woodpile. The rabble has spoken. You are our man. Hold on to the reins till my troops can assemble. And whatever you do, permit no Mormons near the powder magazine!"

In the tape's pause Kurt thought he could hear the rattling of ice.

"By the way," the voice returned, "could you drop that Quiroga book off at the library for me? I found a note in my tickler file saying it's somewhat overdue."

Kurt picked up Omar Quiroga's book from the coffee table, cracked a beer, and went to his father's study.

Though Otto Muller had been dead for fifteen years, Kurt still called the room his father's study. It was attached to the far end of the house like an afterthought, and until a few years ago, when Kurt finally cut a door through the dining room wall, the study was accessible only from an outside entrance reached with some difficulty at the end of a long stony path—Herbert Bayer's clever idea. When they were growing up, the boys were not allowed to enter the study, unless specifically invited, and the ironclad rule of the house was that no one should ever disturb Father while he was at work in his lair.

Kurt sank down in the reading chair, a plum-red leather monstrosity with rounded armrests worn colorless by his father's elbows, and peered out the window into the glaring sunshine. He remembered when he and Bert were children hiding outside that window, spying on their father, wondering what he was doing that required so much time alone. When they dared to peek through the screen they always discovered him in the same pose, bent over his work desk, a pipe smoldering in the ashtray, this lanky, graying European intellectual they loved from afar but didn't really understand, a strange man with odd round spectacles and too much hair, his pen hand forever moving across a page. Sometimes he practiced on the old Steinway piano that still occupied much of the room. The boys marveled at his music. They sat in a tree outside the window and tried to comprehend the amazing flurry of notes the way a child tries to master an unknown language by listening harder, with more effort, more concentration.

Otto Muller wanted his sons to follow in his footsteps but Kurt rebelled early against piano lessons and by the age of eight was running away into the cedar thicket on Red Mountain to escape the daily hour of practice. Bert reluctantly persevered into his early teens, to please their bewildered father, but showed no facility for music and was finally permitted to put away the violin.

Kurt looked around the study at the shelves of intimidating

hardbound books, fat as Bibles, unopened for a score of years and gathering dust, his father's prized library of the great classics, the modern masters. Many volumes were autographed by the dandruff-specked geniuses who had written them and somehow passed through Otto Muller's remote life here in the mountains. Albert Schweitzer, Thornton Wilder, Rudolf Carnap, José Ortega y Gasset. He wanted his sons to read them all, but of course they never did. 'I want you to read Goethe in the original,' he told them once. But of course they never would. They could speak German like Munich schoolchildren, but reading and writing required greater skill, and by the time they reached high school they refused to enroll in the language courses their father implored them to take.

'You have no respect for your heritage,' he scolded them often. 'You are throwing away your birthright. Shame on you for not caring where you come from.'

But hadn't he himself fled to America because he hated the Germans? If their mother had stayed, wouldn't she have perished in the death camps like her father and sister?

'I didn't hate the Germans, I hated Hitler and what he stood for,' he argued. 'There is a difference. But you two, you are trying to deny who you are.'

But they knew who they were. They were Americans. Theirs was a great rugged land of snowcapped peaks and sparkling streams and rich green forests of Douglas firs that towered in the sun. This was their birthright, and this was who they became. Tall, strong, sunburned youths, their playground the Elk Range and the Continental Divide. They took to the slopes in winter, and to the trout creeks late in spring. They backpacked for days into the alpine wilderness and made their meals from what the earth provided, berries and small game. They learned to scale sheer rock walls with ropes and pitons and cleated boots; they rafted the killer rapids at the bottom of lost canyons in the parched, windswept lands known only to a vanished Anasazi.

The Muller boys knew who they were. They had inherited the

earth. For a handful of wild and sheltered years they thought they were invincible.

'You must be Rudi's sons,' their father sometimes teased them. 'He is the great outdoorsman. Go and worry him to pay for all your outdoor toys.'

But the boys would not have traded their father for a dozen Rudi Pfeils. Otto Muller was a reserved intellectual with an eccentric's private laugh and a penchant for stiff, convoluted speech, but whenever he emerged from the seclusion of his study he gave his sons so much affection and attention they could not help but love him. Silly songs, riddles, esoteric jokes. He saved all of his warmth for them.

Kurt imagined his own son sitting with a dinosaur book in a quiet corner of the day care center and wondered if he knew his father was saving the best part of himself for him.

Rousing himself from the stuffy heat of the study, he glanced into his lap and remembered why he'd come here. He opened Omar Quiroga's book and began to skim the early chapters, reading about the excesses of Juan Perón, the years under Isabel, and the historical setting for the military junta of the mid-1970s. When he reached the section about the secret atrocities and how Quiroga was arrested, he thought back to Graciela's story of her own incarceration and the death of her husband.

For another half hour he read Quiroga's account of his torture by the military police. The journalist gave nicknames to everyone, even his fellow inmates. One was a *Dr. Madonna* he had known for many years, since the university. This doctor was eventually assigned to care for dying prisoners.

Kurt sat up, reading quickly:

> *From time to time, if Dr. Madonna allowed the soldier in charge of the night shift to fondle her a bit, the cur would permit the doctor and me to sleep together in the same cot and soothe our aching spirits. As long as he could watch.*

Graciela. He was certain it was her. He closed the book, quietly relieved that she had not lied to him about everything.

He set the book aside and went to the kitchen to make a sandwich. While he was arranging the bread and sliced turkey on the tile counter, the phone rang. He turned up the machine's volume to monitor the message.

"Hello, Lennon," Meg began. "This is Mom calling from Oregon. How are you doing, sweetheart? I miss you bunches and bunches."

There was nothing of the confusion and anguish he could sometimes hear in her voice, that familiar tightness in her throat. This sounded like the old Meg, the bright-eyed girlish Meg, the woman he'd once been in love with.

"I'm feeling a whole lot better now. The doctor says it won't be much longer till I'm completely well. Then I'll be able to come and see you. I miss you so much, sweet pea."

It was all a carefully fabricated lie. There was no doctor, no course of therapy, no quarantine. This was the only way Meg could live with herself, and Kurt didn't have the heart to contradict the story, not in front of Lennon. How else could he explain to a five-year-old that his mother was searching for something more, that she was obsessed with things that couldn't be seen or measured in any way that mattered, and that she'd chosen instead to live with strangers on a soybean farm in another state? Kurt didn't understand it himself.

"How are your friends Justin and Sean? I hope you guys are still good buddies. There's a wonderful book I'm going to send you, and you can share it with them at school."

Twenty years later he could still remember with astonishing clarity the day he'd met Meg at Crater Lake. He had hiked up with Bert and Maya and Zack Crawford to eat acid, lie on his back near the water, and watch the face of God in the clouds. After several hours he nodded out, and when he opened his eyes again, a radiant auburn-haired angel was kneeling over him, snapping photographs of his sunburned face. She had come to the lake on a field trip with her photography program.

"It tells you how to grow your own organic vegetables. Daddy or your teacher can read it to you. Maybe you can talk your father into planting a nice healthy garden."

Kurt lifted the receiver. "Hello, Meg," he said. She sounded so mindlessly joyful he felt like interrupting her.

"Kurt," she said. His voice startled her. "I didn't think you'd be home this time of day."

"I'm going through a career transition," he said, "so there's a little more flexibility in my schedule."

"I'm not sure I understand."

"I resigned," he said. "I'm not the sheriff anymore."

A moment of hesitation. "That surprises me," she said. "I wasn't aware you were thinking about quitting."

"There are a lot of things about my life you're not aware of, Meg."

Another moment passed in which she seemed to be considering his rebuke. "What are you going to do about income?" she asked, that dry tightness creeping into her voice. "Will Lennon be all right? We still have a pretty good stash in savings, don't we?"

"Everything's going to be okay," he said. "We still have savings, and I'll find another job."

"Doing what, for heaven's sake? Working at a tackle shop?" she said, her annoyance growing. "You've never had the training for a real job, Kurt. We've got Lennon's college to think about."

"You know, for a barefoot Sufi you're starting to sound downright middle class, my dear."

"This isn't funny, Kurt."

"Don't stress out on me, Meg, I'll find something. I don't know. Something. Maybe Matt Heron will hire me to teach Conflict Resolution."

"I can't believe you're joking about this. Don't you realize you've just raised the volume of interference in your life to about level ten? This makes the picture very unclear. I don't like the idea of my son doing without."

"Then stop living with Bubba Ram Horn, or whatever his name is, and get a fucking job, Meg. Send the kid some money. Better still, come give him some love."

Kurt could hear the faint white hiss of long distance. She hadn't hung up.

"Does he miss me?" she asked, finally.

"Of course he misses you. You're his mother."

"He asks about me?"

Kurt stroked his face, an old habit. Feeling the smooth skin left him uneasy. "Tell you the truth, Meg," he said, his voice softer now, "he hardly ever talks about you anymore."

Meg began to cry, a gentle grieving. He could hear her trying to clear her throat to speak.

"Take your time, Peaches," he said, using his old nickname for her. "There's no hurry. I've got all afternoon if you want to talk."

He waited in silence. He was willing to listen day and night if it would make their lives better.

"I don't know what's the matter with me," she said when she had recovered enough to speak. "I haven't been happy in a long, long time."

"I know," Kurt said.

"I'm beginning to feel as if nothing is ever going to make me happy again."

"I know. I'm sorry."

"What should I do, Kurt? You were always so good at giving directions. Tell me what I should do."

"I can't, Meg," he said. "I don't know what you should do."

"I'm afraid to come home."

Kurt didn't understand how she could feel this way. Not even in his most angry moments during the divorce proceedings, when the judge was handing away his child to a woman who believed that crystals can cure cancer and bring about world peace, did he ever threaten or try to intimidate her.

"Come on, don't be silly," he said. "You know you don't have to worry about me."

She exhaled a long deep breath, sniffed, cleared her throat. She tried to say something but emotion overcame her again and she hesitated, fighting tears. "It's not you I'm worried about," she managed to say.

With Meg that could mean anything. She might be worried about betraying her beliefs, or returning to the sloughed-off skin of a dead life—to familiar faces and cold, accusatory eyes on the streets of a small town. But then suddenly Kurt realized she was afraid of something altogether different.

"Meg," he said, "is there something you need to tell me?"

He thought her response might take forever. He waited, listening to her troubled breathing.

"Yes," she said at last. "Yes, there are things you ought to know. But I don't think I'm ready to talk about them yet. I need more time. Oh, Kurt, I'm so afraid. I worry so much about Lennon. And you too. I don't know if you'll ever forgive me."

"Talk to me, Meg," he said. "Tell me what it is. We'll all be better off if you do."

She sighed again. "Not right now," she said. "I just can't. Please forgive me, Kurt. Give Lennon a big kiss for me. Hug him. Please."

He held the receiver, waiting. There was a click. Dial tone. Twelve hundred miles between them.

12

SHORTLY BEFORE THE THREE O'CLOCK MEETING WITH Muffin, Kurt returned to Star Meadow. The walking paths were missing their usual meditative strollers; a lone groundskeeper ambled across the lawn in front of the geodesic conference center, surveying a cascade of sprinklers. There was an air of abandonment in the village, and Kurt wondered if the murder had shut down the seminar on Global Unity.

He parked in front of the log dormitory and walked up the steps to what had been Quiroga's lodging. The door was unlocked and the room appeared tidy and uninhabited. The Feds had scoured the place clean.

He knelt down in front of the refrigerator and snapped off the black plastic motor guard. Cheek to the floor, he saw immediately what he was hoping to find—the broken stem of a wineglass still lodged underneath a tangle of grease-caked wires.

Staggs and company must not have small children at home, he thought, or they'd spend more time looking for things on their hands and knees.

He pulled a handkerchief from his pocket and reached in to extract the stem. It was about three inches long, a clear crystal shard with a jagged tip and a tiny piece of the base still intact. Resting in his handkerchief the stem looked like the broken shaft of a dart. When he raised it to his nose he could detect the faint scent of burgundy.

Libbie McCullough glanced up at him from the receptionist's desk, then resumed mixing her usual hideous concoction of honey, brewer's yeast, and aloe vera juice. For years now she had been trying to convert the entire department to the vegetarian life, insisting that the elimination of red meat in cops was the first step toward creating a more peaceful planet. So far she'd won over only one believer, and he had been barbecued in a fiery wreck.

"May I help you?" she asked. She glanced up again, licking honey from her long finger. "Oh my god, Kurt! I didn't recognize you."

Her bewildered smile disappeared and she began to treat him with functionary distance, as though he were a stranger who'd come in to pay off his parking tickets.

"Would you like some refreshment while you wait?" she asked mechanically, holding up the blender.

"No, thanks, Libbie."

"Have a seat, please," she said. "I'll let her know you're here."

So that's how it was going to be, he thought. Eight years sharing a thousand confidences, a thousand petty grievances, meant nothing to her now that he was no longer her boss.

The door to his old office was fifteen feet away but Libbie buzzed the intercom.

"Don't jerk me around, Libbie," Kurt said. He walked over to the door and turned the glass knob.

"No, Kurt!"

He saw now why Libbie was acting so strangely. Neal Staggs sat across the desk from Muffin, his navy-blue blazer draped over the back of a metal folding chair. The shoulder holster strapped to his white dress shirt gave him the appearance of a lantern-jawed G-man out of the Hoover era.

"Darnit, Kurt Muller!" Libbie said, rising from her desk to grab his arm.

"Kurt?" Muffin said, standing, her brow wrinkled.

His beard. He kept forgetting it was gone.

"I'm sorry," Libbie apologized. "I asked him to wait."

"It's okay, miss," Staggs said. He stood up slowly, extending himself to his full height, hitching his chin. Kurt sensed he was being sized up by a slightly smaller man worried about his moves. "Mr. Muller and I are ready to talk."

Kurt chucked back the bill of his baseball cap. "You got that right," he said. "Let's do it."

This sudden semblance of cooperation surprised Muffin, but she recovered quickly and asked Libbie to close the door and hold all phone calls.

"I just want to state right up front," Muffin said, tensely re-arranging items on her desk—stapler, Scotch-tape dispenser, paper-weight—"that I'm not satisfied with Agent Staggs's line of thinking in this matter and I've told him so."

Staggs began to pace the tight office space, hands in his pockets, offering an indifferent smile. He obviously didn't care what she thought.

"The man's paid to come up with theories," Kurt said, barely able to control his contempt. "He's got one about me, I want to hear it."

Staggs continued to pace, his eyes cast downward at his gleaming black shoes. "Yeah, I've got a theory, Muller," he said. "I've got a theory you're up to your jockstrap in dirt, ace, and your fairy fiefdom out here in the mountains is coming down around your ears. You don't have much time left, my friend. We've laid the pieces on the table and they're ready to fit in place for a grand jury. Kurt Muller's looking at a long vacation punching license plates," he said, "and learning fun new games with the boys in the shower."

"Agent Staggs," Muffin said sternly, "this meeting doesn't have to turn into—"

"Look," Staggs interrupted, raising his hand. "I've been patient with this office long enough. I don't see proof one that you or anybody else out here is getting the job done in law enforcement, Miss Brown. And I don't have time to wait for you to sweet-talk this guy while important evidence washes down the river. We've got to move, and we've got to move now. Either you push the man to the wall, or I'm going to push him for you." He glanced at his gold watch, twenty-five years of service. "It's your play, Deputy. Take your best swing."

Muffin looked rattled. The color drained from her face. She was slow to respond.

"The agent thinks you're running a major drug operation in the Valley," she said finally, her eyes shifting to Kurt. "You and Jake Pfeil."

Kurt laughed in disbelief.

"A grand jury isn't going to find this such a yuck," Staggs said. "Not after I play them some nice clear tapes featuring Jake Pfeil on the car phone."

He reached inside a pocket of the blazer and pulled out a minicassette. "To give you a little preview," he said, clicking a button. Jake's voice came on immediately: *"Don't worry about Muller. Muller won't be a problem. He's a standup guy. We've known each other since we were kids. Our families were close."*

Muffin turned a questioning eye on the man who had given her her first job out of the academy.

"What is this shit?" Kurt said.

Staggs clicked off the recorder and smiled at him. "Trust me, there's more," he said. "And the grand jury is going to be real curious about your numbers, Muller. In ten years you've busted maybe a dozen people in this valley for drug possession. All of them coke heads who showed up babbling at their real-estate desks, or waving a gun in a motel lobby—the kind of stoned-out creeps nobody could miss, not even a freaking nun. That's your record, hoss. Check the sheets. In ten years maybe a dozen pathetic sociopaths begging for help."

He slipped the recorder back into his blazer and leaned forward, the veins jutting in his neck. "Nobody busted for pot, and no serious traffickers of any kind. Not one. Fucking kingpins named *Hay-soos* flying in and out of here in their Learjets all day long and the sheriff hasn't noticed them, Muller. What do you think the grand jury's going to conclude, my friend? Especially," he said, "when I give them the details of the Erickson case."

Over the years Kurt had determined that the stories about drug lords and their Learjets in Aspen had been greatly exaggerated. Tabloid fantasies, Hollywood myth. He'd come across little evidence. He also knew that if the stories were in fact true, his department had neither the technology nor the manpower to wage war against a multibillion-dollar enterprise that even Ronald Reagan was incapable of curtailing.

"According to Agent Staggs," Muffin said, "most of the Hispanic workers in the Valley are your foot soldiers. Yours and Jake Pfeil's. He thinks they're doing all your dealing and dirty laundry in exchange for green cards."

Kurt pressed the flesh between his eyes. "And my foot soldiers killed Omar Quiroga because he discovered our ring?"

"So I am told," she said.

Kurt looked up. Staggs was still standing behind the chair. Defiant, composed, cocksure.

"Tell me, Staggs," he said, still unsettled by the tape. "What happened to Graciela Rojas?"

The agent didn't hesitate. "You killed her," he said flatly. "You or one of your boys."

Kurt stood up slowly. Muffin stood at the same time and worked her body halfway between the two men, into that small, uncomfortable pocket of space that kept them apart. She looked worried, but determined to control what happened next. There were too many people here too close together, and one of them was wearing a gun.

Kurt knew all the rational questions he could ask. *Why would I have picked her up at the bar, in front of witnesses? How did I get these stitches in my head? Why did I tell my story to the authorities and then organize a search party out at the Grottos?* But Staggs was a man with a vendetta, and such men had easy answers for everything. It was a waste of time to confront him with the weaknesses in his allegations. That was the job of lawyers.

"Deputy Brown," Kurt said, withdrawing the handkerchief from his parka, "there's something you ought to take a look at."

He spread the cloth on a corner of his old desk and told her where he'd found the broken stem. "It's a disgrace how sloppy the Bureau is getting these days," he said.

Staggs stared at the shard of glass. His mouth parted. Someone was going to lose his job for this. But the gears were already grinding—new rationalizations, another lie.

"I suggest you have it dusted," Kurt said to Muffin. "Good chance there's a print. And I'd be willing to bet, oh, say, my Learjet and the Saab," he said, "that the print you find won't be mine. Or Jake Pfeil's. Or from some poor Mexican busboy shot dead in his kitchen."

Muffin relaxed for a moment and bent over to study the stem. She gave Kurt a tenuous smile. "I'll have it checked out right away," she assured him.

"I wonder," Kurt said, "if our man here's got a theory whose print's going to show up on that glass."

Staggs had gone somewhere inside his head to readjust things. "If"—he spoke haltingly—"*if* what you say is true, that you got this from Quiroga's room"—he cleared his throat, buying time, trying to reorganize his thoughts—"it belongs to the United States government. You're tampering with evidence in a federal felony case." His eyes left the broken glass and settled on Muffin. "You're obligated under the law to turn it over to me immediately."

Muffin began to refold the corners of the handkerchief, carefully covering the stem. "What I've been wondering all along," she said, "is how you found out Omar Quiroga was dead, Agent Staggs? I talked to Matt Heron and his people, and they said they didn't even know Quiroga was missing until your men showed up to search his room. So why don't you tell us," she said, making a small white bundle on the desk, "in the spirit of cooperation between agencies—Who gave you the call?"

Staggs had returned from that far-off floating place. "I strongly suggest," he said, "that you hand that over right now, Miss Brown."

Muffin walked around the desk and placed the bundle inside a drawer. "I'll turn it over as soon as we get a workup," she said. "I'll be happy to share the findings with you."

She stepped to the office door and opened it, showing Staggs the way out. "Now if you don't mind, sir," she said, "I've scheduled an appointment with Mr. Muller for this hour. I would prefer to conduct my interrogation in private."

The agent waited, regarding them both with seething anger, then grabbed his blazer from the back of the folding chair. At the door he stopped and hitched his chin, that familiar gesture.

"Your time is running out, Muller," he said. "We've got a pretty package with your name on it, ace, and we're about ready to tie the bow." He glanced at Muffin. "You can fool this little gal here, and you can fool a lot of flakeheads in this dipshit burg, but you don't fool me, my friend. I've got yards of tape on you and your sandlot pal Jake Pfeil. You've let things slide around here for a long time and you've made quite a cozy nest for yourself. But the party's over, dude. I'm here to turn out the lights."

He slipped on his blue blazer. "I've got a file this thick on you Aspen boys. Affidavits, wire transcripts, glossy eight-by-tens, the whole enchilada. My only regret is," he said, straightening his lapels, shaking out his cuffs, "your brother isn't around to go down on this one too."

A cold chill raced through Kurt's heart.

"Don't look so surprised, Muller," Staggs said, his chin jutting. "I know all about your brother. Truth is, he may be the one I wanted the most."

The agent made a quick pivot and stormed through the reception area toward the courthouse corridor, his stride full of purpose and indignation. Kurt took a step after him but stopped, more baffled than angry. He had no idea what the man was talking about. But the chill remained in his blood.

13

LENNON SWUNG AWKWARDLY AND MISSED, AND THE ball disappeared into the brush at the edge of the yard. "That was a bad pitch," he said, tilting back his head to look out from under the long bill of the Chicago Cubs baseball cap. Kurt's father had brought this cap home for Bert when they were boys. It was still too big for Lennon, but he refused to bat without it.

"Run get the ball," Kurt said.

He noticed a solitary hang-glider high in the thermals, his rainbow wings sailing above the river and the old brick hydroelectric building that now housed a handsome art museum. Some fool tourist half lost, floating aimlessly toward Red Mountain, oblivious to the cloudbursts every afternoon in the summer.

"Over there," Kurt pointed, directing Lennon into the cedar bushes. "More to your right."

Playing ball with his son out here in the yard usually cleared away all the rubbish in his head, but this afternoon he couldn't stop thinking about what Staggs had said: 'He may be the one I wanted the most.'

Across the shallow valley, gray rain clouds were rolling like ground fog over the crest of Ajax, drifting toward the rusticated rooftops of town. A tiny gondola carried tourists up the long steel cable into the mist. Kurt had scattered Bert's ashes on that mountain one rainy afternoon like this one, the clouds low and black above the peak where mourners had gathered in final meditation. His mother was there, frail and wheezing and racked with sorrow. She stayed in the Jeep while the others made their way down the steep grassy slope with the ceramic urn.

Twenty years earlier the two brothers had drunk themselves blind the night before Bert shipped out to Nam. 'Ashes in the wind,' he made Kurt promise. 'I'll probably come back in a million pieces. It won't take much to scatter me.'

In the end, a lifetime from the jungle, Kurt was waiting when the helicopter touched down on the hospital roof. Even now, four summers later, he was still haunted by what he saw when they unzipped the body bag.

"I found it!" Lennon ran back into the yard, waving the baseball in his hand. "Come on, rag arm, fire the old peach! Fire the old pepper ball!"

Kurt smiled. These were the same taunts Bert used to hurl at him when they were kids, playing in this same corner of the yard.

Sometimes it helped to think that his brother had simply gone away somewhere. That they'd lost touch for a few months but would get back together at Christmas if the weather was good. There had been a petty disagreement. A misunderstanding. Brothers were like that sometimes. Bert always took his sweet time about saying what was on his mind. But they would work it out.

Their closest years were the ones after they'd returned home from the army. They knew they had both survived some ancient, hellish rite of manhood and needed to close ranks to protect one another against the old deceptions of God and country. The world was not the same place they had left to become soldiers. While one brother slogged through the bloody rice paddies of Asia and the other monitored radio transmissions at a long gray border coiled with razor wire, their country split apart. Great men were murdered, cities burned. Their rosy childhood was gone.

Kurt remembered how different Bert looked after Nam. His eyes mostly. Dark, hard, weary. At twenty-four he was already a troubled man. He chain-smoked now and spoke the bitter slang of a lifer. He trusted nobody, not even his brother. He tested Kurt, picked on him, brooded over imaginary offenses. It was as though their boyhood knot had come untied and Bert needed to tie it anew. He needed something certain, the familiar wordless comfort between brothers. More than anything he needed a friend who understood the trouble—the pain and loss and vicious brevity of it all.

"Look, Daddy!" Lennon said, lowering his bat. "Wow! That guy's coming right at us!"

Kurt turned to see the hang-glider angling toward them, his belly skimming the green broom-tops of the cedar grove thirty yards away. He was going to crash into the thicket.

"Come here!" Kurt said, racing toward his son. He could already picture those rainbow wings twisted in the dense brush like the shreds of a wind-tattered kite. His friend Bobby Coleman had hit the only tree in a hayfield and now lived in a wheelchair.

"Let's help him, Dad!" Lennon said, his eyes transfixed on the bright wings diving toward him.

Kurt scooped up the boy and backpedaled for the house, watching the glider clear the last cedar by inches. The Cubs cap fell from Lennon's head and he whined, but Kurt refused to stop and pick it up while that madman was plummeting into their yard.

"Son of a bitch," he said in amazement.

For a moment the glider hovered above the clearing as if he could brake in midair. The wings shifted, dragging against an invisible current, defying gravity, and then the contraption floated gracefully to earth like a child's birthday balloon with a slow deflating leak. The flyer's legs touched ground running and he stumbled once, twice, catching himself each time. Kurt was certain the momentum would send him headlong into the parked vehicles, but the man had an athlete's sense of balance, whoever he was, and pulled up beautifully, his heels digging into dirt.

"Yowzer!" Lennon said, struggling to free himself from his father's arms. "He landed just like Inspector Gadget!"

They watched from the porch as the man in the orange Gore-Tex jumpsuit untangled himself from the flying machine. "Wait here," Kurt said.

"I want my cap," Lennon said.

"Wait right here," Kurt said, holding him back by the wrist.

The flyer flexed his legs and arms. He was tall, lean, smiling at them through a trim dark mustache. Kurt guessed the fool had developed trouble and was forced to bring himself down wherever he could. Dumb-shit tourist, he thought. He didn't know there was no decent space to land over here on Red Mountain.

"Got your message, little brother," the man said, squatting, his knees cracking after a deep knee bend. He removed the bicycle crash helmet from his head and dropped his sun goggles into the bowl. "I just happened to be in the neighborhood and thought I'd drop in."

"You freaking lunatic," Kurt said.

Jake Pfeil looked back at the cedar grove and the path of his descent. He seemed as amazed as Kurt and Lennon. "I could use a drink," he said.

When Kurt came back outside with two cold beers, Jake was showing Lennon the harness of the hang-glider.

"Nice kid," Jake said. "Good thing for him he favors his mother."

"Daddy, this man said he can teach me how to fly!"

"Go inside and play Nintendo or something," Kurt said.

Lennon's bottom lip curled. "I want to learn how to fly," he said.

"Go on inside."

Lennon put his hands in the pockets of his Oshkosh jeans and sullenly refused to move.

"Lennon, I told you to go inside," Kurt raised his voice. "Do not argue with me. Just do it!"

He was immediately angry with himself for using clumsy force. But he didn't want his son listening to this conversation.

Jake watched the boy walk toward the house, his head down, disappointed and hurt. "Can't keep him under your wing forever, little brother," he said.

"Here's your beer," Kurt said. "We've got things to discuss."

Jake walked like a man who had just ridden a horse a great distance. He sat on the edge of the wood porch, letting his weight down gingerly, wincing. Kurt remembered Jake's bad shoulder, the convenient old wound that excused his failure at college football.

"I wondered when the Feds would finally get around to you," Jake said.

Kurt propped one foot on the porch and drank his beer. "I want to know what's going on, Jake," he said. He could hear the electronic blips of Nintendo coming from Lennon's window.

"My lawyer told me what Staggs has been saying about you and me and this army of wetbacks selling grass on school playgrounds," Jake said, his forehead wrinkling with amusement. "You were a cop a long time, Muller. Tell me something. Where do they find guys like Staggs? I'm going to have my secretary send him my résumé. I quit dealing pot when the Mafia did away with ten-dollar lids."

Kurt knew that. Everybody in Aspen knew that.

"Now he's saying I had that scribbler whacked. The guy from fucking Tierra del Fuego you dragged out of the river. He says somebody has come forward with a make. You can see how I'm a little confused here myself, little brother. The man is adding insult to injury. First the schoolchildren, now murder one. I'm wondering if maybe there's something here you know that I don't. Like who's this somebody telling stories to the Feds?"

Kurt couldn't be certain of Jake's innocence in the Quiroga murder. He couldn't be certain of anything about Jake. Not as long as there were file photos of Chad Erickson sitting upright in his car, the top of his skull split open like an overboiled egg where the projectile had exited his cranium.

"Staggs played me a piece of the tapes, Jake," Kurt said. "You dragged my name into your slime."

Jake took a drink and licked at the cottony film on his lips. "I'm at a disadvantage here, little brother," he said. "My lawyer and I have only made it through cassette thirty-seven, the Reagan years."

"Listen to me, Jake." Kurt dropped his boot from the porch, a resounding thud. "I don't care if the grand jury drags your bloody carcass through the streets. All I want to know is why you think I'm such a good friend and standup guy I would so much as piss on you if you caught fire."

Jake took his time getting up. He stretched his back, flexed his legs again, then bent down to pick up Lennon's bat. "Here I am coming down in the trees, my life flashes before my very eyes, and all I can remember is that time Bert hit one into your kitchen window," he said, reading the bat's label, feeling its grip. "Remember that? Our mothers were making lunch for one of those awful family picnics and the glass flew all over the potato salad."

Kurt remembered that the three boys were sentenced to help the janitor mop and clean the Aspen Institute building.

Jake took a slow practice swing. "The tapes are bullshit. Forget about them," he said. "I've got lawyers that eat wiretaps for breakfast. By the time they're finished, the grand jury will hear whatever we want them to hear."

"Somehow I don't find that very comforting," Kurt said.

"This isn't about tapes," Jake said, setting his feet in a batter's stance. "If they had good tapes they would've yanked me in a long time ago. This is something else. Somebody's come forward with a make on this murder. I don't know who it is, but he's got the Feds wetting their happy little drawers."

"They want you pretty bad. I can't say as I blame them."

Kurt had tried his best to put Jake away. It was impossible to imagine the man behind bars.

"I didn't take out that scribbler," Jake said. "But somebody hates me bad enough to say I did. I'd like to find out why this individual's got a problem with me."

He unzipped the orange jumpsuit and reached inside to rip loose a wallet Velcroed to his waistband. The wallet contained a substantial stack of hundred-dollar bills.

"I want to talk to the guy," he said, fanning the bills. At least five thousand dollars. "My lawyer has offered to arrange a meeting. Strictly private, no badges. We think we can work things out."

Kurt snorted. "Just like you worked things out with Chad Erickson?"

"I need a name, little brother. That's all. I'm not going to hurt anybody."

He tossed the wallet onto the porch next to an empty beer bottle.

"You were a cop a long time. You learned a few chops, how to track somebody down. I want you to help me with this name. I could bring in a slick PI from L.A., but it'd take the guy a couple of weeks just to get over his asthma. I've got time considerations."

Kurt didn't know whether to laugh or feel appreciated.

"This is only an appetizer," Jake said, nodding at the money. "A little for your trouble, a little to grease the wheels. I'll double what you see there when you give me a name."

Kurt looked over at his son's window. Lennon was standing there, his face close to the screen, watching the two men in the yard. He looked like the most forlorn little boy in all the world.

"You're out of a job, Muller. You could use the work," Jake said. "I'm not going to hurt anybody. My lawyer just wants to know what the Feds think they're doing hanging this bullshit on me. He wants to find out if Staggs has a case or he's just passing gas."

Kurt stared at the wallet. With that kind of money a man could trade in his Jeep, buy an old van, pack up his son, and hit the road. Maybe take the boy to visit his mother in Oregon.

"Look, man, I know you hate my guts," Jake said, "but like it or not, whoever's fucking me over is fucking you over too. I guess growing up in the same town with Jake Pfeil was a federal offense. I can't change that. I'm just trying to find out who the players are."

Kurt suspected that if he found out something and gave Jake a name, whoever it was would have serious trouble starting his car.

"It's pretty simple, little brother. You help me, you help yourself." He gave Kurt a rueful smile. "Like the old days, one big family picnic."

Kurt put his hands in his hip pockets and looked away at the mountain. "You're forgetting something, aren't you, Jake?"

Jake shrugged. "Tell me."

"The glass in the potato salad."

They stared at each other. In spite of who Jake had become, in spite of who he had always been, Kurt saw in him at that moment a little piece of all that was left. They were the last surviving inheritors of a dream. Everyone else was either dead or living in Arizona.

Kurt regarded the wallet of hundred-dollar bills. "I've got to know something first," he said.

Jake appeared unexpectedly pleased. "Name it," he said.

"Why were you and Bert spending so much time together those last few months?"

Jake cracked his neck with a slight move of the head. The smile evaporated. "We played racquetball at the club a couple of times," he said. "We did a little coke together. That what you're after?"

The last year of his brother's life Kurt was so fogged by depression and lack of sleep he was only vaguely aware that something was wrong. Lately, though, looking back four years, he realized he'd been blind to many things. But who could blame him? There was a first child, a strained marriage, a murder investigation he couldn't solve, pressure from the FBI.

He knew now that Bert had withdrawn gradually, in small hurtful ways. He stopped calling. He stopped coming over to watch the Broncos play football on Sundays, their most sacred ritual. He made lame excuses to miss holiday get-togethers and weekend skiing and good bands in the clubs. Kurt understood, of course, that it was hard to be around him and Meg while there was a new baby in the house and so much tension. The place was a mess. Lennon cried hour after hour with colic. Kurt and Meg argued constantly about the thousand niggling obligations of baby maintenance, how to wash this, when to prepare that, whose turn it was. They were exhausted, nervous, shrill, boring. It made perfect sense, at the time, that Bert would choose to stay away.

At the funeral, as Kurt carried the urn down the grassy slope to scatter his brother's ashes, he struggled to remember how long it had been since he'd last seen or spoken to Bert.

"I can't take your money, Jake."

Jake glanced toward the house and saw Lennon standing at the window. "Think of it as an investment for your boy," he said. "A college scholarship."

"There's more," Kurt said. "With you there's always more."

Jake had a dreamy look in his eye, and for a moment Kurt remembered that expression on a much younger face.

"Can you believe that two guys named Pfeil and Muller still own the high school stats in this valley?" he said, raising his face to the sky. "Most completions, most yards in the air for a single season, most passing touchdowns. It's hard to believe, all these years." He waited, his eyes closed to the sun. "Goes to show you what kind of sorry-ass teams they've fielded since the old days. Acid must've ruined the gene pool around here."

Kurt sat down on the edge of the porch and thought back to when he was a big wet-nosed sophomore at defensive end, trying with all his might, scrimmage after scrimmage in those cold autumn afternoons, to knock Jake Pfeil on his butt. Jake was still the most elusive son of a bitch in the world.

"Maybe you didn't know your brother as well as you wanted to," Jake said.

He was probably right, Kurt thought. He had known the burned-out young soldier who'd come home to the noisy confusion of a new world, but that was twenty years before. Bert was a very different man at the end.

"He got tired of being poor," Jake said. He opened his eyes and gave Kurt a sober look. "Every sweaty little sausage grinder in the country with a wad of money in his back pocket was buying a second home in Aspen and Bert got sick of watching them take over our town. I know you think I've turned out to be a bad boy, little brother, but let me tell you something. A lot of the fat cats with swimming pools up here on Red Mountain and in Starwood and the West End have buried their share of bodies back home in their quiet little suburbs. They've made their money over somebody's grief."

Kurt wondered how many bodies Jake had buried in his time.

"It bothered him," Jake said. "He'd see some fucking moron with a bad toupee and gold chains, some guy who owned delis on Long Island, fly in here a couple of seasons with his squeeze secretary and then start acting like he was best friends with Jack and Warren. A few inquiries, a lot of liquid assets, the right realtor, and bingo"—he snapped his fingers—"instant property, instant status, instant Hollywood suck. It's hard to recognize this place anymore. Remember when you could drop into the Paradise on a Tuesday fucking night and hear Cher—*Cher*, for Chrissake—singing her heart out to twenty locals in muddy Sorels? No more, little brother."

"I always hate it," Kurt said, "when the sausage grinders chase off a class act."

"You asked," Jake said, "so I'm telling. Bert hated what was happening here. He couldn't figure out why they were rich and he wasn't. And why they owned his town and he could barely make rent teaching their ugly kids how to ski."

Kurt stared down between his knees, watching a single black ant crawl across the scuffed toe of his hiking boot. "So you were going to help him out," he said. "For old times' sake."

Jake shrugged. "Bert was no different than anybody else," he said. "He needed a little financial stability. He didn't want to wake up one morning, twenty years from now, and have to walk down a cold linoleum corridor to piss in a toilet with a bunch of toothless old men."

Thunder rumbled over Ajax and Kurt could see the rain approaching. He thought about his mother living in Scottsdale among the blue-haired widows who nodded off every night after their clonidine.

"How were you going to make him financially stable, Jake?"

Jake held his ground. Even when wide hulky bodies were flying all around him, the pack pressing closer and closer, he always stood his ground and waited till the last second, scanning the entire field, watching the options unfold, holding out past any sensible margin of safety, before making his move. The best stats in the Valley. No one was ever going to catch him.

"You always were the Boy Scout in the family, weren't you, little brother?"

There was something dark and slightly malicious in Jake's smile.

"Tell me about it," Kurt said, rising to his feet. "You've never done anything in your life unless there was something in it for Jake Pfeil."

They faced each other now, only a few feet apart. Jake was not going to flinch, not in this century. You could knock him down and he'd get up laughing. Kurt had seen it happen too many times. He'd get up laughing and the next time around he'd make you pay. The next time around he'd give you a good hard knee to the head when nobody was watching.

"Did you offer him investment counseling, Jake?" Kurt said, nodding at the wallet. "Maybe some kind of employment opportunity? I'm curious to know how you were going to make an old ski bum like Bert a wealthy man."

"You're still thinking like a fucking cop," Jake said bitterly.

They studied one another, the changes wrought by age, listening to other voices, laughter distant and forgotten, their own lost echoes in the yard. Slowly, unexpectedly, something softened in Jake's face, that dreamy, faraway look again.

"Tell you the truth, little brother, it never went very far," he said in a quiet voice. "I had some ideas, sure. Some opportunities for him to move into. Nobody was in a rush. Then one afternoon I got a message from my answering service. Miles Cunningham called to tell me Bert had dropped off the Bells."

Kurt remembered what it was like when he phoned his mother. The hardest thing he'd ever done in his life. His windpipe had felt as though someone had knotted a wire around it. He kept clearing his throat, struggling to get out the message. She began to sob even before his first choking words. She knew. Mothers always knew.

'Mein lieber Sohn,' she cried over and over. *'Mein lieber Sohn.'*

Kurt heard soft footsteps on the porch and turned. Lennon was standing there, looking down at the wallet.

"Can I come out now, Daddy?" he asked in a tiny sad voice.

"Sure you can, sweetheart," Kurt said, walking over to hug him. There was a lump in his throat. All this talk about a dead son.

"What's that, Dad?" Lennon said, pointing to the wallet.

"That belongs to Mr. Pfeil."

Lennon looked at Jake, then at the hang-glider resting near the Jeep. "Daddy, will you let Mr. Pfeil teach me how to fly?" he asked.

Kurt ran his hand through Lennon's silky red hair. "We'll talk about it sometime," he said.

Not a chance in hell, he thought.

"You've got a great kid there, little brother," Jake said. "He's growing like a weed. Last time I saw him he was in one of those papoose hippie things on his mother's back."

Lennon shifted out of his father's arms. "My mommy is getting well," he said.

Kurt and Jake exchanged glances.

"She still in Telluride?" Jake asked.

Kurt shook his head. "She's moved on," he said.

"I always liked her," Jake said. "She was a smart girl."

He ambled over and squatted to meet Lennon eye to eye. The Velcro wallet lay at the boy's feet. "This is for you and your daddy," he nodded, his hands on his knees. "Your daddy knows what to do."

Lennon looked up at Kurt with one eye squinted, as if he, too, were gazing drowsy-eyed into the sun. He smiled a sly, unsure smile at his father, an accomplice in a secret he didn't understand.

Jake straightened up and stretched. In spite of his fanatical daily workouts at the Nordic Club he always carried himself like a man who'd just taken a beating.

"Think it over, little brother," he said, rubbing the back of Lennon's head, giving his neck an affectionate shake. "It's only a name. Everybody will go home happy."

Kurt wasn't going to lift a finger to help Jake eliminate another enemy. But he was curious now if there was someone out there linking his own name to the Quiroga murder.

Jake picked up his crash helmet and started out across the rocky yard. "I'll stay in touch," he said over his shoulder.

The rain was closer now, sweeping across the bowl of land this side of Hunter Creek. Kurt sat down on the edge of the porch and hooked an arm around Lennon's waist.

"Aren't you forgetting something?" he called after Jake. The wallet hadn't moved an inch.

The old quarterback waved an arm lazily over his head like a seasoned ballplayer signaling for a fair catch. "Keep the glider," he said, tramping off toward the dirt road that trailed into town. "I'm petrified by the damn thing."

Lennon dropped to one knee and jerked his arm, an imaginary gearshift. "Yesss!" he exclaimed.

Kurt glanced at the wallet. He should have stuck it back in Jake's jumpsuit, he thought.

Five thousand dollars. Double that if he uncovered a name.

He should have tossed it back.

14

THAT EVENING HE DROVE OUT CEMETERY LANE PAST THE deck-lit suburban enclave on the edge of the golf course, the strange lumpish pyramid of Red Butte jutting up in the dark just beyond the shingle roofs and two-car garages. The road dropped low to cross the bridge over the Roaring Fork, and as the Jeep climbed toward the scrubby pastures of McLain Flats, Kurt switched on the ultrasonic signal to warn any wandering deer that he was approaching at high speed. Off to the left he could see lights from the airport twinkling through the wide river gorge like distant stars visible in a black tunnel. A hundred years ago bearded men in drooping hats had blasted open that deep fault-line gorge to lay track for the old Denver and Rio Grande Western Railroad, now another forgotten passage in history's back pages.

The unmarked turnoff to secluded Starwood looked like an ordinary country road going nowhere. The residents preferred it that way. Movie stars, rock singers, retired lobbyists, investors with a little property in Costa Rica. The elite of the elite. Aspen itself was not exclusive enough for them.

The road curved up a boulder-pocked hillside without a single mansion in view. A security station was the first sign that visitors were entering another world.

"How's it going, Harley?" Kurt said to the uniformed guard who stepped out of his glass booth to greet him with clipboard in hand.

"I recognize the Jeep," the guard grinned at him, "but who's that clean-cut dude sitting at the wheel?"

"Shoot any autograph hounds lately?" Kurt said, amused by the huge ivory-stock Colt strapped to Harley's hip in a Western holster.

"I used to have a beard myself," Harley said, stroking his chin. "My old lady left me 'cause I shaved it off. She said it was like living with a raw oyster."

His name was Harley Ferris and they played on the same softball team every summer. Harley was a big, sweet, slow-talking left-fielder with a rocket arm. Third-base runners thought they could tag up and make it home on a deep fly ball. Harley laughed like a mean little kid every time they tried.

"What brings you up to my chateau?" Harley asked. "This police business, or you out roaming around?"

Apparently he hadn't heard that Kurt was a civilian now. But then Harley probably hadn't heard that Gerald Ford was out of office.

Kurt nodded at the clipboard in Harley's hand. "Put down I came to shoot pool with Barry Manilow," he said.

Harley rolled his eyes. "I gotta put something," he said. "Sorry, man. They run a tight ship around here."

"I'm going to the Rostagno party," Kurt said.

Harley straightened his thick shoulders and began to write on the clipboard sheet. "I'm supposed to ask for the invitation," he said. "No matter who, I gotta ask."

Kurt opened the glove compartment and feigned a search through the junk. "What do you know about them?" he asked, rattling dead batteries and wire.

"Not much," Harley said, glancing up from his clipboard. "The girl's home for the summer. She's a real popular item, if you know what I mean. Takes to rich boys with funny hair and old

Corvettes. When Daddy's out of town, they start showing up with appointment slips." He jerked his thumb at the guard station. "I'm thinking about installing one of those pick-a-number things they got at Baskin-Robbins." He paused and grinned at Kurt. "You trying to get in her shorts too?"

Kurt clattered screwdrivers in the glove compartment. "Gee, Harley," he said, "I can't seem to find that damn invitation."

The guard leaned forward again and spoke in a quiet, conspiratorial voice. "She's a wild one, Kurt," he said. "She gets a line of toot up her nose, she likes to come flying by with her top down, if you know what I mean. Always gives me a nice peek at her set. One of these days she's going to kill somebody in that little sports car."

"Do you know which place is theirs?" Kurt asked. "I can't find the invitation."

Harley Ferris produced a map of Starwood and circled the address. "You're not going to get me in trouble, are you, Kurt?" he said, noticing the stitches above Kurt's eye.

"Relax, Harley," Kurt said, putting the Jeep in gear. "I'll wear a ski mask."

Beyond the security station the country road became an impeccably maintained street with proper curbs and gutters. Ivy and smooth green carpet grass replaced the arid hillside terrain, and the unnamed lanes of Starwood sundered off in their own secret designs. It was like Beverly Hills up here. Concealed in elaborate arboreal landscaping, the homes of the ultrarich sprawled across the mountainside, vying for the best view of the Valley, each one a fussy architect's favorite wet dream. Kurt had been here on several occasions. Celebrity New Year's parties, fund raisers for his campaigns. From time to time he brought minors home to their brittle parents —rich kids caught smoking dope in the park gazebo, or panhandling for money on the mall. He once drove to Carbondale to retrieve a Starwood girl who'd tried to rob a convenience store using a silver letter opener as a weapon. Fourteen years old, she couldn't stand her latest stepfather and was running away to the Coast.

In the dark it was impossible to find an address. He cruised down a narrow lane enclosed in dense hanging vines, the jungly foliage illumined by delicate Japanese lanterns that cast a green botanical hue over this thin ribbon of night. The only sound was the steady ticking of lawn sprinklers, their soft spray on leaves. He stopped to turn on the map light and check the directions, and realized he was lost. But he knew if he kept circling the cloistered streets he would eventually find a trail of parked automobiles. Within a half hour he came upon a platoon of young preppie valets arranging Volvos and BMWs along a wooded cul-de-sac.

He followed a handful of arriving guests across a redwood footbridge over a gurgling stream. Near the entrance to the Rostagno home there was a garden of carefully displayed rocks, an impressive assortment of shapes and colors. One of the guests explained to his friends that the rocks were not rocks but expensive ceramics produced by a Hopi artist from Taos.

The usual hired servers greeted them in the foyer, pretty blond women who lived to ski. They looked stunning in male tuxedo shirts, black trousers, bow ties. The young woman who took his suede jacket had danced with him one night at the Paradise.

"Isn't your name Steve?" she smiled, trying to place where they'd met.

Another girl offered to get him a drink, and he went to lean against a massive white column, searching for Cecilia Rostagno among the clusters of guests making conversation in a sunken living room with the monumental proportions of an ancient forum. Like most parties in Aspen this one promised its share of faded celebrity, the lesser has-beens who'd once held court near the margins of fame but who were now dissipating further into obscurity. They clung to this society for the gouty food and drink and the vain possibility that an adman from Cleveland might remember who they were and offer them a steady job endorsing cat food.

He recognized an aging actress who had starred in several forgettable spy movies in the sixties, and at least one forgettable television series where she played somebody's testy wife. A surgeon's scalpel had kept her cover-girl features intact, but her thick platinum hair, the hallmark of her screen presence, looked as though it was now maintained with the aid of high chemistry. Wineglass in hand, she was speaking to an eccentric screenwriter with wild devilish eyebrows who had collaborated with her on a picture fifteen years ago, the last time either one had worked. Kurt vaguely remembered the film as a lame jet-set romance shot on a Caribbean island. The tabloids had made a field day of the alcoholic binges, the pills, the mysterious suicide of her lover found hanging in a shower stall.

Sitting on a sofa next to his young wife, the mother of their two-year-old, an over-the-hill novelist, now in his seventies, was entertaining a group of graying matrons who still read his books. He was an imposing figure—large, overfed, Buddha-like, his hair nearly gone except for long frosty wings combed back over his ears. In spite of great wealth he always wore the cheap sport jackets and checkered pants of a small-town Rotarian. He held uncompromising opinions on every conceivable subject and was known to browbeat dissenters. A dozen of his books had been blockbuster best-sellers, nearly all of them made into movies. But the younger generations were not interested in the war in the Pacific, or endless rehashes of Nazi intrigue. His sales figures had been slipping for twenty years, and it was rumored he was deeply depressed and unable to write anymore. Over drinks one evening in the Jerome Bar, Kurt had learned from the man's research assistant, a Princeton woman who'd probably written his last three books for him, that the great novelist's publishing house of five decades was trying to dump him. Tonight, however, he carried on in fine form, lecturing and laughing and waving the glass in his hand. The elderly admirers were hanging on his every word.

The waitress brought Kurt a vodka tonic and he moved on, circling the periphery of the party, looking for Cecilia. Near the master fireplace, chatting with the dignified reserve of gentility, stood several people who had known Kurt's parents. They were Institute folk, harmless highbrow millionaires who had escaped to Aspen in the fifties to avoid the rat race and live off their prodigious fortunes. Observing them now, he imagined how his father might have appeared had he survived—erect, tan, sparse of hair, his flesh a little loose at the neck. One man was a Russian who had defected after the war to work for the CIA. Kurt's father liked him because he was well read in four languages and played a fair jazz clarinet. At a Christmas party one year, when the Muller boys were home from college and feeling unusually hostile toward the older generation, Bert had asked the retired agent, in front of a house full of Institute cronies, to account for his whereabouts on the day John Kennedy was assassinated. It was meant as a joke, an awkward attempt at humor after a few drinks, but the old fellow was not amused. As Kurt recalled, the man sputtered a bit, contradicted himself, then grew angry and stormed out of the party. Their father glared at Bert, then laid a forgiving hand on his son's shoulder. 'I never realized until my boy's interrogation,' he said to his puzzled colleagues in the circle, 'that poor Yulie knew Oswald.'

Kurt watched the silver-haired Claudio Rostagno stride down the marble steps into the living room, making his way toward tennis rival Bob Graeber and the other hotel developers. Rostagno glad-handed the men, gripping their upper arms with a virile tug, and bent to kiss the wives on each cheek. His manners were courtly, European. From time to time he punctuated his conversation with a stiff-shouldered nod. Kurt wondered where the man's daughter was and how long he could remain unnoticed in these outer shadows. He hated parties and didn't relish the idea of getting caught up in this gathering and its idle conversation.

Rostagno handed a drink to his wife, the belle dame Patricia Graham, now enjoying the flawless plasticity of her fourth face-lift, one for each husband. Kurt suspected that this house belonged to her. She was a New Orleans girl with family money from a banana empire in Honduras and with each marriage had acquired even greater prosperity. Kurt had met her some years ago when she came to his office to request a restraining order against estranged husband number two, the alcoholic Texan with the world-renowned gun collection who'd made a habit of abusing the poor lady at social functions. Kurt had thrown the sorry bastard in jail one snowy night for taking drunken pistol practice on her Mountain Valley mailbox.

Patricia Graham was speaking with a ravishing young brunette the locals called the Merry Widow. Though not yet thirty, the woman had been widowed three times, all of them reckless men prone to accidents with hunting rifles and fast cars. Tonight she was escorted by a glamorous male model wearing a gem earring, chic Italian shoes, and an expensive Armani suit. She had no doubt picked him up in New York, where she kept an apartment in SoHo. The young man seemed unaware of how ludicrously overdressed he was for an Aspen party.

Kurt finished his drink down to the ice. It was only a matter of time before someone recognized him and came over to talk. Where the hell was Cecilia?

Meg had taught him that on painful occasions like these, when trying to avoid social interaction, one should always look passionately at the art. It was wise advice. The homes of the Aspen rich were filled with strange abstract noodlings, vast canvases of drips and splatters, art by the square yard. Kurt turned his back to the party and chewed his ice and gazed at a colossal rectangular painting composed of two angry slashes of color, red and black.

'What's this stuff all about?' he had once asked Meg on one of their early dates, a gallery opening below the old Opera House. She was an amateur photographer and had studied art history in college.

'It's about art supplies,' she'd said with a cunning little smile.

Sometimes he missed her. Seventeen years together, a wonderful child. Maybe they should have tried harder to live with the differences.

"This Gottlieb is strange and very beautiful, don't you think?" a voice behind him said. "I've always felt there is something terribly disturbing about it."

Cecilia had found him. Tonight she looked more enchanting than ever, her strapless dress a striking aquamarine color that brought out the rich creaminess of her skin. The fluff of black hair on her bare shoulders reminded him of Graciela.

"Would you care for another drink?" she asked.

He swallowed the ice in his mouth. "Yes, thanks," he said.

Cecilia looked over the guests milling about the living room and signaled to a server. "Do you know any of these people?"

"Not my crowd."

"Mine either," she said with a mischievous smile. "Shall we make a change of scenery?"

She took the server aside and whispered something, then turned to Kurt. "She'll send down a bottle," she said.

She stepped closer and looked up into his face, at the small row of wiry stitches in his forehead. She touched a button on his shirt, fingered it, feeling its roundness. "I wasn't sure you'd come," she said in a quiet voice, her eyes fixed on the button. "I'm glad you did."

"I take my private consultation very seriously," he said.

She placed a warm hand flat against his chest. "Good," she said, a naughty smile brushing her lips. "Let us go find out what you have in mind for my little room."

They went downstairs to a cavernous wing buried in the cliff. Huge white columns gave the space the gloomy, vaulted coldness of a temple ruin. Cecilia escorted him through the arcade and out onto a marble balcony for a view of the stars. It was a crisp summer evening in the mountains and she pressed close to him. Down below, on the dark floor of the Valley, lights clustered in unknown constellations. Headbeams inched along a far-off highway.

"You were very impressive at the club today," she said. "Do you enter competitions?"

"I just like to stay in shape," Kurt said. "An old man like me never knows when he'll need a little extra endurance."

A thin dark eyebrow lilted. "I like older men," she said. "They're more entertaining."

She was clutching her elbows now, shivering from the cold, and he suddenly remembered the moment in the Grottos when he covered Graciela with his jacket. "It's chilly out here," he said, placing his hands on Cecilia's bare shoulders.

"Yes," she said, her shoulders relaxing. "Shall we go inside?"

She took him to a small *fumoir* with wood paneling and a stone fireplace and poured pinot noir into two long-stemmed glasses.

"So, my friend," she said, shifting closer in the antique French love seat. "What do you do when you are not working out at the club?"

Kurt sipped the dark wine. "I'm an instructor at a place called Star Meadow," he said. "Massage, yoga, t'ai chi." He watched her eyes for the slightest response. "It's a retreat for old hippies who can't cope. We do lots of seminars. Have you heard of it?"

Cecilia smiled at his description. "Yes, of course," she said. "It's that place run by Matt Heron, isn't it? What is he like?"

"Helluva guy," Kurt said. "Real down to earth. We just had a very unfortunate thing happen out there and Matt handled it great. Did you read about that South American writer they found floating in the Roaring Fork? The guy was attending one of our conferences." Kurt shook his head. "The potential for a major PR disaster. But Matt handled it like a pro."

Narrowing her eyes as if recalling something that had happened years ago, Cecilia made a deliberating nod. "I did read about it, yes," she said. "The authorities think there was a drug ring involved."

Kurt laughed. "Matt told me that's all a lot of jive. The cops know who's behind it, but they're keeping it quiet. The murder didn't have anything to do with those Mexicans in Emma."

Cecilia lifted the wineglass to her lips. Her dark eyes studied him. "I hope everything works out for you," she said in a husky voice.

"It's okay," he said. "We're off the hook. Matt says the cops will arrest somebody soon." He glanced down at his glass, turning the stem. "I really shouldn't be talking about this, but they think it happened in the guy's room at the Meadow. They found a broken wineglass with somebody's prints all over it."

She rubbed a finger slowly, absently, around the lip of her glass, tracing its shape with a nail the color of an exotic fruit. After a moment she placed the glass on the coffee table, stood up, and crossed the room to lock the door.

This could get interesting, Kurt thought.

She watched him, her shoulders against the door. A wave of soft black hair fell across that dazzling face which was so capable, in the smallest momentary drama, of mischief and sexiness and trouble.

"I'm trying to decide if you are a man who can be trusted."

Graciela had wondered the same thing. He drank his wine and waited.

She studied him for a few seconds longer, then sauntered across the room to the fireplace. She knelt on one knee, exposing a muscular brown thigh, and reached back into the hearth. Underneath a loose stone there was a small, ornate jewel box. She brought the box back to the coffee table, set it before them, and opened the brass-hinged lid.

"I must be cautious," she said. "I have my little secrets."

Kurt hadn't done cocaine in years. He had given up drugs altogether, mostly to play it straight around Lennon. He didn't want to live with the hypocrisy anymore.

"My father does not approve, to say the least," Cecilia said.

She dipped a tiny silver spoon into a plastic bag and brought the coke to her nostrils for two dainty sniffs, pinching her nose. She offered the spoon to Kurt but he hesitated, considering for a moment what to do.

"Do you?" she said.

He knew if he declined, their night together would be woefully short and unrevealing. He had no choice.

The coke burned straight through his sinuses and into his brain. The rush was immediate and breathtaking. There was no doubt about the purity of her stash. This was high-grade cocaine.

"Let me show you something," she said, pushing a button on a console by the love seat.

A faint whir sounded across the room and the wood paneling began to slide away, exposing a large video screen. Cecilia touched another button and a view of the upstairs living room flickered into focus. More guests had arrived. The aging novelist was still pontificating to his audience around the sofa.

"Father likes to keep an eye on things," she said, flipping to another room. Two men wearing starched white jackets and chef hats fussed over an assembly of hors d'oeuvres. Waitresses darted in and out with trays of drinks. Cecilia used the control device to direct the surveillance camera around the kitchen. She zoomed in on the girl Kurt had danced with at the Paradise.

"What do you think of this one?" Cecilia asked. "She's very pretty, isn't she?"

The girl had stopped at a work station to arrange a stack of napkins on her tray.

"Yes," Kurt agreed. The coke had gone to his throat, numbing his vocal cords.

Cecilia curled her lip in mock jealousy. Her eyes wandered over the stitches in his forehead. "You like her?" she said.

"I've seen her around town," he said. "She's a great dancer."

"Is she good in bed?"

Before he could devise an answer she bent over the jewel box and had another spoonful of coke. She flipped past several empty rooms of the house, cold palatial chambers filled with cold colors and cold furnishings, until she located a bedroom where two people were roaming about on their own, examining objects—the books on a nightstand, feminine bottles and lipsticks and a mess of jewelry left on a vanity. It was the Merry Widow and her escort.

"Whose bedroom?" he asked.

Cecilia focused the camera on the young man as he sniffed a perfume bottle and then sprayed some on his neck. "It is mine," she said, somewhat dismayed.

The Merry Widow opened the drawer of an antique chiffonier and ran her hands through slinky lingerie.

"Do you know these two?" Cecilia asked.

"No."

"I have heard that this woman is quite bizarre," she said. "We mustn't let her out of our sight."

The Merry Widow ventured into an adjoining room and called to her date. The young man put down the tube of lipstick he was tasting and followed after her. Cecilia clicked another channel and found them in a large gleaming bathroom, her private dressing area. Marble steps led down into a round marble tub spacious enough for a bacchanal of Roman gods. The Merry Widow knelt in her tight black dress and turned on the shining spigots. The young man brought over a tray of bath beads and beauty oils. Soon frothy white bubbles lathered the tub and they began to undress.

"And how about this one?" Cecilia asked. "Does she excite you?"

"She's nice."

He had to keep his head on straight, but the coke was giving him such a rush it was hard to focus on anything except the Merry Widow's lovely nude body stepping into the bath. So far he had made absolutely no progress engaging Cecilia about Quiroga and Graciela.

"Do some more with me," Cecilia urged, touching her nose, scooting closer to him. She retrieved the spoon and filled another nostril.

"I'm okay like this," he said.

This whole deception left him hollow. He was beginning to feel ashamed of himself.

"Come on," she nudged Kurt with her shoulder. "Do a little more for me."

Trapped now, helplessly compromised, stricken with indecision, he snorted another spoonful and closed his eyes while the coke blazed through him, slicing raw every nerve end. He didn't know where any of this was leading and he felt paralyzed, unable to follow the strange receding arc of the evening. As he watched the couple on the video screen embrace in the thick white foam, Cecilia rested her warm hand on his knee and began to scratch him gently with her long nails.

Find a way, he told himself. *Get her to talk*.

The young man cupped foam in his hands and stroked the Merry Widow's breasts, massaging them, sudsing her dark nipples. They leaned forward to kiss, an exchange of tongues. Her hand searched under the foam, taking him. A delicate fist rose to the surface, disappeared, rose again, a fine knowing rhythm.

Cecilia stared at the screen. "Does this amuse you?" she asked, her nails making the lightest scrape against his knee.

"It's better than the Playboy channel," he said. He was hard as a pillar and certain she knew it.

Cecilia picked up a phone on the console and touched two numbers. "Rafael," she said, her voice stern, "we have a problem. Two people have left the party and are intruding where they do not belong. You must go to my bedroom at once and ask them to leave." She listened to the voice on the other end. "Yes," she said, her nails scraping gently. "In my bath. Please have them removed."

She replaced the receiver and squeezed Kurt's knee. "Come," she said. "We must not forget we have business to take care of."

"Funny," he said, "I was just thinking the same thing."

She latched the jewel box and returned it to the hiding place under the hearthstone. They walked out through the arcade past a still swimming pool whose eerie, aqueous light cast phosphorescent reflections against the columns. At the end of the long archway there was a stairwell winding down to a dim basement. Cecilia unlocked a door at the bottom of the stairs and led him inside an unfinished room with a single bare bulb dangling from the ceiling, its meager light suffusing the place in a ghostly gray pallor.

"The first thing I shall do," she said, "is install professional lighting." She pointed. "Track lights, don't you think?"

She began to question Kurt about Cybex machines and free weights and bicycles and treadmills and whirlpool baths. Pacing the empty floor space in a jerky, erratic ramble, she suggested where each piece of equipment might be located.

"Well," he said, trying again to focus, "you know what you want after all. You don't really need me, then, do you?"

Cecilia wandered into an unlit corner and sat down on a weight bench, the only object in the room. "Come," she said, patting the leather. A barbell was set in the rack, forty pounds, enough for a routine workout.

"I can tell you are a man of considerable experience," she said. "I'm sure you can teach me many things. I am always eager to improve."

He stood before her, looking down at the barbell, at her darkened face. She rose and began to unbutton his shirt. "So let us begin the lesson," she said.

She pulled apart the shirt, baring his chest, and ran her fingers through the thick brown hair. Her nails welted his skin. She leaned forward and opened her warm mouth over an erect nipple, circling it with her tongue.

Interrogation gets a whole lot easier, Kurt thought, *when you're not a cop.*

They kissed hard, clacking teeth, a hot edgy cocaine kiss, dry and furious. Their embrace had a grudging anger about it, yet he was aroused, his skin damp and tingling.

"Let me watch you," she said, pinching his nipple. She gave him a push and he tripped backward, sitting hard on the bench. "I want to feel your muscles working."

Go with this, he thought. *But remember why you're here.*

"Lift," she said, her hands on his shoulders, forcing him to lie back on the bench. "Show me what you can do."

He scooted into position to grip the barbell and lifted it off the rack. He began to bench-press the forty pounds, taking his time, sweat dripping down his arms, his ribs.

Cecilia hiked up her dress and straddled his thighs, sliding her hands through the wet hair on his chest, massaging his pecs. She caressed his face, her nails nicking the stitches above his eye. "What happened here?" she whispered. "Did one of your women hurt you?"

Kurt remembered that final moment in the Grottos with Graciela, someone standing over them. The blinding light. He extended his arms and set the barbell in the rack, then lay back, exhausted from the workout and the coke and the entire wasted evening.

"Do you like it when your women hurt you?"

She took his wrists and forced his weakened forearms underneath the bench. Something attached to the bottom of the board made a loose rattling noise as her hands fumbled about beneath them. He had no idea what she was doing until the rattling thing clamped tightly around one wrist, then the other. Instantly he recognized the snap of cold stainless steel. He'd handcuffed a few miserable bastards in his day.

"Tell me about them," she said, raising herself upright, her hands braced on his sweating chest. "I want to know all about your women."

Kurt wriggled his wrists, testing the cuffs. They were the real thing. She sat on his belly, rubbing herself against him in a slow circular motion, her coarse hair bristling his bare skin. He rocked his shoulders, testing the bounds of mobility, but found himself trapped beneath her.

"That girl upstairs. The little blond whore who brings the drinks," she said. "Is she one of them?"

Kurt felt like a complete fool. He couldn't believe he'd let her handcuff him to a fucking weight bench.

"Don't lie to me," she said, flicking a long nail across one of the wiry stitches in his forehead. It was not a pleasant sensation. "I want to know who they are, these precious whores of yours."

This is your moment, he thought. *Your only chance now.*

"I meet them at the Meadow," he said.

"The ones you massage?" she asked. "They put themselves at your mercy?"

"Yes," he said.

"And then you fuck them in the ass."

She took hold of a stitch between her nails, like a nurse with a tweezer, and gave it a quick little tug. A sharp white flash of pain hit him behind the eyes. He struggled against the cuffs.

"Tell me about them," she said. "These foolish women who come to your mountain meadow to save the world. Do you fuck them all?"

"Only the Latin ones," he said.

She tugged at another stitch and he winced. "Tell me," she said, grinding her teeth, her face flushed and wet.

"There is a new one from Argentina," he said. "Her name is Graciela. I take her to the Grottos at night and we fuck in the rocks."

He didn't know what to expect now, only that he needed to lead her further, to reel out more line until something struck.

"I was with her at Andre's," he said, "when I saw you there with Jake Pfeil. She told me she knew you. Do you remember her? A beautiful woman from Argentina."

The muted light veiled the confusion in her damp face but he could feel the sudden terror toiling and turning behind those dark eyes, working its way out, moving from uncertainty and doubt into a small safe discovery. She didn't like what she was hearing.

"You're a bad boy," she said in a soft voice. "A very bad boy. You have lied to me."

She kissed his forehead gently, his eyelashes. Long black hair fell from her shoulders, concealing everything but those piercing eyes. "You told me you were alone, my friend. Instead you were there with your fat whore from Argentina. I am unhappy when I am lied to. It makes me very angry."

She kissed his cheeks, soft nibbling kisses. He couldn't move. Her strong legs were locked against his ribs.

"And now you want to fuck me," she said, "like you fuck all the others. You pick me up at the club and tell me lies and want me to be your whore."

Her fingertips delicately touched his stitches, as though counting each one. "You're a very bad boy," she said. "And bad boys must take their punishment."

There was a quick blinding prick of pain, like a hot needle inserted into his eye. He cried out, hurt, his stomach churning sudden nausea. She'd yanked loose one of the stitches. Blood was trickling down his face.

"You fucking crazy bitch!" he gasped, rocking from side to side.

"Now we'll find out," she said, "who is the whore."

She lifted the skirt of her dress and slid herself onto his face, dropping the folds like a hood over his head. Darkness enveloped him and he struggled to breathe, his nostrils stuffed with musky hair. Her athletic thighs managed him, directed his resisting mouth. Just when he thought she might suffocate him, break his windpipe, she released a long shuddering moan and went slack, resting her full weight on his face. He began to gag. Blood from the torn stitch was dripping into his ear.

She finally raised her dress and crawled off of him. "*Gusano!*" she said, rubbing at a small bloodstain on the skirt. "Look what you've done. Now I must go upstairs and change."

The room's basement air was a cool relief to his lungs. He felt like a prisoner given a momentary reprieve from the guards.

"You revolt me," Cecilia said bitterly. "I ought to have you beaten for this."

Kurt wriggled his arms, his shackled wrists. He tried to blink away the blood in his eye.

"Here," she said, tossing a key that bounced off his chest onto the concrete floor. "Let yourself out through the servants' area. I don't ever want to see you again."

When she reached the door Kurt shouted her name. "Why did Graciela think she knew you?" he asked in a hoarse voice. "And Quiroga?"

Cecilia hesitated, then turned to peer at him through the dusky light. She seemed to understand now that she had been set up. Anger coiled around her like heat from an exposed wire. "I don't know who you are or what you want," she said, "but I intend to find out." She slammed the door behind her.

Kurt felt drained, humiliated, in pain. He lay there for some time, trying to shape his scattered thoughts. The cocaine was wearing off and he felt hot and shaky and inexplicably annoyed with his entire life. He realized he was chewing his lip. He couldn't believe he'd let some little bitch handcuff him half naked to a weight bench.

Jerking wildly at the cuffs, Kurt finally managed to pull loose the lynch screw. He squirmed to the bottom end of the bench and slid his butt off onto the cold concrete, then rocked the legs until the bench turned over. The barbell crashed to the floor with a loud rattling clang and rolled away. It took considerable effort to maneuver his cuffed wrists under his feet and around in front of him, and he grunted and strained and cursed the girl for doing this to him. Finally he crawled over to the key and unlocked the cuffs. He pulled a handkerchief from his pants and applied it quickly to the bleeding stitch. His face and hair were wet with blood.

Groping his way through the dark basement, he found the stairs. At the swimming pool he knelt down to soak the handkerchief, leaving a red bloom in the motionless water.

"*Perdóneme, señor,*" a voice said above him. "Mr. Rostagno would like to see you in his study."

Kurt looked up to find a short, barrel-chested Hispanic man in a pressed white guayabera shirt gazing down at him. Kurt had seen this man somewhere before, but with the pain in his head, the ripped stitch and gnawing cocaine crash, he couldn't remember where.

"Let me guess," he said. "Mr. Rostagno wants me to play happy-hour piano."

The man was trying to place Kurt as well. He cocked his large head, studying him. Ancient acne scars pitted his face.

"If you please," he said, motioning toward the arcade with an open hand. "It would be better if we go quietly."

Claudio Rostagno was waiting for them in his study. Distracted, grim, he paced the soft carpet in what Kurt recognized as familiar court behavior, a tennis pro angry with himself, going deep inside to deliver the next serve. Kurt's arrival brought him around.

"I want to look in your face," he said, setting his drink on the large rosewood desk. He was close enough to breathe expensive

Scotch on Kurt, his arms locked behind his back like an officer examining a troop. "I want to see what kind of man would come into my home uninvited and insult my daughter."

Behind the thick black frames of his horn-rim glasses were the eyes of authority, the cold, confident eyes of someone who was used to being obeyed. There was a dark ferocity that suggested guile and perhaps other, more chilling qualities.

"I'm going to have you arrested," he said. "Rafael, please call Starwood security."

Kurt grinned weakly at the barrel-chested man standing near the double doors. "Go ahead, Rafael," he said. "I'll be happy to show them where Cecilia keeps her stash of coke."

Rostagno exhaled a long breath, his shoulders slumping, his chest caving slightly. Clearly he had heard this sort of thing before.

"I don't even know your name," Rostagno said. "What do you want from us?"

Kurt looked around the room. It was not unlike his father's study, Old World and male and sealed off with a timeless antique air that hinted of stale tobacco and aging brandy. There were shelves of hefty volumes and overstuffed reading chairs and a large leathery globe of the kind no one had manufactured in thirty years. But something about this place struck Kurt as odd. For a man who had rendered decades of political service to his country, there were no plaques of recognition, no framed certificates of honor and achievement, no flags or engraved cigarette lighters, not the usual wall of photographs of the ambassador with other distinguished men of international repute. It took Kurt a moment to understand what was bothering him. The study appeared curiously false.

"I've lost a friend," Kurt said finally. "I came here tonight because I thought your daughter could help me find her."

Rostagno placed a hand in one pocket of his blazer, a dapper gesture, and went to his desk to retrieve the drink. "I have no idea what you're talking about," he said. His bearing was rigidly perpendicular, his shoulders thrown back. "Rafael, would you please see to it that this man is escorted off the premises. He seems to be another one of my daughter's disgusting distractions. I don't want him mingling with the guests."

Rafael left his post by the doors and came forward. "Yes, sir," he said.

Kurt recalled now where he'd first seen Rafael. The powdered pool cue, the *Más Mota* T-shirt.

"Somebody thought he knew your daughter and he ended up floating in the river," Kurt said to Rostagno. "A woman I admire very much thought she knew her too. Now she's missing and my guess is she'll turn up dead. Maybe it's just a coincidence about your daughter. Maybe one and one don't really add up to two murders. You better hope so, Mr. Rostagno."

"Rafael." Rostagno nodded angrily at Kurt.

The barrel-chested man reached out and took Kurt's arm, but Kurt jerked away. "I can find my own way out," he said.

At the door Kurt turned to regard the Italian diplomat. "I have a feeling this isn't the last time we'll see each other."

Rostagno stared at him with a cold hatred, with a feudal sense of insult, of family honor violated. In his darkest moments Kurt's father was capable of this same outrage.

"You have made a grave mistake coming here tonight, my friend," Rostagno said. "For your sake you had better hope our paths never cross again."

Kurt leaned against the railing of the footbridge and stared down into the moonlit stream. Arriving guests passed behind him, and someone was complaining about the food at a ritzy restaurant in town. "Too much cilantro," she kept repeating. "Too much cilantro, don't you agree?" Although the stitch had stopped bleeding he was still crashing from the cocaine, in a foul mood, unsure what to do next. Maybe he should talk to Muffin, but he couldn't face her reaction to how stupid he'd been. Always letting the little head do the thinking.

Suddenly there were loud, angry voices in the private drive. He turned to see Cecilia storming down the gravel pathway, crying, shouting at the man following after her, arguing in a language Kurt didn't understand. She slammed the door of a sports car and cranked the engine. Her father stood over her, fuming, his hands clamped down on the window frame as if he could restrain the sleek little automobile by force. But the tires screeched rubber, knocking him backward, and the car weaved out of the driveway and into the night.

Kurt raced for his Jeep and followed her taillights down the deep, vine-choked lanes of Starwood. She might have lost him had she not slowed for the guard station, where Harley Ferris came out to watch her creep by, a hand on his hip, grinning from ear to ear.

Kurt kept pace more by sound than sight. He could hear the Miata squealing around the hairpin curves of the gorge below and knew she was not yet out of reach. Harley had said that someday she was going to kill someone in that car, and Kurt thought it might be tonight. He pushed his old Willys for all it was worth, but the Jeep was no match for her. He felt like a crude amateur telescope searching for the quick flash of a meteorite in the vast nighttime sky.

Swerving down from McLain Flats he saw sparks shower the darkness near the Rio Grande trailhead and figured that she'd bucked onto the narrow river-bridge, her tailpipe scraping hard against the concrete bed. He floorboarded the Jeep past the old cemetery where his father was buried and finally caught a glimpse of the sports car when it ripped through the red light at Highway 82.

The sight of town itself seemed to sober her driving and she slowed past the quiet West End neighborhood, the dark empty park, the red brick buildings still glittering in June with ridiculous white twinkle lights. He was able to catch up near Carl's Pharmacy and follow her sharp, last-second turns through the small busy streets near the pedestrian mall. It did not surprise him when she skidded to a stop in front of the Blake Building.

He parked across the street and watched her walk hastily to the intercom at the building's glass entrance. She jabbed a suite button several times and ran an impatient hand through her windblown hair.

"I need to see you!" she said to the intercom, her shrill words audible to Kurt across the street. "Are you alone?"

There was a long silence and then a buzzer sounded, permitting her into the building.

Kurt didn't have to read the nameplate to know who Cecilia had come to visit. He looked up at the windows of Jake Pfeil's corner suite. Light seeped softly through the drawn curtains. The old quarterback was home.

He sat motionless in his Jeep for some time, feeling wasted, muddleheaded. He was coming down hard from the coke and the hot surliness had now given way to an eye-burning exhaustion. He could smell his own body odor, a sour funk that stained his shirt. He rubbed his salty face, the tiny bristles of a fresh shave like steel wool irritating his skin. He needed a drink to dull the blade inside him that made little slices at his patience. He needed to talk to somebody who could tell him something useful.

On the corner there was a bar in an old bank building from the mining era, its entrance the original iron vault door imprinted UTE CITY BANK AND TRUST, 1885. Kurt ordered a shot of tequila and a beer and took them to a pay phone in the rear, near a barred teller window where a pretty girl checked coats.

The phone rang ten times before Miles picked up the receiver.

"Hello, Mr. Cunningham," Kurt said. "This is the Supreme High Elder of the Church of Latter-day Saints in Salt Lake City. I was just calling to assess the status of our military vessels at harbor in the creek near your property."

"Fuck you, ex–law man," Miles blubbered into the receiver. "I won't stand for this feeble mockery. I'll feed your entrails to my hounds."

"Listen, Miles, I know it's late and you're probably blown out of your skull, but I need your help, man. I really do."

Silence, a crackle of labored breathing.

"I have to know what a Spanish word means and I think you can probably tell me."

Kurt heard the sound of a man choking on his drink.

"Am I hallucinating," Miles said, "or are you calling me up in the middle of a perfectly transcendental veejay interview with Snoop Doggy Dogg to ask what a fucking *word* means?" Kurt could almost feel the spray of spittle. "Didn't they teach you how to use a dictionary in that podunk Aspen school you went to?"

Kurt downed the tequila and chased it with beer. The place was packed with beautiful strangers arranging their evenings together. He noticed a young man sitting at the end of the bar, hunched over his drink, listening with sullen indifference to an older fellow at the next stool.

"I think it might have something to do with Omar Quiroga," Kurt said. "You've been to Argentina. You know Spanish."

Kurt said the word.

"It means 'dry toast,' " Miles said. "It's a favorite party food in Buenos Aires."

"This is serious, Miles. Don't fuck me around, man. I'm in no mood right now."

"How the hell should I know what it means, Muller? You're probably not pronouncing it right, you moron."

Kurt spelled it for him. "Is it somebody's name?" he asked. "You've been down there, Miles. You took pictures at those trials. Does it ring a bell?"

"Christ," Miles breathed. "You're making me miss the part where Snoop discusses his favorite German philosophers."

"You fucking sot!" Kurt screamed into the phone. He banged the receiver against the wall. "Don't dick me around, man. This is important. So straighten your ass up, goddammit, and give me your undivided attention!"

Complete silence on the line. Kurt thought he might've broken the phone. He looked up to find several party cruisers raising their eyebrows at him. Even the sullen young man at the bar glanced his way. Turned-up collar, coal-black hair glistening with gel, skin the color of bronze. As unlikely as it seemed, Kurt felt he knew him.

"There's an old Portuguese aphorism my dear departed mother once taught me," Miles finally spoke. "Roughly translated, If you want a sailor's eye, don't piss in his ear. What the hell have you been snorting, anyway?"

As Kurt began to tell Miles what he wanted him to do, he finally recognized the young Romeo at the bar. He let go of the receiver in midsentence and stood up. The young man stood up at his stool.

"Angel?" Kurt said.

Dressed for an evening on the town, Angel Montoya looked older, more sophisticated. The little fool hadn't taken his advice to leave the Valley.

"Stay right there," Kurt said to him. "I want to talk to you."

Angel turned quickly and headed for the bank-vault door.

"Excuse me," Kurt said, elbowing people aside. He bumped someone's arm and she spilled her drink on her date's tasseled loafer.

"Asshole," the date said.

"Angel!" he said, shouldering his way through the jam of drinkers. "Hey, don't run, I'm not going to bust you."

Every face in the club turned to regard him.

"Get out of the fucking way," Kurt said, shoving a tall nosy fellow into a crowded table. They all began to yell at him.

Out on the street he caught a glimpse of Angel disappearing into the swarm of evening strollers on the pedestrian mall.

"Angel, wait!" he shouted.

He wanted to ask him what he knew about Rostagno's man, the barrel-chested pool player in the *Más Mota* T-shirt. But Angel was gone. Passersby were looking at Kurt the way everyone had looked at him tonight. As if he were a homeless drunk babbling to himself on a public street corner.

Kurt sat on a curb next to his Jeep and watched the drowsy light soften the curtains of Jake's suite. There were no shadows, no furtive figures gliding past. He kept thinking about Cecília and Jake, the two of them up there together. They were meant for each other.

"Hey, Muller, you all right?"

The city cop named Mike Magnuson was standing over him, amused. "We got a report some drunk was sitting on a curb bleeding like a stuck pig," he said.

"I'm not drunk," Kurt said.

Magnuson grunted and bent down to examine Kurt's face. "Jesus, man," he said, "you been in a fight or something?"

Kurt didn't realize that the stitch had started to bleed again. The side of his face was sticky with blood.

"Come on," Magnuson said, extending a hand. "We better get you to a doctor."

"I'm all right," Kurt said. "It's just a torn stitch. I'll get a Band-Aid."

"Why the hell are you sitting here, anyway?"

Kurt grabbed Magnuson's hand and pulled himself to his feet. His legs had lost their feeling. They were the legs of someone else.

"I don't know, Mike," he said. "Trying to figure out where everybody's gone."

He could imagine Lennon sleeping peacefully on the sofa in Mrs. O'Carroll's den. Right now all he wanted in this life was to hold that sleeping boy in his arms, to feel his sweet soft cheek against his own. Then the bleeding would stop and every wrong in this sad old world would almost be right again.

15

KURT ARRANGED THE BLANKET AROUND LENNON'S shoulders and kissed him gently, then went to the fridge for a beer. Sitting in his favorite armchair in the dark living room, he closed his eyes, drifting into that weightless nebula between consciousness and dream, poking absently at the Band-Aid Mrs. O'Carroll insisted on applying to the stitches. It had been a long strange evening and his body had finally given out.

He wondered if Cecilia was involved with Omar Quiroga's murder. Could the broken wineglass stem mean that she had spent the evening with him at Star Meadow and things got a little too rough? But what about the bullet behind the ear? Professional work. And what had happened to Graciela?

He could still see the two of them sitting together at Andre's, baring old bruises, an intimacy he hadn't felt with a woman since his best years with Meg. Perhaps that was why he was so drawn to Graciela. She reminded him of someone he had once loved.

Alone in the dark, half asleep, drinking, he felt an aching coldness, a sudden and inexplicable sensation of being washed aground in a quarry of sharp rocks, his skin softened by days in the water, sliced open, a sack of broken bones. Then he realized it was not his body but Graciela's. He was never going to forgive himself.

The phone rang. He sat up quickly, startled. For a fleeting second he forgot where he was.

"Hello, darling," the voice said. "Did I wake you?"

Fifty years in America and she still spoke with the unmistakable accent of an immigrant.

"Mom," he said. "What are you doing up this late?"

"An old lady doesn't sleep so much," she said. "Is my little dumpling in his bed?"

"Hours ago," Kurt said, a partial truth.

"He's probably as tall as his grandmother now," she said. "When I see him next he'll be driving a car."

"Mom, he's only five."

"*Ach, mein einziges Enkelkind.* Does he still play in the trunk?"

She had left her stage trunk with them, the stickered, rusty-latched repository of her life in the German theater. Masks, slippers, a gauzy costume dress, colorful playbills crumbling like ancient parchment. He and Bert loved to dig through the junk when they were kids. It was all that was left of their mother's world before she married the bespectacled composer from Salzburg and fled to America.

"He likes those damn greasy face paints," Kurt said. "They're impossible to wash out of his clothes."

"Do you show him that picture of his grandfather? I don't want him to grow up not knowing."

"He has a picture of you both, Mom. The one where you're side by side on skis at the foot of Little Nell."

His mother had looked a hundred years younger then. Tan, fit, her hair short and tousled, smiling that self-mocking theatrical smile, exhilarated from an afternoon on the mountain.

"And Meg?" she asked. "Does the little dumpling hear from her?"

"No, not very often," he said hesitantly. "She's still in her ashram in Oregon. He's better off without her right now. There's no telling what kind of life he'd be living. Meg's smart enough to know that."

"A boy needs a mother," she said with mild accusation.

Kurt sighed. "I do what I can, Mom."

"I know you do, darling. The two of you should come live with me. I know how to take care of my boys."

It had been a year since he'd seen his mother. Last summer he and Lennon drove down to Scottsdale to visit her in the comfortable suburban bungalow, its pristine lawn kept alive by a computerized sprinkler system. He was certain her monthly water bill exceeded the gross national product of a small emerging nation.

"How are you feeling?" he asked. He was concerned about her heart condition.

"Don't worry about the old gal," she said. "I couldn't be better. The tests were very encouraging."

"Tests? What tests, Mother?"

Too often she called to tell him the results of tests he didn't know about.

"My heart, dear."

He sat up straight. "Are you having problems?"

"So at seventy-seven I'm not a spring chicken. Dr. Fischman is taking very good care of the old gal. You shouldn't worry so much."

But he did worry. "We're coming to see you," he said, a sudden inspiration. "August. Before Lennon gets started in kindergarten. I'll let you know."

"I would move heaven and earth to see Aspen for a few days," she said wistfully. "I miss the place. I miss my boys."

They both knew that was not advisable. The last time she'd come, against the wishes of her doctor, she was hospitalized for dizziness and heart palpitations and sent quickly back to Arizona. The altitude was too much for her now. Her home of forty years, the place where she'd raised her children, buried a husband, scattered the ashes of a son, had finally begun to choke the life out of her.

"Why don't you and Lennon get on a plane tomorrow and fly

down to see me?" she said. "My treat. I have a plastic credit card, you know."

"We'd love to," he said, "but this isn't a very good time right now."

"Ten years a sheriff and they can't give you a few days off to see your mother?"

At this late hour he didn't have the energy or the courage to tell her he'd resigned. Or to bring up what had happened to Chip.

"I'm working on a tough case and can't get away just yet."

"I hope it's not like that Ted Bundy mess," she said. "I saw a television program that showed how simple he got away. Your name they didn't mention, thank god. But you could tell they thought you were an idiot."

"Thanks, Mom. I appreciate the encouragement."

"I always thought you would make a good instructor. Skiing— or backpacking even better. Sheriff is not for you. You're too nice a boy to be talking every day to killers."

"You're such a stage mother. Always looking out for me."

He could hear her take a secret drag on her cigarette. Even a heart condition hadn't broken her of the habit she'd acquired decades ago as a young professor's wife in Chicago. One of these nights she was going to fall asleep with a lighted cigarette and set her cozy bungalow on fire.

"Guess what I have in my lap?" she said. He could actually hear the smile on her face.

"A .357 Magnum with a custom-built silencer?"

"Such a funny boy," she giggled. "Always the joker."

It made him feel good, her giggle. This late at night it soothed him like a warm glass of milk.

"I know what you have in your lap, Mom. Give me a hint which one you're looking at."

She kept the old photo album by her bed and phoned him sometimes, when she was turning casually through the sticky, tarlike pages and came upon a picture she needed to talk about. He was the only person alive who understood the common language of those yellowing family hieroglyphs.

"Your father called it the architecture of the gods," she said.

The smile was still there in her voice. Sunlight slanting through her memory.

"Ah, yes." He grinned. "Mesa Verde. We had a woody station wagon as big as a PT boat."

"Do you remember the year?"

"Uhhh. About 1956."

"*Wunderbar!* A gold star for the tall Muller boy!"

On one page, he remembered, there were a half-dozen photos of Bert and him climbing around the dusty stone balconies of the Cliff Palace.

"The Pfeils were there on that trip too," his mother said. "Have you forgotten? Poor little Katrina ate something that didn't agree with her and she threw up on her brother, that Jacob."

"I knew there was a reason I liked Katrina," he said.

The halcyon years, before the feuds, the lawsuit, the eventual wall of ice between the two families.

Kurt didn't realize he'd drifted off, lost in those sweeter days of crew cuts and coonskin caps, until her sniffling brought him back around. "Mom, are you okay?"

"I manage," she said, an old woman softly sobbing. "There's so much that's gone, darling. The old gal has outlived a husband and a son."

Kurt felt awful. He was powerless to make her life any better.

"Mom, we're coming to see you, I promise. In August."

She sniffed, catching her breath. "Something was bothering him," she said. "I don't know what, Kurt. Something. A mother feels these things."

He had heard her talk like this before.

"Yeah," he said, a slow nodding confirmation.

"He should have talked to me. We were always so close. When he was a little boy he loved to touch my hair. Some children had a special doll, a blanket. Your brother had my hair. I sometimes thought I should make him a wig to hold."

Kurt smiled.

"I don't understand why my boy didn't come to me and tell me his troubles. Something was wrong. I could have helped."

He didn't know what to say to his mother. She had been grieving like this for so long.

"Today I was trying to remember the last time I actually talked to him," Kurt said.

She took a deep breath and sighed, holding back the tears. "You're the only one I have left in this life," she said. "You and my little dumpling. Come to me if there is something," she said. "Whatever it is, Kurt, promise me you'll come and talk."

Kurt made the promise she needed to hear.

"Now put out that cigarette and get some sleep, Mom," he said. "It's very late."

"An old woman doesn't sleep so much," she said.

"I love you, Momma. Everything's going to be all right."

"I love you, too, darling. I love my two precious boys."

He hung up the receiver, dragged himself to his feet, and went to check on Lennon. His son was a hot sleeper and had already kicked off the covers. Kurt knelt on one knee, straightened the sheet, and bent to place a kiss on the boy's forehead. Lennon moaned and brought an arm around his father's neck, grabbing a handful of hair.

In the middle of a deep sleep Kurt heard something. A footstep on the stairs, perhaps. He told himself to wake up. To open his eyes and reach for the gun in the night-table drawer. He had had this dream many times. He needed to wake up but he couldn't. Something terrible was going to happen if he didn't wake up, but he just couldn't do it.

He thought he heard Lennon's voice. "Daddy," the voice said, a sleepy mumble.

Kurt sat up in bed. He was reasonably sure this wasn't a

dream, but he could barely focus, keep one eye open. He found the cold flashlight on the night table, got up, and stumbled to the stairs.

"Daaa-ddy."

This time he was certain the voice was real. Lennon was having a nightmare. Kurt lumbered down the stairs, yawning, still trying to open the other eye glued shut with sleep.

His son was standing in his bedroom doorway. White moonlight washed through the room behind him, outlining his silhouette. "Daddy," he said, "is that you walking around?"

"Yeah, sweetheart," Kurt grumbled. "Do you need a drink?"

Suddenly a dark figure stepped from the shadows and grabbed the boy, and Lennon screamed like Kurt had never heard him scream before.

"Lennon!" he shouted.

A blunt hard whack dropped Kurt to the floor. He rolled quickly and came up swinging the flashlight, striking someone, batteries scattering like marbles across the pine boards. The assailant cried out and fell backward onto the coffee table, splintering wood.

"Daaaaddy!" Lennon screamed, squirming and kicking.

Kurt lunged for his son, but another solid blow put him facedown on the rug, the life gone from his legs. A hand snatched his hair, smashed his face to the floor. Everything went numb, his nose, his cheekbone.

The man holding Lennon barked orders in Spanish. There were three of them, maybe four.

Kurt reached up, gripped a loose shirt, and slung the guy off his back. He swung and missed, swung wildly in the darkness.

Lennon was crying hysterically, calling for his father.

"Let him go!" Kurt bellowed.

He scuttled toward the bedroom door, his arms thrashing, a diver searching frantically through muddy water for a drowning child.

Two men tackled him at once, smothering him in a grunting heap of knuckle and bone. The blows to his head had weakened him but he fought hard, landing punches, biting, a taste of salt and blood in his mouth.

"*¡El cloroformo!*" instructed the man struggling with Lennon.

A wet, harsh-smelling handkerchief slapped against Kurt's face. *Cloroformo* was the last word he heard.

He came to in a close dark place, choking on gasoline fumes and the heavy smell of singed oil. He was cold, his feet bare, the pajama bottoms wrapped around his ankles like a cord. His hands and mouth were taped. The car's jerking downshift had brought him around and he realized they'd stuffed him into a trunk and were driving him somewhere, probably to kill him.

"Lennon," he gagged, rolling over, stretching his legs to feel for his son.

The boy wasn't in the trunk. A hot queasy panic churned his stomach. What had they done with his little boy?

The car stuttered up a sharp incline, slowing, the driver downshifting again to find a better gear. The muffler backfired like an old bazooka. Kurt worked at the tape on his wrists, stretching his forearms, yanking with all his might. In a few moments he managed to free himself and then ripped the tape from his mouth.

Definitely not professionals, he thought. *I would already be dead.*

He tried to find the trunk latch, his fingers fumbling over loose wires and flaking metal. He would jump if he had to. Fifty miles an hour, he didn't care. He jiggled the latch but it wouldn't open from the inside.

The car surged upward along the smooth road, the grade so steep Kurt could imagine only one place like this in the whole range. They were taking him up Independence Pass to the Continental Divide. A desolate place above tree line with many awesome crevasses in which to dump a body.

Think, he told himself. *Think.*

He gripped the trunk matting underneath him and peeled it back, groping into the spare tire well. He ran his hands over gritty rubber and found a gas can lodged in the same cavity. He shook the contents. Two, maybe three inches of gasoline. If only he had a lighter. When these bastards opened the trunk he'd fry their faces.

The highway leveled out and the huge old car began to drift silently through the darkness. *We've reached the top*, Kurt thought. *We're at the Divide*. His stomach turned again when he realized they were pulling off the road.

He shifted around to a kneeling crouch and searched for the trunk light, finding the smooth little bulb near the latch, breaking it off with a quick snap. The engine shut down, clattered, and then the car was still. A fierce night wind blew over them, shuddering the old junker in its tracks. One door opened, then another. Footsteps crunched in the gravel, coming for him. In a panic he clawed about for something else to use, anything. A greasy tire jack squatted in a corner of the trunk, the handle of a lug wrench wedged against it.

Two men stood by the trunk and spoke to each other in Spanish. One of them laughed, a chilling, raspy sound deep in the chest.

Kurt crouched, the gas can in his left hand, the lug wrench in his right. A key clicked in the lock. There was a sudden pop, a vacuum release, and the lid swung upward with a rusty squeak. Cold air rushed into the trunk.

"*Vamos a trabajar*," the man said, reaching into the darkness.

Kurt rose up and doused him in the face with gasoline. The man screamed and grabbed his eyes and stumbled backward, falling to one knee. His companion reached for the pistol in his belt but Kurt smashed him across the forehead with the lug wrench. He groaned and collapsed deadweight to the gravel.

The first man was crawling around in the dirt, wailing, rubbing at his eyes. Kurt leapt from the trunk and clubbed him in the head.

"*Where is my son?*" he screamed.

The driver was out of the car now, yelling something, running back toward them. The darkness exploded with rapid fire, a burst from his automatic pistol. Kurt dove for the ground and rolled against the back wheel on the passenger side. He could hear the loud snap of another clip being loaded into the piece.

It was so dark up here, the cold blustery peak of the Divide, that he couldn't see more than five yards. Wind howled over the barren landscape, making it impossible to detect movement. He peered around the tire, looking under the car to locate the driver's feet. There was a long silence. Kurt didn't know where the man was. He drew his legs to his chest and listened hard, hearing only the pulse throbbing in his ears. He waited, praying for the man to give himself away. The sharp wind flapped his loose pajamas and he shivered. His bare feet were already numb.

Nothing. No footsteps. Only wind gusts raking the thin line of chaparral off the shoulder. His back pressed against the tire, he could feel the chassis of the old Chrysler rock in the icy current. One of the men lying on the ground began to moan.

He'd lost the lug wrench in the roll. It had to be somewhere close by, within arm's reach. He leaned over and slid his hand through the powdery dirt, searching for it. Where the hell was that thing?

A door creaked and the dome light went on in the car. Kurt withdrew his hand quickly from the spread of light and hunched closer to the tire. Now he saw the lug wrench a few yards away, but he couldn't risk crawling for it.

He heard a footstep and looked again under the car. A pair of legs was positioned by the rear license plate, only a few feet from him. There was a loud slam—the trunk lid—and more light shone on the two prone bodies.

"¡Chingao!" the gunman spat. He kicked the lug wrench out of his way and took three slow steps toward the chaparral, firing a blurt of bullets into the dark brush.

Kurt sprang up and blindsided him, and the pistol clattered onto the asphalt. The move had come back to him instinctively, the way you drive your shoulder into the ball carrier's gut when he's down, planting your entire body weight into him, a somersault spin.

The gunman choked up his dinner, a foul smell, something

ruptured inside. He tried to roll over and get to his feet but Kurt leapt back on him and pinned his shoulders to the gravel.

"Where's my son?" he demanded, smashing the man's face with one fist, then another. "Where is he?"

In the weak light from the car he could see that this was not a man at all but another Mexican boy.

"I'll kill you right here if you don't tell me something fast."

The kid coughed up more stale food. "We don't hurt him," he said.

"Where is he?" Kurt said, slapping his face.

"We leave him there," he said.

Kurt knew this kid. He was the surly young goateed *vato* from the pool hall.

"Why did you do this?" Kurt shook him. "Who put you up to this?"

Blood trickled from the corner of his mouth. "Don't kill me," he begged.

"Tell me who put you up to this," Kurt said, slapping his face again.

The young man began to cry. "A man say you kill our friends," he said. "He give us money to take you out."

"Who was it? What's the man's name?"

The boy's eyes filled with tears. Kurt turned him on his side so he could spit out the blood and vomit. It was going to take a long time to get an answer out of him. More time than Kurt had. He needed to find his son.

"Talk to Angel Montoya," he said, giving the kid another shove. "He knows I didn't kill anybody. But if I ever see you again, you son of a bitch, I'm going to kill you."

He picked up the cheap Accu-tek .380 automatic lying on the road and then the little Saturday Night Special that had dropped near the rear bumper.

"You boys need to learn who your friends are," he said, tossing the weapons into the backseat of the car.

One of the Mexicans was sitting up now, holding his head,

whining like a run-over dog. The other one was still knocked out cold.

"Better not leave that guy here overnight," Kurt said as he opened the driver's door. "He'll freeze to death."

The old tail-finned Chrysler handled like a halftrack, but Kurt forced it back down the dark narrow switchbacks of Independence Pass, roaring toward Aspen. At a bend near Lost Man Campground loose rocks had spilled onto the highway, and the car skidded across debris he could feel like a land mine set off underneath him. He careened into the other lane, the huge old vessel taking on a wild pendular rhythm of its own. Just then a bright red Wagoneer rounded the bend toward him, blared its horn, and swung wide, grinding to a stop on a shoulder above the deep river gorge. By the time Kurt reached town he was trembling uncontrollably, his pajama shirt drenched with sweat.

Please let him be alive, he prayed as the Chrysler rumbled over the bridge near the art museum. *Please, dear God.*

From Red Mountain Road he could see that the house was dark. He didn't trust what the kid had told him. There was another one, an older man with a deep, commanding voice who had held Lennon and given the orders. So where was the bastard now?

Kurt stopped the car at the turnoff, forty yards from his property fence, and cut the lights. He grabbed the little .22 from the backseat and dashed barefoot across the rocky terrain to the side of the house, where he peered in a living room window. Everything was dark. Quiet. He ducked below the windows and scurried around to his father's study. He poked the nose of the pistol through the screen and slit it open, then wrapped his pajama shirt around the stock and cracked a pane. Glass fell inward, sprinkling onto the carpet. He reached in and released the latch.

Slipping quietly around the old Steinway he opened the door to the dining room, listening, letting his eyes adjust to the darkness of the house. He thought he could hear something, a faint sobbing. The sound tore at his heart.

"Lennon!" He rushed into the living room, the pistol wiggling in front of him like a blind man's cane. "Lennon, baby, is that you?"

There was no answer. Blood pulsed in his ears. He tripped over the broken coffee table, fell to his hands and knees, and jerked up, pointing the gun in one direction, then another.

"Lennon!" he called. "Where are you, son?"

"Hands up, you're under arrest!" The toy gun.

He ran into the boy's bedroom. "Lennon!" he said. "It's me! —Daddy!"

"Daddy?" A tiny sparrow's voice under the Roy Rogers bunk bed.

Kurt dropped to his knees and reached under the bed, feeling a thatch of soft hair, a small face wet with tears.

"Is that man still here?" he whispered, pulling his son out and gathering him up in his arms.

"Daddy, I'm scared," Lennon cried. He was clutching the plastic gun.

"I know, sweetheart, I am too," he said. "Is anyone still in the house?"

"The bad guys?"

"Yeah, the bad guys," Kurt said. With one arm he held the boy to his chest, squeezing him tight. The pistol was aimed at the door, his finger resting nervously on the trigger.

"I don't think so," Lennon said.

"Oh, baby," Kurt said, hugging him close. "I'm so sorry."

He kissed his son's hair, smelling the warm meadowy smell that was Lennon and no other child.

"You look terrible, Dad. Did they hurt you?"

Kurt had a bloody nose, a cut lip, a couple of knots on his head, skinned knuckles, feet he couldn't feel anymore. The stitches above his eye had begun to bleed again. He sat there holding his son, half naked and shivering from the cold.

"No, sweetheart," he said. "Nobody can hurt me when I've got you."

His son clung to him, a muscular little grip, his face buried in

Kurt's neck. After a few moments Kurt set the gun aside and leaned back against the bed.

"Come on, champ," he said, fighting exhaustion and tears. "Let's go make a phone call."

16

MUFFIN ARRIVED IN TWENTY MINUTES, HER EYES SWOL-
len from sleep, and raced up the porch steps with a
pump shotgun in her hands. Lennon was happy to see her and left
his father's arms long enough to hug.

"Are you all right?" she asked, placing a kiss on his forehead.

"I chased them away with my weapon."

Muffin embraced Kurt and stood back to examine the cuts and
bruises. "You keep this up," she said, brushing dirt from his cheek,
"you'll earn enough face-lifts to join the gals in Les Dames."

Soon the patrol cars began to appear, Sheriff's Department
and Aspen municipal police. Red Mountain was out of the Aspen
jurisdiction, but law-enforcement officers in the Valley pulled together like family.

Mike Magnuson made coffee, and his partner, the rookie cop
from Durango, gathered up pieces of broken furniture and helped
straighten the living room. The Aspen chief of police, Gerald Ryan,
showed up within the hour in his Saab. Ursine, graying, professo-
rial, Ryan had once taught history at the University of Montana. His
soft fleshy neck flowed out underneath a weak chin. He was known
for slow, relentless pacing with an unlit pipe, a mannerism left over
from his years in the classroom.

"What steps have been taken?" he asked in his usual fustian manner. Everyone knew that Ryan was better suited to slide presentations and computer printouts.

Muffin explained that two Pitkin County units had been dispatched for Independence Pass. Six heavily armed deputies.

"The Mexicans won't get far," Kurt said. "Not in the shape they're in."

It was three o'clock in the morning. Lennon settled into his father's lap on the living-room couch, his eyes drooping, and tried to remember what had happened for the questioning officers. He'd watched the bad guys fight his daddy and drag him out of the house, then he was shoved into his bedroom and told to go back to sleep. He ran to his toy chest to get his plastic gun, but when he came out, everyone was gone.

"I hid under the bed with Michaelangelo," his favorite plastic Ninja Turtle. "He protects you from the bad guys."

Ryan scratched his neck with his pipe stem and paced the living room, offering little in the way of discussion, looking very much like someone's befuddled uncle reaching an important decision. Soon he left, still lost in thought, remote, his face the unhealthy flush of a man suffering from high blood pressure.

The three remaining policemen went outside to assume their sentry posts for the night, and Lennon eventually drifted off to sleep in Kurt's arms.

"You think that Mexican kid was telling the truth about a payoff?" Muffin asked.

She was walking around the pine-paneled living room, turning off lamps, dimming the house. Everything was dark now except for one kitchen light, whose milky glow made little difference.

"Somebody bought them," Kurt said, resting his chin on Lennon's warm head. "Somebody's spreading bad bullshit about me all around the Valley."

Muffin sat down in an armchair. "Any idea who it is?"

He shook his head. He had a strong hunch, but it was too

early to say. Jake Pfeil was offering good money to find out the same thing.

"We'll know more after they pick those kids up," he said.

Through the window he could see Dwight's blazing tow truck hitching up the old Chrysler. The boys at the garage would tear it apart screw by screw. On a night like this they had nothing better to do.

"I called you tonight," Muffin said, her voice hushed in the room's sleepy silence. "I called you a couple of times."

Kurt hesitated, calculating how much to tell her. "I was out," he said.

"So I gathered."

He was exhausted. He sucked in a deep breath, let it fill his lungs. "I went to a party," he said.

"Well," she said. "I wish I had the time."

He would have to tell her something or the room would get colder in a hurry. She wasn't going to let him off that easy.

"What do you know about Patricia Graham's latest husband?"

The question seemed to distract her. She moved in the chair, straightened her shoulders. "Zip," she said. "Does this one beat her up too?"

"This one's daughter knows something about Omar Quiroga."

Muffin leaned forward, clasped her hands, rested her forearms on her knees. "Go ahead," she said.

He didn't want to tell her his suspicions. Not until he'd met with Miles.

"It's complicated," he said. "Give me another day and I'll lay it all out for you."

"We don't have another day, Kurt. The reason I called you tonight was to tell you the results of the lab tests. We dusted that wineglass stem for prints."

Kurt lifted his chin from Lennon's head. "And?"

Muffin's voice dropped down in a low register of fatigue. "A partial," she said. "We faxed it to Denver to run through their computer. But it's a partial, Kurt. A pitiful little smudge. Those things don't mean squat in court."

Kurt felt the building blocks giving way underneath the thing he'd been constructing in his mind.

"In three or four hours the follow-up story on Graciela Rojas is going to hit the streets in the *Daily News*," she said. "I tried to sit on it, but there was nothing I could do. In about six hours Neal Staggs is coming by my office for the lab results—the wine stem, the sweater. This is not going to be a good day for you, Kurt. I suggest you give Corky Marcus a call first thing."

Corky Marcus was Kurt's attorney, a good friend and a major contributor to Kurt's last two election campaigns. Over the years Corky had advised him on legal matters in the Sheriff's Department and had even represented Kurt during the divorce. Corky's youngest son was in Lennon's group at the day care center.

"Staggs is not clean," Kurt said. "Don't make his case for him."

Muffin stood up and walked to the window to watch the tow truck at work. "How's this going to end, Kurt?" she asked in a quiet voice that betrayed her own lack of resolve.

He was too tired and beat up to consider the possibilities. "I don't know," he said. "But I need more time."

She came up behind him and placed her hands on his shoulders, a gesture of friendship. "You haven't done yourself any favors," she said, squeezing the tendons between his shoulder blades and neck. "I hate to be the one to tell you, mister, but for a long time now you've been wearing a sign on your back that says 'kick me please,' and just about everybody's taken their turn. The media, the county commissioners, the Feds."

"I've made some mistakes," he said, closing his eyes, trying to enjoy her hands.

"Staggs has some pretty good reasons for thinking you're dirty. You've done your best to make him a happy man."

Lennon shifted in his sleep, clinging like a kitten to his father's chest. "Give me till noon," Kurt said. "I'll have some answers we can both live with."

"Let me take a wild guess," she said. "Something to do with Patricia Graham's latest husband."

"You'll be the first to know," he said.

She circled the couch in the dusky light. When she wasn't in a hurry she had a nice sensuous gait about her, a ranch girl's stride, as if at any moment she might take a quick hitch-step and leap bare-back onto a horse. She hadn't bothered to brush her hair and long chestnut bangs fell in her eyes. Some men found her plain, unappealing, but Kurt liked the way she looked. He liked the smile that made her brown eyes sparkle.

"You know, Kurt, when you were my boss there was something that pissed me off about you," she said, sitting beside him. "Every case we worked, you always liked to keep one little revelation to yourself. I'm wondering what it's going to be this time."

Her expression was distant, veiled in shadow.

"We tested the blood on the sweater," she said. "There were two makes. Hers"—she paused—"and yours."

For several minutes they sat in silence like quarreling lovers, each one waiting for the other to give in.

"She's dead, Muffin," he said finally. "She's in the river somewhere. I didn't do it."

The telephone rang and Lennon jerked in his sleep, moaning gibberish, clutching at his father.

"Yes?" Muffin said quietly into the receiver. "Yes, this is Brown. Who is this?"

She held the phone and regarded Kurt with the professional seriousness he'd seen her use often in the line of duty. "All the way to the switchbacks?" she asked.

She kept watching Kurt.

"Okay," she said. "Let's wait for light."

She put down the receiver and ran a hand through her hair. "They couldn't find them," she said, closing her eyes, tired and impatient. "They drove up and down the Pass and didn't see a soul."

"That's fucking impossible," Kurt said.

"Believe it," she said. "They're going to make one more run and then come on in."

Sweat rushed down Kurt's rib cage. "Did they check the turn-off at the Divide trail?"

"Yes, goddammit," she snapped at him.

She stood up and strode toward the door. "I'm going outside to spell Perkins. Get some sleep," she said, snatching her parka from the wall peg. "We'll talk in the morning."

Impossible, Kurt thought. How the hell could three people in their condition disappear up there?

"And Kurt," she said, turning, zipping her parka. "Call Corky. Soon."

He sat holding his son in the solemn darkness of the living room, the boy's warm lumpy body comforting him like one of Meg's handmade feather beds. In spite of the early hour chill Lennon's hair was wet with perspiration. Kurt carried him up to his own bed and arranged pillows around him, the only passable substitute he could think of for a mother close beside him in sleep.

Nobody is ever going to separate me from this beautiful child again, he thought, looking down at his son.

He trod slowly back downstairs and went to his father's study. Concealed behind a large, slightly surreal portrait of the Muller sons, painted as a gift by Ben Shahn in the 1950s, was an old wall safe with a combination lock. Kurt ticked the numbers he knew by heart and cranked open the heavy iron door. On a mound of ledgers and yellowing, string-tied family papers lay the wallet with Jake's money, and next to it, Graciela's woven handbag.

'You always liked to keep one little revelation to yourself.'

He counted the money again. Five thousand dollars for a name. He removed the small spiral notebook from the handbag and thumbed to the last page.

PANZECA?

17

AT EIGHT O'CLOCK, A COOL, CLOUDLESS SUMMER MORNING from ridge to ridge, Kurt parked his Jeep in front of the Woody Creek Tavern and went inside. The place was dark and deserted except for the figure seated at a table near the window. Miles Cunningham came here every morning to take the edge off his night with a couple of bourbons and read his mail, which arrived in hefty bundles at this small, wood-stove roadhouse north of Aspen.

College photography students wrote to tell Miles they'd discovered his work and it had changed their lives. Museum curators wanted to arrange retrospective exhibitions. Magazines requested permission to reprint his images. Aging bureau chiefs begged him to take another assignment. The occasional psychopath asked if a certain photograph carried a secret message etched in the emulsion. Miles read every correspondence with a stoic detachment and stuffed the print-fee checks in the pockets of his camo hunting vest. He sorted through the photos sent as homage from admirers around the world but kept only the nudes, which he stapled to his bathroom wall in a growing erotic collage. On principle he never answered a single letter.

"Morning, Miles," Kurt said, dragging back a chair to sit down.

Miles rested a forearm on a pile of envelopes, sipped his bourbon, and studied Kurt's face. "Jesus, Muller," he said, "you look like you've been in a cockfight."

The tavern carried the morning-after smells of stale beer and fried meat and the faint suggestion of broken toilet pipes. Kurt could hear somebody rattling cases of liquor bottles in the storeroom behind the bar.

"So the Feds are all over your ass again," Miles said, giving the morning newspaper a little shove across the table.

The headline read MULLER UNDER INVESTIGATION FOR MISSING ARGENTINE WOMAN.

"Hoover's mutant progeny. They're sweethearts, aren't they?" Miles said. "The swine have broken into my photo files so many times I went ahead and gave them a key."

This morning Miles seemed relatively composed, his speech clear and clipped with precision. Perhaps this was how he always appeared before the day wore on and he sank deeper into his vices. The tics were less pronounced now, that awful twisting of the mouth as he formulated biting phrases, the stiff, arthritic angle of his neck. Kurt didn't know what to make of him in such a temperate state.

"The Feds are drawing their own cartoon," Kurt said. "It doesn't have much bearing on reality as we know it."

Miles picked up a tarnished silver lighter engraved with a map of Vietnam and lit a cigarette. There were already a half-dozen butts mashed in the tray. He squinted at Kurt through a plume of smoke, studying the damage to his face. "I think this is what you want," he said, sliding a large manila envelope to the middle of the table.

Kurt reached out to take the envelope but Miles clamped a strong hand over his wrist. "First," he said, "I'd like to know why I spent half the freaking night digging through my files for this. What's going on here, little brother?"

Kurt looked him in the eye. "Let go of my wrist," he said.

Miles released his grip. He tapped ash into the tray, took another drag, and sat back in his chair, watching Kurt open the envelope.

The photograph showed a man in full military dress. Tall, regal, late middle age, his hair and neatly kept beard turning silver. Miles had cropped out the other officers standing around him, but it was clear that the man was engaged in lively conversation with several of his peers in the armed forces.

"Colonel Octavio Panzeca," Miles said.

In spite of the cosmetic changes, Kurt knew who he was. The black horn-rim glasses gave him away.

"I didn't remember him," Miles said. "I had to plow through a lot of stored-away shit to find something. That's all I've got. He was strictly small time compared to the killer barracudas at the top. He never went to trial—at least while I was down there. He wasn't one of the junta leaders they ran through the belt line." He sipped his drink. "Who is he?"

Kurt stared at the photograph. "He lives in Starwood," he said. "I think the Feds are holding his hand in some kind of protection program." He glanced over at Miles. "Any idea why they'd go to so much trouble for a two-bit colonel from a Third World country?"

Miles shrugged. "Who can figure the fucking State Department?" he said. "I called an old pal of mine in Austin who teaches Latin American studies. We hung out in Buenos Aires during the trials. He said Panzeca was the officer in charge of their weapons research. They were working on the Bomb. Maybe nasty chemicals too. Sounds like he knows some dirty little secrets."

Kurt slipped the photograph back into the envelope.

"This prick have anything to do with Omar Quiroga?" Miles asked, flicking ashes in the direction of the tray.

Kurt didn't know how much he wanted to tell Miles. "That's my guess," he said. "Details to be worked out in a future trade."

Miles's hand disappeared under the table. There was the sound of ripping tape, and then he withdrew a pistol. Kurt was wearing a shoulder holster underneath his parka, but there was no way he could get to it.

Miles placed the pistol on the table between them. A Baby Browning. Tape still clung to the stock.

"Take this," Miles said. "If I know you, you probably aren't packing adequate fire protection."

Kurt relaxed a little and smiled at his old friend. "You always read your mail with a gun taped under the table?"

"Ever since the CIA killed Elvis," Miles said. "A man can't be too careful nowadays. It's best to trust no one."

Kurt pushed the pistol back toward Miles, picked up the envelope, and rose from his chair. "I'll keep that in mind," he said.

Miles sipped the last of his bourbon. "Hey, look, Muller," he said, "we've been down a lot of long dusty roads together, man. You need my help with this thing, I'll be there. I've got special resources. We'll leave carnage stacked up like cordwood through the whole farking Valley."

Kurt stood there observing the living legend. The bourbon was restoring his usual bravado, the ugly twist to the mouth.

"I was talking to Jake Pfeil yesterday and he told me you were the one who called him when my brother was killed," Kurt said. "I don't know why I find that strange, Miles. I guess I didn't realize you and Jake were so tight."

Miles regarded him without expression. The cigarette smoldered from his fingers. "I liked Bert," he said. "He knew how to have a good time. He tried to teach me the joys of cross-country, poor dude."

"I guess you liked Jake a lot too. It was very considerate of you to let him know."

Miles leaned forward and snuffed out the cigarette, absently poking at the butts in the tray. He spoke without raising his eyes. "If there's something bothering you, Muller," he said, "why don't you cut to the chase."

Kurt tapped the edge of the envelope on the table. "What's bothering me, Miles, is you think I'm your little brother."

Miles poured bourbon into his glass and peered up at him.

"You make a phone call to Jake anytime soon," Kurt said, "tell him he owes me five thousand dollars."

As he drove back down the farm-to-market road toward Aspen, Muffin paged him on his CB.

"We've been looking for you all over the county," she said. "You need to come in. Some kids at the Free School found a body down by the river. I'm fairly sure it's her."

Sweat speckled his top lip. "Twenty minutes max," he said.

"Kurt," she said. "Prepare yourself for this, okay? It's not an easy ID. Some animals got at her."

Muffin met Kurt at the courthouse steps and walked him down to the basement morgue. "They were on a field trip," she told him.

The Roaring Fork River rambled like a gentle brook through grassy meadows near the Peaceful Valley Free School. With tambourines and fifes and tall sticks laced with flowing ribbons, the children had marched down to the water to look for mushrooms and wild medicinal herbs.

"She wasn't in one piece," she said. "I've already arranged counselors for the school."

When they entered the morgue they found the coroner, Dr. Paul Louvier, drinking coffee by the examination table. Louvier was a short, muscular, humorless Canadian who had once been the team doctor for a pro hockey club but lost faith in steroids and moved to Aspen in the seventies to ski and treat knee injuries in a makeshift clinic near the library. In those days the county had no budget for a coroner, so he volunteered when he was needed.

The smell of human decay was overwhelming. "You'd better put those on," Louvier said, indicating the two masks on a tray next to various probing instruments.

The body lay under a sheet on the examination table. Louvier raised his mask, sipped coffee, pulled it back in place.

"Kurt, this isn't pretty," he said. "I'm just going to show you the upper torso and the head. Luckily, the animals didn't chew up the face too bad. I think you can make an ID."

The coroner lifted the sheet. A rotting odor escaped like fumes from a sealed room, and Kurt's eyes began to tear. He stepped closer to the table, forcing himself to look. They were right; he wasn't prepared for this. Her long gray-black hair was clotted with mud and a piece of scalp had been gnawed away above one ear. But except for three deep bite marks on her face and shoulders, and a bluish swelling, her features remained remarkably intact. The icy river water had prevented too much deterioration.

"Yes," Kurt managed to say. "It's her."

He remembered standing here with her at this same table while she examined the bullet hole in the skull of her old friend, Quiroga. Kurt began to tremble. This was harder than he had thought. He took a deep breath, trying to pull himself together, but the floor softened underneath him like undulating rubber.

"Why don't we talk in the office?" Muffin suggested.

Upstairs, Kurt sat in a folding chair and drank cold water from the bottle dispenser while the coroner described his preliminary findings.

"No apparent bullet entries," Louvier said. "At least not anywhere I can find. But bear in mind we don't have a complete corpse here."

He speculated that death had been caused by a broken neck. "But there's no trauma associated with, say, a blunt instrument. The massive injury to the neck and the hemorrhaging lead me to believe she took a fall. Maybe onto some rocks. My guess is she was dead before the water filled her lungs."

Kurt remembered what Miles had said about that river in Buenos Aires. You wanted to see your friends, you just stood on the banks and waited for one of them to float by.

Muffin paced the area near her desk. "So you're saying you don't see any signs of foul play," she said.

"No, I don't," Louvier said. "But I'm going to take a break

and have some breakfast and then go at her again, just to make sure."

After the coroner left, Muffin walked over and touched Kurt's arm. "I'm sorry, Kurt," she said.

He was still absorbing the shock. Several moments passed before he realized Muffin was speaking.

"I was wrong," she said. "I should have listened to you."

"Forget it," he said. "You did your homework. You had your reasons."

She looked pale, uncertain. "Staggs is coming by in half an hour to discuss the case. He doesn't know we have a body. This is going to give him a big hard-on, Kurt. Did you call Corky Marcus?"

Kurt finished the cup of water. "Either somebody pushed her," he said, still trying to puzzle out what had happened, "or she was running in the dark and fell into the gorge."

Muffin returned to the desk and sat down, dropping her head back against the leather rest. "Kurt," she said, "I know this is tearing your heart out. But there's a police investigation under way here, and I'm in charge of it. You were the last guy to see her alive, by your own admission. Your blood is on her sweater. Staggs will want me to lock you up."

Kurt crushed the paper cup and stood. "Did you find the Mexicans?" he asked.

Muffin shook her head. "The boys went back about five-thirty and searched the area for two hours in the daylight," she said. "Not a trace."

There were too many things Kurt couldn't explain. Too many things that didn't make sense. He looked at the young woman sitting behind his old desk and remembered how well they had worked together, how loyal she remained through the tough times. As far away and unlikely as their night together had been, he recalled it now with a melancholy fondness.

"If Staggs wants me, tell him to come get me himself," he said. "I'll be in the Jerome Bar at noon. I've got something to show him."

18

HE CROSSED THE COURTHOUSE LAWN AND WALKED toward the Blake Building, wondering if Cecilia and Jake were still together this late in the morning. A city crew rolled by in a flatbed truck, placing orange no-parking cones along Main and Galena, clearing the streets for the annual fifty-kilometer bicycle race. Spectators were already unfolding lawn chairs, claiming turf, watching bored teenage daughters flirt with the local high-school boys careening barechested through the crowd on skateboards. In another hour the racers would appear, sleek blurs of color following the course through town and onward, upward, to the Continental Divide.

"Sheriff Muller!"

He looked back over his shoulder to discover Hans Gitter hobbling after him. Kurt was surprised that the old professor was still here. Everyone else at Star Meadow had packed up and gone home.

"I saw you leave the courthouse just now. May I have a word with you?"

Hans Gitter appeared frail and dispirited, his face a diagram of intricate lines in parchment. The thin white swoop of hair rose magnificently from his scalp.

"I don't have much time now, Professor," Kurt said. "Can we talk later?"

"I know who killed them," the old man said.

Kurt froze. He wasn't sure he had heard this.

"Do you mind if we sit?" Gitter huffed, struggling to catch up. "This altitude leaves me a bit winded."

Kurt led him to a wooden bench where someone had stashed an ice chest, beach towels, a bottle of sunscreen.

"I took a room across from the courthouse. I have been keeping vigil from my window," Gitter said in a voice warbled by fatigue. "This morning I saw them bring in a body. It was Dr. Rojas, was it not?"

"Yes, it was," Kurt said. "Now tell me what you're talking about, Professor."

"This has not gone well," Gitter said. "Not well at all."

Bright sunlight shone on the display windows of the chocolate shop across the street, a long unbroken mosaic of blinding light. Hans Gitter blinked, squinting, a slight palsy in his head and limbs.

"I regret that I was not entirely honest with you," he said. "You see, Sheriff Muller, I came to your office with the story of the young woman because I thought it would help you uncover the truth. I needed your help desperately, but I was uncertain how much to reveal."

He spoke from the dark place deep inside his sorrow. "I am quite distressed with myself over this. Dishonesty runs counter to my nature. But we have had unpleasant experiences with the authorities from time to time," he said, "and I have learned to respect caution."

Kurt leaned forward. "Professor Gitter," he said, "please get to the point."

The creases deepened around Gitter's mouth. "My colleagues and I have known each other for quite some time. I met Quiroga and Dr. Rojas at a conference in Paris several years ago. We are part of an international organization. The world is an unkind place," he said, "and we are trying, in our way, to do something about the cruelty."

"Your group was meeting at Star Meadow?"

"No. The seminar was our cover," he said. "It had nothing to do with our work or why we came."

He reached into the pocket of his trousers, a pair of badly pressed dress pants that must have matched a rumpled jacket hanging somewhere in a closet, and withdrew a stained handkerchief. "There is a man we were trying to find," he said, wiping his mouth, "and our sources led us here to Aspen."

Kurt was beginning to understand. *Graciela, Graciela,* he thought, *you poor deluded romantic.*

"What in god's name were you going to do with this man when you found him?" Kurt said. "Ask him pretty please to go back and stand trial?"

He felt a sudden stab of impatience. What did three soft-skinned academics think they could do to a man who was protected by the United States government and armed with his own body-guard?

"Or were you just going to put a bullet in his head?"

Hans Gitter tilted his face slightly and studied Kurt. There was a measurable pride in the way he straightened his narrow shoulders. "We are not that kind of people, Sheriff."

"You're damn fools is what you are," Kurt said, heat prickling the back of his neck. He stood up and began to pace back and forth in front of the old man. "And because of your naive stupidity, two of you are dead. What kind of intelligence did your operation have, Professor Gitter? Did you people think you could go after a professional soldier—a man who's spent his entire life with a pistol strapped to his leg—and throw a sack over his head?"

Hans Gitter raised his moist eyes to Kurt. "Sit down, young man," he said, patting the bench with a long venous hand. "There is much you do not understand."

Kurt glared at him, his heart laboring in anger.

"Sit down," Gitter said. "I'm afraid you have the wrong impression of who we are. We did not come to Aspen to apprehend the colonel and send him back to Argentina. We came about the young woman."

Kurt tried to control his breathing, slow himself down. He looked up at the hot air balloons suspended like kites in the blue sky, more spectators jockeying for the best view of the bicycle race.

"Many years ago, just after the war, I was a university professor in Amsterdam," Gitter began. "One day, while I was preparing a lecture in my study, our son was kidnapped from the street in front of our home. Seven years old, a precious boy." He halted, struggling to formulate the words. Forty years later the pain was still raw. "The police searched the city for two weeks and finally found our son's body in a trash heap near a canal. The killer was never apprehended. This tragedy destroyed my marriage," he confessed. "It very nearly destroyed my life. After many years of grieving in vain, I vowed that I would do something about the harm that comes to children."

He explained that their organization was dedicated to the health and well-being of children around the world.

"Quiroga and Dr. Rojas introduced me to the peculiar abuses that occurred in Argentina during the Dirty War," he said. "Because I am considered an authority in genetics, they enlisted my services."

Kurt had read in Quiroga's book that many of the orphaned children of *los desaparecidos* were given away to friends of the junta.

"These children have grown up in the homes of the ruling military elite," Gitter said, "and they do not know who they are. They do not even know they are orphans."

Kurt closed his eyes. "My god," he said. The circle of sweat on the back of his shirt grew cold against his skin. "Cecilia," he said.

"Exactly," Hans Gitter nodded.

Kurt shook his head slowly, thinking about last night. The handcuffs, the blood, the stinging pain in his brow.

"Whose daughter is she?" he asked.

Please, he thought. *Please not Graciela's.*

"We feel certain she is Quiroga's niece," the professor said. "Omar's brother was murdered in the Dirty War."

Kurt released the breath he held deep in his lungs, then opened his eyes. "Doesn't she remember?" he asked.

"She was four years old," Gitter said. "She remembers something, of course. But a child's mind is like a delicate jewel box. How much of the trauma of her parents' disappearance still lingers? How much is forever repressed?"

"And now you want to tell her who she is."

The professor nodded again. "She has a right to know," he said.

Kurt thought about Meg in her ashram in Oregon. He wondered how much longer she could rely on convenient lies before Lennon stopped believing them. *God damn this world*, he thought. *Everyone is lying to the children.*

"After all this time, how can you be so sure she's Quiroga's niece?" Kurt asked. "How do you know she's the girl you're looking for?"

"Ahh," the professor said, the smallest suggestion of a smile around his withered mouth. "That is where I excel."

Gitter explained that he and a scientist in Berkeley were the ones who had developed a computerized gene test that could positively identify members of the same family. "Genetic fingerprinting," he said. "You have perhaps used it yourself. In this case I have already worked out the genetic code from the girl's grandmother and from Omar as well. With a little blood from Miss Panzeca I can prove with absolute certainty that she is their relative. We are doing this throughout Argentina. The test is remarkably successful."

Two skateboarders whizzed by in front of them, their rollers clattering across the sidewalk. More spectators were massing at the curb, spreading blankets, a mindless diversion on a hot summer day in the mountains.

"So you met the girl and told her these things," Kurt said, "and she told her stepfather you wanted a blood sample. And it made him mad enough to kill."

Gitter considered his reply. "Not exactly," he said. "Omar made contact with the young lady, yes. They arranged to meet in his lodging at Star Meadow. He was to tell her then about her parents and ask for her cooperation in the test. Dr. Rojas and I waited till midnight for word of their conversation but did not hear from him," he said, "so we went to his room. The place was entirely dark and the curtains were drawn. We discussed informing the seminar facilitators or Matt Heron, but it is difficult to explain the nature and scope of our work to outsiders, you see. And we did not want to risk alerting Panzeca. After all, he has been living here under the protection of your government for quite some time, and surely he has friends in high places. We assumed he is being treated as a special guest of your town, and we did not want to run afoul of his protectors."

Kurt understood now why Graciela had been so cautious and vague. She was trying to figure out if the sheriff might be one of those friends in high places.

"Our only alternative was to wait until morning," Gitter said, wiping his lips with the handkerchief, "and then find someone who could help us. Someone," he paused, "we could trust."

Kurt thought about Graciela's first appearance in his office. She must have known something bad had happened to her friend. If only she had told him everything.

"After spending time with you, observing you carefully, Dr. Rojas felt you were our man. Frankly, I argued that we needed more proof of your integrity," he said, raising an eyebrow. "But Graciela was willing to take the risk. If you will forgive an old man his unsolicited observation, I think she had developed a special fondness for you, Sheriff Muller. She said you reminded her of her late husband."

So the story was true. "The one who hanged himself during the Dirty War?" he asked.

"Why, yes." The professor looked surprised that Kurt knew this. "Her first husband, the father of their daughters. It was such a beastly business, that ordeal in Argentina."

Kurt saw Graciela's face on the examination table, the bite marks deep to the bone. She had been through so much only to end like this. Dead in a foreign country, ravaged by wolves.

"Are you in contact with the family?" he asked. He wondered how old her daughters were now and what they would do with the rest of their lives.

"Carlos Rojas is in Berkeley working with my colleague on the genetics program," Gitter said. "I reached him by phone."

Kurt knew how her husband would feel. Devastated, enraged, helpless. He had been feeling that way ever since Bert's death.

"As you surely observed," Gitter said, clasping his hands, touching them to his lips, "Dr. Rojas was a remarkable woman. I shall miss her intelligence and her dedication." The old man was suddenly overwhelmed with grief. "I shall miss her great heart."

Tourists ambled by toting designer shopping bags filled with booty. A juggler named Willie the Wizard was entertaining an audience near the steel sculpture on the corner. There was an air of cheerful euphoria in the crowd gathering for the race.

"Colonel Panzeca will pay for what he's done," Kurt said. He gave the old man's shoulder a consoling squeeze and stood up. "And there's a journal Graciela wanted back from the FBI. It was Quiroga's. You'll have it before you leave town."

Gitter gazed up at him, squinting into the harsh white sunlight. "And what will you do about the young woman?" he asked.

Kurt had no idea how any of this would play out. Had Quiroga gotten his chance to tell Cecilia about her parents and the Dirty War? Only one living person knew the answer to that.

"If she doesn't know already," Kurt said, "I'll tell her myself."

He left the old professor sitting on the bench and made his way down the busy sidewalk to the Blake Building. Cecilia's forest-green Miata was still parked at the curb where she'd left it, and Dwight the tow-truck driver was hitching the rear bumper to his rig.

"Say, Muller," Dwight greeted him. "Can you believe this

asshole? Signs up all week for the race. Must have their face deep in somebody's cobbler."

More spectators were arriving to stake out sidewalk space with their lawn chairs and coolers. Kurt peered up at the windows of Jake's corner suite and saw that the curtains were still closed. He stepped to the glass entrance, read its tidy row of intercom buttons, and pushed the one for *Pfeil*. A few moments went by. He pushed the button again. There was a white hum from the wall speaker.

"*¿Papi, sos vos?*"

Cecilia's voice, distressed, in tears. Kurt didn't know what to reply.

"*¿Sos vos, Papi?*" she repeated, her words distorted by the speaker.

He waited, giving her time. And then the buzzer sounded, opening the door for him.

19

HE MOUNTED THE STAIRS AND WALKED DOWN THE carpeted hallway to Jake Pfeil's suite. The door was ajar a couple of inches so he gave it a cautious push and stepped inside. He looked around the elegant foyer at the antique vases, the Oriental throw rugs. Someone was sobbing in another room, the bedroom where he and Jake had had their conversation. He thought about drawing his gun but decided against it.

She was sitting on the floor next to the bed, one leg tucked underneath her, wearing nothing but a man's white dress shirt. Her face was buried in the rumpled black satin sheet hanging off the edge, her sobbing now a mournful, breathless moan.

"*¿Papi?*" she said, raising her head to look at him. A dark greasy snarl of hair covered her eyes. Mascara had dried like streaks of charcoal on her beautiful face.

"*Papi*," she said, "*algo terrible ha pasado.*"

A nude body was lying facedown on the bed. The body of a shapely young woman with skin as flawless as October snow. Her thin wrists were handcuffed to the brass headboard. She wasn't moving. A plastic Baggie of coke was split open on the nightstand next to her handcuffed wrists, the powder spread across the surface like baker's flour. Two thousand, three thousand bucks of blow.

Kurt knelt down and turned the lifeless face toward him, pushing aside ringlets of blond hair. It was the girl from Jake's party, the one who'd pulled out a handful of beard. A small puddle of vomit had caked on the sheet by her slack mouth. He reached out and touched the lovely sway of her back and recognized the cold, unmistakable texture of death. She had been lying like this for at least two hours.

He stood up and surveyed the room. The place was a mess. Lingerie and gaudy sequined gowns were strewn everywhere, across armchairs, on the floor, as though the women had been playing some cabaret costume game. Empty champagne bottles littered the carpet like knocked-over bowling pins. Near the bed there were several half-eaten cartons of take-out Chinese food, a disgusting odor.

"Where's Jake?" he asked.

Cecilia stared at him, her eyes bloodshot, teary, doomed. *"Vos,"* she said in a strained voice, *"no sos mi papi."*

"In English, Cecilia," he said, bending down to brush the hair from her eyes.

She studied his face. A tiny flicker of comprehension struggled to hold pilot somewhere deep inside those suicidal eyes. She slapped his hand away and scooted against the bed. "I know who you are," she said.

"Yes, you do."

"You're the one who is trying to kill my father."

He rested back on his haunches. "Your father has done some terrible things," he said. "But I don't want to kill him."

"You people are *gusanos*," she said, her streaked face tightening with hatred. "You tried to destroy him in our own country but you failed. Now you pursue him here."

"There are a lot of things you don't know about your father," Kurt said.

"¡Mentiroso!" she said. "Liar! You *gusanos* twist the truth."

"What happened to your friend?" he asked, nodding toward

the body. "Did you and Jake get a little too kinky with her? Or was it the toot?"

Cecilia's face held her anger another moment, then collapsed again in tears.

"Is that what happened with Omar Quiroga?" he said. "You went out to Star Meadow and had a few drinks with him, and then you got a little rough?"

"No!"

"Or maybe you slipped something in his wine," he said, "and then hauled the poor drugged bastard out to the Grottos and put a bullet in his head."

"No." She shook her head, weeping louder now.

"No, you're right, Cecilia. You couldn't do something like that all by yourself, could you, darling?" he said. "Lug around a big man like Quiroga. Stick him in the trunk of a car." He reached over and grabbed her chin, forcing her to look at him. "Drop his body off a cliff into the river."

She jerked her face away.

"Even a pretty little weightlifter would need some help for a job like that," he said. "So who was it, child? Who helped you get the job done?"

He heard a footstep in the doorway behind him and turned quickly.

"That's quite enough," the man said. It was her stepfather. Rafael stood beside him, pointing a .22 Beretta automatic.

"*¡Papi!*" the young woman shrieked. She sprang to her feet and ran to him, throwing her arms around his chest.

Panzeca seemed embarrassed by her lack of dress and this desperate outburst of emotion, but he kept his gaze focused fiercely on Kurt. "*Quítale la pistola,*" he ordered the bodyguard.

"Up!" Rafael waved the gun at Kurt. He reached into Kurt's parka, withdrew the Luger from his shoulder holster, and stuck it in his belt. Then he turned Kurt around and patted him down, his legs, his crotch.

"You were right, my friend," Panzeca said. "We meet again."

The bodyguard stepped back from Kurt and spoke to his boss in Spanish. Kurt recognized the low, gravelly voice now, the deep resonance in the man's native tongue. He could hear this voice bark the words *el cloroformo* in the dark living room.

"Colonel Panzeca," Kurt said. "Does she know the real reason why you murdered Quiroga?"

Panzeca glared at him through the black frames of his impenetrable hornrim glasses. Without the slightest movement of head or shoulders, he instructed Rafael in Spanish and the bodyguard took Cecilia by the arm and led her away into the bathroom.

"Don't leave now," Kurt said, "it's just starting to get interesting."

Panzeca withdrew a small ivory-stock .32 caliber pistol from the pocket of his sport jacket and raised it at Kurt. "You have made some foolish mistakes, señor," he said.

"Yeah," Kurt said. "You got that right."

The colonel stepped toward the bed and peered down at the handcuffed body. "My daughter is a very sick young woman," he said. He raked the fingers of his left hand gently, lazily, across the girl's bare back. "She needs professional help."

Kurt watched the man stare at the body. "I'm tempted to say it runs in the family," he said. "But in her case it depends on which family you mean."

Panzeca turned and looked at him, the .32 set firmly in his hand. "She had nothing to do with Quiroga," he said. "She did not go to Star Meadow."

Kurt shrugged. He should have known the old man wouldn't use his daughter. He didn't want the girl within ten miles of Quiroga.

"That's too bad," Kurt said. "She might've learned the truth about herself."

Panzeca straightened his shoulders, lifted his chin. "You have no idea how much I adore my daughter," he said. "My late wife was barren, God rest her soul. For years we tried in vain to have children. The little girl brought so much joy to our lives. I will not let anyone take her from me, señor."

"And so you sent Rafael to Quiroga's room."

The colonel made no reply. Behind the heavy lenses his eyes appeared distorted, coldly implacable, larger than life. A few feet away, in the dim-lit bathroom, his stepdaughter was stooped over a marble basin, retching her guts out.

"And then what, Colonel?" Kurt asked. "You called your friends in Denver—the Feds, who always take good care of their boy when things get hot and heavy. The people who are helping you live a nice private life in a nice cushy resort town, far away from dirty wars and dirty trials and the persistent little worms who just won't let you live in peace."

"This conversation is over, señor," Panzeca said icily.

"What did you tell Staggs when you called him?" Kurt rushed on. "That Quiroga had tracked you down? That it was kill or be killed?"

"My friend," Panzeca said, "you have dug your own grave."

"You served up those Mexicans to the Feds, didn't you, Colonel? You told Staggs that Quiroga hired them to take you out. It seemed like a good story at the time, just enough to keep the suits off balance. But then you got too ambitious, didn't you, amigo? You went for it all. You decided to take down the guy who was sticking powder up your stepdaughter's nose."

Panzeca lowered his proud chin for a moment and the gun sagged in his hand. He appeared absorbed in thought. *"Ese demonio,"* he said distantly. He glanced down at the silt of cocaine on the night table and in a flash of rage swiped at it with his free hand. A white cloud drifted over the dead girl.

"Where is he?" the colonel asked bitterly.

"I have no idea," Kurt said. "He wasn't here when I came in."

"¡Rafael!" he shouted. *"¡Ven!"*

The bodyguard left the girl and came into the bedroom. Panzeca gave the man his orders in Spanish.

"You must go with Rafael," he said to Kurt.

Kurt realized that the talking was over. His throat grew tight. Fear made him cold. He knew he might never see his son again.

"I have a child too," he said. "A little boy."

"I am very sorry," Panzeca said.

"Talk to Staggs," Kurt said. "Use that phone right there and give him a call. Talk to him before this gets out of hand."

The colonel nodded to Rafael.

"Come," the bodyguard said, wagging the Beretta at Kurt. Probably the same gun that had given him those stitches in his head.

"Don't do this, Colonel," Kurt said, trying to control the panic in his voice. "Talk to Staggs. We can all work something out."

Rafael took Kurt's arm and shoved him toward the door. "*Vámonos*," he said. "We go for a little ride."

Kurt glanced in the bathroom at the girl leaning over the sink, her heaving now dry, convulsive, painful to hear. "I know you're doing this for her," he said. "But sooner or later you'll have to face something, Colonel. She already knows. Somewhere inside her she's already figured out who she is," he said, "and it's killing her."

For the briefest moment Kurt thought he saw a shadow pass over the man's face, an unsettling recognition of the thing he most feared and denied, the nightmare that troubled his sleep. Then just as quickly it was gone. Shoulders back, his stance rigidly erect, the very definition of military grace, Panzeca studied Kurt, another insect he was having removed from the garrison of his new life. With a flick of his hand, an officer's impatient gesture, he dismissed the entire affair.

"Take him," he said.

Rafael seized Kurt's arm, thrusting the Beretta against his ribs.

20

IN THE HALLWAY OUTSIDE JAKE'S SUITE, RAFAEL TUCKED HIS gun hand in the pocket of his blue nylon windbreaker and told Kurt to walk ahead of him.

"Don' do nothing stupid," he ordered.

Kurt took his time walking toward the stairwell. "Where are we going, Rafael?" he asked over his shoulder.

"Don' turn around."

"You taking me out to the Grottos, like you did the writer? Or is it up the Pass again? Drop a body in one of those ravines, they won't find it till the next Ice Age."

"*¡Cállate!*" Rafael said, poking the gun barrel in the small of Kurt's back.

"What happened to your boys, Rafael? We had such a good time together last night, and then they disappeared on me. I guess they didn't like the cold. Next time, hire a better class of losers."

Rafael nudged him again. "Stop talking and keep moving."

"Do your boys know who you work for, *carnal?* Do they know your boss is the one who dropped a dime on their brothers to the FBI?"

They reached the stairwell. Rafael gave him a push and Kurt

stumbled down a couple of steps. "Shut up or I shoot you right here," the bodyguard said.

"I don't think so," Kurt said. "I don't think you want a lot of noise and blood and another dead body lying around the building. Not while your boss is upstairs trying to clean up his stepdaughter and get her out of here."

"Don' be too sure, smart boy."

Kurt turned enough to see the man slip a silencer from his baggy jeans.

"Don' be too sure I don' blow your focking head off right here."

A hard flat circle of steel touched the base of Kurt's skull, a cold metallic kiss. The silencer pressed against his head the way it must have pressed against Omar Quiroga's.

Rafael leaned close. "Too bad about the woman, eh, hombre?" he whispered in Kurt's ear. "Too bad the bitch have to jump. Before I do her I wanted to fock her first, like you was going to."

Kurt looked through the beveled glass doors. Out on the sidewalk the crowd was cheering the first bicyclers whirring past them in a stream of iridescent colors.

"She got away from you, didn't she, asshole?" Kurt said. "You tried to chase her down and she jumped."

The silencer pressed harder into his skull. Rafael made an intimate sucking sound through his teeth, his warm rotten breath in Kurt's ear. "Such a waste for us both, no?" he said.

The muscles tightened in Kurt's neck. He wanted to kill this man.

Rafael pushed him toward the doors. "Now be a good boy and walk nice and slow around the corner," he said, "or they find your focking body right where you stand."

Kurt wove his way slowly through the crowd, hoping someone would recognize him and stop to talk. People stood around drinking beer stuffed into Huggers, their attention focused on the race in the street. A shout went up for a pack of bicyclers locked neck and neck, their bodies arched forward, legs churning, a whiz of bone and light metal.

Rafael grabbed Kurt's arm and steered him toward the alley between the Blake Building and a row of shops. "Here," he said.

A bright red Wagoneer was parked in the alley. Kurt stopped, his mind struggling to remember.

"Move," Rafael nudged him. "You drive."

Kurt had seen the vehicle before. He had nearly forced it into the gorge below Lost Man Campground. This was how the three Mexicans had disappeared into the night.

"I'm not getting in the car, Rafael," Kurt said. A steady flow of passersby parted around the two men. "You'll have to kill me right here."

Rafael jerked the Beretta in his windbreaker. "*¡Vámonos, pendejo!*" he commanded.

A small girl chasing her sister noticed the shape in the windbreaker and said, "Hey, mister, is that a gun?"

Heads turned. Rafael swiveled in a half circle, surprised by the attention, and tried to conceal the .22 deeper in his pocket. Kurt lunged for his wrist and a muffled shot blew a hole through the windbreaker, splattering concrete. Bystanders screamed and dropped to the sidewalk. Rafael swung his elbow into Kurt's jaw, a teeth-grinding blow, but Kurt grabbed some blue nylon and dragged the man down. He had a lock on a shoulder, a leg, he wasn't sure. He waited for a bullet through his lung but suddenly realized that the gun was on the ground a few yards away. People were shouting, running in every direction, but no one had picked up the gun. Rafael slipped from his hold and crawled toward the weapon on his hands and knees. Another second and he would have it.

Kurt knew he couldn't get to him in time. He lumbered to his feet and ran, leaping over a picnic cooler as a bullet ripped through the Styrofoam, spewing ice and water. Suddenly he found himself in the street, speeding bicyclers bearing down on him. He froze, trapped in the rush of wind, a hundred wheels zinging by at forty-five miles per hour. He heard another muffled shot and looked back to see Rafael standing at the curb, the pistol raised. He aimed at Kurt and fired again and a racer went down, the bike crashing away underneath him, spinning off into the crowd. Brakes squealed, riders swerved, skidding, piling into one another, a loud collision of metal. Loose spokes pinwheeled toward Kurt, missing him by inches. Bodies were all over the street.

He stumbled to the far sidewalk and turned to see Rafael dodging through the wreckage, forearming an Asian racer to the ground. The bodyguard kicked a twisted bike out of his way and stopped to squeeze off a shot that went wide and shattered the plate-glass window of a pharmacy.

Kurt ran to the doorway of the pool hall and rumbled down the stairs into the smoky club. All motion slowed suddenly into a soft hazy swim of faces, brown-skinned men relaxing around the tables, drinking from long-neck bottles, considering their next play. He was outside of himself now, hearing someone with his voice scream for help, seeing the faces turn leisurely, a long ash dangling from a cigarette.

"Thur-man!" his voice stretched out the name.

Thurman Fisher was leaning back against the bar, watching a baseball game on the TV, immutable in his routines, a laconic uncle listening with one ear to a couple of wisecracking regulars. The three men shifted their eyes slowly, torpidly, to see who was making all the noise.

"Thurman!" Kurt shouted again, running toward him. "Where's your gun?"

There was one final moment when everything became as slow and unfocused as a nightmare. Thurman pushed away from the bar, stood up straight, squinted in confusion, his mouth opening. He didn't understand what was happening until Rafael reached the bottom of the stairs and silencer bullets spat across the bar, popping the glass mirror, splitting open stately liquor bottles arranged in a row.

In full stride Kurt flopped belly first onto the smooth bartop, rolled, and landed on the damp floor near the far end. Thurman was crouched down several yards away, panting, his chin wedged into his chest. Broken glass covered his hair and shoulders. He groped about without his bifocals, found the .38 in an old cigar box, and slid it along the tile floor in Kurt's direction.

Lying on his elbows Kurt peered around the brass footrail and saw Rafael throw down the Beretta and pull out the Luger he'd taken from him at Jake's place. He fired two loud rounds into the walnut siding of the bar, splintering wood just above Kurt's head. Kurt ducked back, reached around the corner with his left hand, and blindly pulled off three shots, demolishing a fake Tiffany lamp hanging above a pool table. He waited, anticipating return fire, then gazed out through the thick smoke. Rafael had disappeared.

Kurt scurried in a crouch to the closest pool table. A shot rang out, hit the chrome strip, ricocheted off. The next bullet struck solid wood. Where was that asshole? All Kurt could see were the terrified faces of young Mexicans huddling under every table. But no Rafael.

Squatting low, the .38 against his cheek, Kurt scrambled to the far end of the table and counted four pool shooters down on their knees beside another table, staying clear of fire, cue sticks clutched in their hands. One of them was staring back, his dark eyes frightened, questioning. Kurt motioned for him to keep down. *Don't do anything stupid, Angel*, he thought, giving him a nod of recognition. *Don't do anything to get us all killed*.

He heard boot soles scratching from one position to another, a squabble in Spanish, someone cursing. He worried about these kids hiding under the tables. Whose side were they on? *Goddammit, Thurman*, he thought, *get somebody on the phone*.

Hunkered down like this, his bunged-up ski knees hurt like hell and his calves began to cramp. He shuffled a few steps to relieve the pain and, pistol raised, peeked around the table's edge.

He almost missed the first quick move, the way Rafael reached around the corner of a pool table and grabbed Angel by the back of the hair and pulled the boy against him as a shield. All Kurt would remember later was Angel's scream, the cue snapping in half, two wild bullets coring into the table near his own face. He rolled onto his belly, stretched his arms, and steadied the .38 for a clean shot. But the gunman held the struggling boy in front of him, a muscular arm locked around his throat, and squeezed off another round that lodged in the wall.

"*¡Pinche cabrón!*" Angel gasped, fighting for breath, his hands searching the floor for the broken cue. He found a long piece and jerked it over his shoulder, grazing Rafael's head. Enough to distract the man, loosen his grip.

"Roll, Angel!" Kurt yelled.

Angel was free, crawling for cover. Rafael whirled on his knees and aimed the Luger at Kurt, but Kurt shot him three times in the chest.

After it was over, Kurt stood up slowly, set the .38 on the green cushion next to a cluster of striped balls, and exhaled the longest breath of his life. He walked over and looked down at Rafael. Blood splotched his windbreaker, pooled around his still body. This was the man who had put a cap in the back of Omar Quiroga's head and four stitches in Kurt's, who had muscled his little son around in a sleepy dark world the boy would never forget. This was the man who had chased a rare and wonderful woman to her death.

"Take a good look at this son of a bitch," Kurt said to Angel.

The young man had risen to his feet and was staring at the blood. Sweat poured down his face.

"I want all of you to take a look at this man," Kurt spoke loudly to the others who were crawling out from under the tables, moving cautiously toward the dead body. Eighteen, twenty years old, the hardworking elder sons who had come north to make some decent money and take it back to their families living like dogs in dirt shacks.

"This man was a liar. He was not your *hermano*," Kurt said. "Because of him, Angel, your brother died in that house in Emma."

Angel looked at him, his eyes filled with fear and caution.

"This man got your friends killed," Kurt said, staring hard into the faces of the young men gathering around. "You tell those other guys, the ones who tried to kill me last night, that they made a bad mistake. I don't want to see them in this town again. You tell them to go back home. Because if I ever catch them, they're going to jail."

The lean faces studied him, their eyes dropping to regard the man lying facedown in his own blood. They were still in shock, awed by the violence, frightened and exhilarated. Kurt knew they were good boys with the courage to cross rivers in the dead of night just to wash coffee cups for minimum wage. He knew most of these boys had never committed a sin worth confessing to a priest.

He bent down and started to pick up the Luger that had fallen from Rafael's hand, then decided he should leave it for Ryan's men. He could hear a siren in the distance.

At the bar Thurman Fisher set out four shot glasses and filled them with Kentucky bourbon. Behind him only one jagged shard still clung to a corner of the mirror's frame; a stream of expensive liqueurs trickled from the shelf. Ashen, disheveled, the two stool patrons dusted off their clothes and reached with shaking hands for the Jack Daniel's.

"Do me a favor, Kurt," Thurman said, squinting through cracked bifocals. "Next time somebody's chasing your ass, please run into a freaking T-shirt shop."

He swallowed a shot and slid the last glass toward Kurt.

"Don't let those boys touch anything till the city cops get here," Kurt said, tossing back the drink. "That Luger belonged to my father, Thurman. I don't want anybody walking off with it."

He made his way up the stairs and into the sunlight. The street was swarming with responsible citizens giving comfort and medical assistance to the fallen racers. Tourists milled about in the wreckage, pale and disbelieving. Several bicyclers and a handful of volunteer firemen were trying to clear the street, disentangling bikes, leading the walking wounded over to rest in lawn chairs. An ambulance rolled slowly, insistently, through the stunned crowd, the driver blowing his horn at people in his way.

When Kurt reached the sidewalk, a woman wearing a halter

top pointed at him and said, "That's him! That's the man!" She was scooting ice into the gutter with the side of her bare foot. "Somebody get his name!"

He entered the Blake Building and returned to Jake's suite, slipping quietly through the front door and into the bedroom. They hadn't bothered to clean the place. Everything remained as it was, the gowns strewn on the floor, the Chinese food rotting in paper containers, the cocaine spread across the night table, the girl's body facedown on the bed. The only difference was that her handcuffs had been removed.

It won't matter, Colonel, Kurt thought. *The coroner will notice the skin rubbed raw on her wrists.*

He covered the nude body with a black satin sheet, then pulled a handkerchief from his pocket and used it to hold the phone receiver. "Libbie," he said, "I need to talk to Muffin. It's urgent."

"Sorry, Kurt. Muffin had to dash to Galena Street. There's been some kind of crazy accident at the bicycle marathon."

"This is important, Libbie," he said. "I want you to beep her and tell her there's a body in Suite 205 at the Blake Building. A young woman is dead."

"Oh, Jesus," she said.

"Suite 205," Kurt repeated. "Write that down. It's Jake Pfeil's place."

After he hung up he looked around the room one more time. The colonel was no doubt very pleased with the way everything had worked out. The two Argentines were dead. Rafael was taking care of a meddlesome intruder who had discovered the family secret. And the demon who was ruining his stepdaughter's life would soon be brought down as a coke user with a dead girl in his bed. Everything had worked out splendidly.

Kurt glanced at the clock radio. Twenty minutes past noon. Someone was waiting for him in the Jerome Bar.

21

A S KURT APPROACHED THE HOTEL HE SPOTTED A FEDERAL agent leaning against the red brick wall near the entrance. Banana Republic shorts, clean new hiking boots, his face buried in a Forest Service trail map like a tourist planning his day. Kurt walked up to the picture window of the Jerome Bar and peered in. The Victorian parlor was packed with architects and city planners from the Design Conference. Neal Staggs sat by himself at a small table in the corner, wearing casual slacks and a short-sleeve Izod shirt, nursing a drink. He looked like a pampered golfer waiting for his caddy to cart him off to the first tee. Kurt noticed two other agents, a broad-shouldered man with a red mustache sitting at the bar and the tough little grunt who was guard-dogging Quiroga's room when this whole nightmare began. His meaty hands wrapped around a beer stein, chewing gum with the grace of a Jersey hood, the grunt stuck out in the arty crowd like a dime-store number-painting in a gallery of Matisses.

Kurt left the window and walked over to the agent examining the trail map. "It's no wonder you guys couldn't find Patty Hearst," he said.

The man raised his eyes and looked at Kurt through tinted sunglasses.

"Tell Staggs I'll talk to him in the dining room," Kurt said. "But tell him to leave the kids in the car."

At this time of day the hotel's formal dining room was unoccupied, an ornate still-life in white tablecloths, crystal goblets, preciously arranged silverware. Summer light bathed the corridor outside the frosted glass that isolated this quiet place, but the room itself held the shadowy chill of a wine cellar. Kurt chose a table with a view of the outdoor pool, where tanned hotel guests read *The New York Times* at umbrella tables and ordered drinks from college waiters in uniform T-shirts. He could remember when the hotel was owned by Jacob Rumpf. The old man allowed the town kids to swim whenever they wanted in a primitive heated pool that was now buried in the foundation beneath a new ballroom.

In a short while Neal Staggs appeared in the doorway. He looked around the room, assessing its seclusion, then strode across the floral carpet in silent deck shoes.

"Okay, it's your party," he shrugged, pulling aside one of the high-backed mahogany chairs. "I was beginning to wonder if I got all dressed up for nothing."

Kurt touched the pointed silver tines of a salad fork. "I had one of those unavoidable delays," he said. "I had to kill a man."

Staggs stopped himself halfway into the chair and gave Kurt a hard look. He seemed to be considering whether to sit or call in his men.

"He was the first man I've ever killed, Staggs," Kurt said. "He deserved it, but I still don't feel very good about it."

Staggs dropped down slowly to rest on the edge of the seat. His hands were braced against the side of the table. He could get away in a hurry if he had to.

"I think you probably know the guy," Kurt said. "I know you know his boss. He's an old friend of yours."

He took the photograph from the manila envelope and slid it across the tablecloth. Staggs stared down at the picture of the military officer. Color left his face. His eyes remained riveted on the image, his jaw grinding, an old habit his wife probably complained about to their marriage counselor.

"I know who Rostagno is," Kurt said. "The man I just shot was trying to wash out his dirty socks for him. The fuck killed Omar Quiroga, and he did his best to kill Graciela Rojas. So how do you want to do this, Staggs? I'm about twenty minutes from going to the DA with what I know. But it gets even uglier. There's this young kid in town who writes for the daily newspaper. Just out of college, read too much Woodward and Bernstein, you know the type. He's been busting my hump for a year, trying to win his Pulitzer prize. Except now I've got a real story for him. It involves South American military creeps and dirty wars and foreign-policy protection for an asshole killer the FBI is helping to live the good life under another identity in America's poshest resort." Kurt paused. "Just because the man knows something about chemical warfare."

The agent's eyes flashed up from the photograph. He seemed offended by the suggestion.

"That's what it's all about, isn't it, Staggs?" he said. He pressed his finger against the sharp tines of the fork until there were four deep indentations. "You people don't want somebody like Iran or Iraq to get their hands on Panzeca's dirty little mind."

Staggs frowned, the long furrows on his forehead drawing together his thick black eyebrows. He pinched the corner of the photograph and tossed it back at Kurt. "What does it matter?" he said. "We do what we do."

Kurt shook his head slowly. "Are you that fucking brain dead it doesn't bother you when a gumball like Panzeca jerks your agency around by the nose, murders somebody, and then makes you his cover?"

Staggs slumped back in the chair and scratched at his ear. "Go ahead, break my heart," he said.

Kurt leaned forward and gazed into the agent's face. He knew he was dealing with a man whose soul had been locked away long ago in the deep freeze of his profession.

"Kill a few spics without green cards, who's going to weep?

That how you figured it, Staggs?" he said, twirling the fork between his fingers. He thought about plunging it into the man's heart just to see if there was one. "Point a finger at them, fill out the report nice and neat, dot all the *i*'s, cross the *t*'s, bullshit the media, and wipe your hands of a murder."

Staggs propped his elbows on the chair's delicate arms and laced his fingers, raising them to his chin. "The problem with guys like you, Muller, is you don't appreciate a man's deeply held religious views," he said. "What you don't understand about me, my friend, is I believe in karma. Oh, it's probably not a kosher karma, but I've worked it out over the years in this job and I can write a fucking treatise on it. What goes around comes around. You've probably said it yourself a couple dozen times with a joint stuck in your mouth."

He dropped his hands to his lap. "The way my cosmic karma works is very simple," he said. "Those little pricks out in Emma were doing something bad, sitting on a bunch of cannabis plants, collecting weapons for who knows what, and their time had come. Nobody was going to punch their clock, sure as hell not a dick-water hippie cop like you. So they got what they deserved, if maybe for reasons that look blurry under the glass. In this job I have to live with that. Your cosmic chit comes up, you got to pay it."

His eyes widened. He was enjoying this.

"You don't have to worry about the colonel, my friend. His time is going to come. Go ahead and pat yourself on the back if it'll make you feel like a hero. We'll have to move him tomorrow to some other locale so Geraldo doesn't show up with a camera and disrupt his tennis game, but sooner or later, in some tony country-club hideout, he's going to fuck up again and somebody will make him pay. It won't be us, of course. Some little greaser will come up behind him in the manicurist's chair and slit his throat with a barber scissors. And you know what, Muller? I won't give a damn. I don't like the cockroach any more than you do. But I let the bureaucrats on Capitol Hill sort out the policy. I do my job and take my vacations with the little wife and raise my kids to stop at red lights."

Kurt set down the fork and looked at him. "How does Jake Pfeil fit into this mystical experience of yours?"

Staggs cocked his head, a questioning smirk on his face.

"You couldn't nail him on the Erickson hit so you tried to drag him in on this one," Kurt said. "The world of karma according to Neal Staggs."

The agent smiled tepidly. "Tell you the truth, Muller," he said, "I was hoping Pfeil and the colonel would kill each other over the daughter. You can't imagine how relieved I would feel."

Through the picture window Kurt could see a boy about twelve years old bounce once on the diving board and cannonball into the pool.

"You've got a journal I want," he said, picking up the photograph and studying the image of Colonel Octavio Panzeca. "I told Graciela Rojas I would return it to Quiroga's family. Give me the journal and you can have the photograph and the negative."

Staggs began to laugh, his All-American prep-school face contorted into something hideous. "Okay, fine, Muller," he said, wiping an eye. "You need a little victory out of all this, you can have it. I'll get the fucking book laminated for you. We've already photocopied it forty times and sent every page to one bullshit expert or another. They've picked over every comma to see what it all means. Yeah, sure, you can have it back. If it'll make you feel like a hero."

Kurt knew that retrieving the journal was little more than a gesture. He hated Staggs for making it so explicit.

"And you can go ahead and keep your pictures and your negatives." Staggs nodded at the photograph in Kurt's hand. "I don't think you're going to talk to the DA, or to the fucking press, or to anybody else for that matter. You know why, my friend?" he said, the laughter disappearing abruptly from his face, leaving behind an uncompromising hardness that seemed to settle in the bone itself. "Because we know the whereabouts of an old lady living a quiet life in Scottsdale, Arizona, and I personally would get my rocks off calling her up and telling her a few things she wouldn't want to hear about her darling son."

Kurt dropped the photograph onto the tablecloth. "You don't have any dirt on me, Staggs," he said angrily. "Those tapes are horseshit. Jake Pfeil is a proven liar."

"You?" Staggs said, raising an eyebrow. "Those tapes aren't about *you*, my friend. They're about your brother, the demolitions expert."

It was there again, that sudden chill in the blood. "What the fuck are you talking about?" he said.

Staggs rested his shoulders against the chair and crossed his legs, a man relaxing, ready to exchange pleasantries. "Come on, Muller, it's time you dropped the Mayberry routine," he said. "We know what your brother did in Nam. We've got a book on the tactics he and his unit were trained for. You want *photographs*, I've got a nice set of black-and-whites showing what happened to an ARVN captain they suspected of collaborating with the VC. Guess where they found his brains when he sat down in his Jeep one muggy morning in Saigon? A beautiful job, Muller. A variation of the old Malaysian Door, a wood projectile set off by the man's own body weight. Asshole to brainpan in two seconds. I've got to hand it to your brother and his buddies, they appreciated simplicity."

Kurt swallowed. His throat was dry.

"I've got other pictures too. South Vietnamese politicians leaning the wrong way, hookers who talked too much to their johns. They met with a very messy demise," he said. "We've read your brother's reports. He wasn't the best, but he was good enough. Quick, efficient. He showed a lot of promise in biomechanical engineering."

"You fucking liar!"

Kurt wanted to grab Staggs by the neck but instead grabbed the white tablecloth. Silverware and goblets crashed to the carpet. Staggs stood up quickly and backed away, knocking over his chair. The red-haired agent materialized instantly and dropped to one knee, his 9-mm Ruger trained on Kurt. The waiters' door flew open and the man in Banana Republic shorts dashed in, his weapon raised.

"It's okay, fellas," Staggs said, catching his breath. He rolled his shoulders, straightening the Izod shirt. "Our friend Muller here is just showing a little frustration with something he's been trying to deal with for a long time."

Kurt didn't move from his chair. His heart was beating so fast his chest felt overflexed and tight. He stared at the mess he'd made on the floor. Something in him had finally broken, floated loose, and he was never going to get it back.

"You know, Muller, I almost believe you," Staggs said, composed now. "I almost believe you didn't know anything about Pfeil and your brother and Chad Erickson. But nobody could be that blind."

Kurt couldn't force himself to look away from the photograph lying in the glass.

"You got some anger here, take it up with Jake Pfeil. He's the one who knew how to make use of your brother's talent. And while you're at it," he said, "why don't you ask your old pal why Bert Muller suddenly fell off a mountain the very day we were going to bring him in?"

He nodded to the two agents and they holstered their guns.

"By the way," Staggs said on his way to the door. "I just came from the morgue. I got a good look at the Rojas woman. You must be a pretty rough date, Muller."

His colleagues laughed. Then all three men were gone.

Kurt sat for several minutes longer, an aching pressure constricting his chest. He breathed deeply, trying to recall the calming rhythm Meg had taught him years ago, but he had a darkening sense that nothing could help him now. All he could see in his mind was a snapshot of two brown-haired boys climbing around sandstone ruins in the shadow of an immense overhanging cliff. They had left behind the tower steps and rope-tied ladders and were scaling higher and higher, digging in with their nails, finding toeholds in the red clay. Their mother called after them, entreating them to come back down. They had gone too far, she cried. They were going to fall.

22

KURT WENT HOME, COLLAPSED INTO HIS FATHER'S ARM-chair, and brooded for nearly an hour in the quiet study, trying to wrap his mind around what Staggs had told him. The phone kept ringing but he didn't want to talk to anyone, especially Muffin Brown, who would have serious questions about the shootout in the pool hall and the nude corpse of an unidentified young woman. The only person he wanted to see was his son, so he forced himself to get up and go to the kitchen, where he made peanut butter sandwiches and filled a canteen with Gatorade. He packed a change of clothing for Lennon, his sunglasses, the Cubs baseball cap. At the last minute he added packages of trail mix and Ninja Turtle fruit gummies to the backpack. The phone's message light was still blinking when he left the house.

Surrounded by an army of fierce sebaceous mutants, Lennon sat on Mrs. O'Carroll's parquet floor, making explosion noises, lost in play. "Daddy, guess what?" He waved an ooze-covered figure. "Ozone Destructo is the bad guy, but he gets slimed by Eco Man."

This was the safest place for Lennon today. Private, unknown.

"The planet is in grave danger," said Mrs. O'Carroll, looking up from her book, "but Lennon and Eco Man have it under control."

He took his son to Hunter Creek, one of their favorite hiking trails. The path began behind a large complex of red-roofed condominiums that had once served as employee housing units, the city's attempt at affordable living quarters for its many worker bees. In recent years the condos had been expensively remodeled and sold off to airline pilots and cold-eyed urologists who used them six weeks a year.

What Kurt liked about the trail was that once you walked a few yards into the dense grove surrounding the creek, there was no trace of condos or county roads or the Victorian spires of small-town life. Today the only visible hikers ahead of them were three outfitted women from somewhere else, determined nature-lovers with short butch hair and solid bodies and the plain, strong-jawed faces of men they lived happily without. Lennon had established his rituals on this trail, the places he stopped, the things he did every time. Children depended on the familiar. To suggest another way was to threaten the small safe steps they took to claim the world inch by cautious inch.

"The pirate's plank, Daddy!" Lennon called out excitedly.

They left the path where a downed trunk jutted into the creek and ventured out onto its pale barkless surface, holding hands to keep balance over the water, then tiptoed back to look for long sticks and have a mock sword fight. At the boardwalk over a gentle runlet—a finger of spill-off that sloped into a clear shallow pool—Lennon stopped to kneel down on the sagging boards and study the gold flakes glinting beneath the water on a bed of sand.

"Daddy, maybe we should become miners," he said. "Then we won't ever run out of money."

Though Kurt had not spoken with his son about resigning as sheriff, the boy had picked up something.

"There's nothing to worry about, sweetheart," he said. "We're never going to run out of money."

They held hands, something Lennon still liked to do, and walked up the path through leafy foliage, hopping from one flat stone to the next across another runlet, brushing away mosquitoes near secret pools of stagnant water in the deep still woods. They eventually emerged into a garden of boulders just before the bridge.

"Let's go watch the creek," Lennon said, scurrying over the rocks like a ground squirrel.

"Wait for your dad!" Kurt yelled after him.

On the wooden footbridge over Hunter Creek they stood side by side and peered silently into the hurling snowmelt waters. Kurt had learned long ago that you could stare into moving water and get lost for hours. The roar shut out everything, forced you inward. The dancing illusions of water had a calming, hallucinogenic effect on the soul, took you to another place. Ever since he was a boy roaming these trails with his older brother, this was the sight that soothed his heated blood.

A young hippie couple, second generation—the boy ponytailed and bare to the waist, the girl in a bikini top and cutoffs —crossed the bridge with their black Lab, a handsome animal with heaving lungs and a beautiful coat wet from a roll in the stream. Lennon patted the dog, rubbed his smooth damp hair.

"Daddy, when can we get a dog?" he asked as they left the bridge and turned onto the next leg of the trail, the high, exposed path that rose steeply up the mountain into blistering sunshine. "Let's go to the pet shop and get a big one like that."

There wasn't a pet shop within a hundred miles, but Lennon had seen a music video about children visiting one.

"I like the idea of having a dog," Kurt said, "but we need to talk about it some more."

Lennon was probably ready for a dog, he thought. When he and Bert were young they owned a mutt named Ute that followed them everywhere. Bert named him after the Indian tribe that settlers had chased from this valley.

"Okay," Lennon said, "let's talk about it."

"I've got a better idea," Kurt said. "Let's stop and eat some grub."

The trail was a tough negotiation from here, upward at thirty-five degrees through rocky moraine and across another bridge into tall timber and alpine meadows where a couple of dilapidated shacks marked an early miner settlement. But this was about as far as Lennon's legs could take him. Already his fair cheeks were crimson with heat and exertion, and his lungs struggled like the panting Lab's. Kurt spread their lunch on a flattened boulder in the sparse shade of a fir tree and handed the boy the canteen of Gatorade.

"Here," he said, removing Lennon's cap. His red hair was pressed flat, soaked with sweat. Perspiration pooled in the sprinkle of freckles below each eye. He lifted Lennon's plastic sunglasses and wiped his face with a hand towel from the backpack and tried to dry his hair.

"Your mother would have my hide," he said, "if she knew I'd forgotten to put on the Water Babies."

He squirted lotion into his palm and rubbed it gently on Lennon's flushed cheeks, his arms and legs, the back of his tender neck. Such a beautiful child, he thought. His face in repose, a little worn from the hike, had the serenity, the flawless innocence, of a Pre-Raphaelite figure. It was easy to see why, at first glance, people sometimes mistook him for a girl.

"Daddy," he said, his eyes as blue as the waters of a coral grotto, "is Mommy going to get well?"

"Yes," Kurt said. "And when she does, she'll come and see us."

"Is she almost well?"

"She's getting better every day."

Lennon was quiet for a while. "I worry about her," he said.

"I worry about her too."

"Know what, Daddy? I miss her."

Kurt took out the sandwiches and some cloth napkins. "I know you do, sweetheart," he said. "But don't worry too much. She's going to come and see us. She just needs a little more time."

"At the hospital?"

"Yes," Kurt said, unwrapping a sandwich.

"Why don't we go visit her?" Lennon said. "We can take her some presents to make her feel better."

Kurt thought this over. "I'll have to ask," he said.

"The doctor?"

"Yeah, the doctor."

Lennon was a messy eater and in a very short time had separated the bread slices and was licking off the jelly.

"Know what, Daddy?" he said with a mouthful of food, a brown smear across one cheek. "When I was a baby my mom used to read me a story every night before I went to bed."

"I know," Kurt said. "And now I read them."

Lennon nodded, agreeing, humming with pleasure over the sandwich. "When I was a baby," he said, "she used to watch cartoons with me."

Kurt reached over and brushed a strand of damp hair from his son's forehead. He could smell the boy's salty scalp. "I'll ask the doctor if we can go see her," he said.

"Yesss!" Lennon said, gearshifting the air.

As they ate, they watched the hot air balloons drifting leisurely above town. Lennon said he could see a unicorn painted on one canvas. From this high vantage Aspen looked so small, so contained, a place still confined to the perimeters of the old mining camp, when it was just an obscure name on a silver company's dog-eared map. Kurt thought about Bert and how their childhood had been wedged into this remote valley like the town itself. Their parents wanted them to grow up in the rarefied mountain air, far away from the corruption of cities and a civilization doomed to war and annihilation. This was the best life the Mullers could imagine for their children, for any children. An idyllic existence, pure, untroubled, free.

When Bert graduated from college in Boulder and was drafted, their father, an ardent pacifist, hired a prestigious Chicago attorney to help his son win a CO deferment. But Bert refused to cooperate, viewing his father's position as one more embarrassing European eccentricity, a quaint philosophical pose, the same antiquated principle that led the man to use a straight razor with a leather strop.

In the years after Vietnam the brothers talked from time to time about Bert's decision and ultimately decided he'd gone in just to prove that, unlike the two foreigners who'd raised him, he was a full-blooded native son beholden to something they couldn't understand or be part of.

'But I wish to hell I'd listened to the old man,' Bert said on more than one occasion. 'I wish I'd talked to that lawyer.'

When Kurt dropped out of college to enlist, hoping to hitch up with his brother in Southeast Asia, their father was so distraught he couldn't discuss the subject without becoming emotional. 'Albert I understand,' he said over the phone, his voice a tremor of disappointment. 'But you, my dear boy—you have more time. You have other choices.'

Kurt watched the balloons float in the clear blue sky and thought about his son's last birthday party, and all the birthday parties when he was growing up, the promise that innocence would never end, that someone older and wiser would always be there to serve the cake. He wondered what would have happened if he and Bert had stayed at home in this valley. If they had taken jobs as ski instructors or trail guides, as their mother had wanted, and left Boulder to the barefoot intellectuals and the U.S. Army to the bullies who enjoyed blowing up strangers in faraway places.

He closed his eyes and remembered the Bert before Nam, the muscular, brown-skinned mountain boy who dragged him over Pearl Pass every winter on cross-country skis, who spent his summer days fly-fishing the Fryingpan River, who loved nothing more than to hammock under a shade tree reading Ian Fleming and Ray Bradbury. How did that innocent boy get from there to the bloody photographs in Neal Staggs's file?

He turned over in his mind those last few months before Bert's death and thought he understood now why his brother had withdrawn from him. Bert didn't want his little brother, the sheriff, to suffer implication in any way. He didn't want him to get hurt by what he'd done.

Goddammit, Bert, he thought. *What happened to you?*

"Daddy," Lennon said, "are you all right?"

Kurt opened his eyes. "Yeah, sure," he said.

"Are you crying, Dad?"

"No, sweetie," Kurt said, wiping his face. "The sun got in my eyes for a minute."

He scooted over and wrapped an arm around the boy's narrow shoulders. If he kept him this close, he thought, and never let him go, maybe his son wouldn't have to face the next dirty war.

23

IN THE CORRIDOR OUTSIDE THE SHERIFF'S OFFICE TWO DOZEN news reporters from around the state were clamoring about, exchanging information, complaining to the deputies posted by the door. The ESPN camera crewmen had given up for the evening and were breaking down their equipment, disgruntled that the acting sheriff refused to appear and answer questions. Kurt hadn't seen the place this packed with reporters since the Ted Bundy escape.

The hotshot from the *Aspen Daily News* saw Kurt coming down the corridor. "Mr. Muller!" he said. "You've been mentioned in connection with the gunplay at the race. Were you involved?"

Tim Rollins was a pleasant-looking lad, twenty-five and eager, sandy blond hair long over his ears and curling onto his collar. He wore jeans and hiking boots and a faded Western shirt with rolled-up sleeves. He looked more like an out-of-work country musician than a Dartmouth grad.

"I saw your article about me," Kurt said, shifting the box in his hands. "Where'd you get that mug shot? My high school year-book?"

The other reporters smelled blood and moved quickly to surround Kurt, who pushed through their ranks to the office door.

"Evening, Kurt," said Dave Stuber, one of the deputies standing guard. A couple of years ago Kurt had given the young man time off, with full pay, to work through a difficult alcohol rehab. Now he was one of the department's most reliable investigators.

The reporters pressed in close, barraging Kurt with questions. "What's in the box?" someone asked.

Stuber chewed gum, casting a cynical eye over the gathering.

"It's your call, Stube," Kurt said above the voices. "Fire hose or Mace?"

"I'm thinking stun gun," the deputy replied.

Inside the reception area Muffin stood by the cooler drinking water from a paper cup while she conducted a somber discussion with Libbie McCullough and three other deputies. Muffin looked pale, worn, a ranch girl unaccustomed to testy college grads wielding tape recorders.

"Jesus, Kurt," she said, rolling her eyes, "why the hell do you keep disappearing?"

"I went for a hike up Hunter Creek with Lennon."

The deputies exchanged impatient looks. No one was in a good mood. Libbie rushed back to her desk and opened two bottles of vitamins, scattering grainy pills over her blotter.

"Who needs some A?" she asked nervously.

Kurt could tell by the way Muffin regarded him, tense, unamused, that this wasn't going to be a pleasant occasion. She ushered him into her office, closed the door, and extended her hand toward a large stuffed chair with patterned fabric, something that might occupy a maiden aunt's musty reading parlor.

"Already making home improvements, I see," he said, shoving aside a stack of folders on the desk to make room for the small cardboard box he was carrying.

"Kurt," Muffin said, "you were in this office ten years and you never had a chair anybody wanted to sit on."

She began to pace in a wide loop around the desk, hands on

her hips, trying to contain her anger. Kurt had seen her this way only once or twice.

"Let's cut to the chorus, shall we?" she said. "What the hell's the matter with you, man? You left the scene of a crime. No, make that two crimes. Three, if you count endangering behavior at a bicycle race televised on a major cable network. Eight riders have gone to the hospital on stretchers. Not to mention bullets flying around people in the street, a man shot to death in a pool hall, and another body stone cold dead in your old friend's suite."

"He's not my friend," Kurt said.

She stopped abruptly and squared around to face him. "The mayor and the commissioners are all over my ass, Kurt," she said. "ESPN and the distinguished gentlemen of the press are camped on my doorstep. The phone is ringing off the hook. And the guy who caused all my troubles is taking a hike in the woods. Is there any reason why I shouldn't kick you in the nuts?"

Kurt studied her body language, the way she shifted the weight of her hips. The last time she was this worked up she hand-cuffed a drunk biker to a urinal in the Conoco john on Highway 82 and left him there for two hours.

"I needed some time," he said. "I wanted to be with Lennon for a little while before the shit hit the fan. I didn't know when I'd get a chance to see him again."

Muffin closed her eyes and rubbed her forehead with the heels of her palms. "Okay, you win the Ward Cleaver prize for father of the year," she said in a more composed voice. "Now I want to hear the whole goddamn story from start to finish. I want to know how a guy who's already in shit up to his chin can keep wading in deeper and deeper."

He glanced out the window into the softening haze of blue light. Ajax Mountain had become a dark irregular outline in the mottled dusk, more shadow than stone. He remembered this as his mother's favorite time of the day, how she loved to walk among the trees in the quiet, fading light. Now he saw her resting in her air-conditioned bungalow, leafing through pages of the family album, her swollen feet propped up on pillows. He saw her rise slowly from the sofa to answer the door, where two men in plain gray suits produced their shields and asked to speak with her about her deceased son.

"I went to see Jake," he began, calculating how to phrase the story, what to leave out. "The door was open and there was a body in the bedroom and a Hispanic male standing there with a gun. He lifted my piece and walked me down the stairs. When we got outside I tried to take him but the guy was a lot better than I thought. We wrestled around on the sidewalk and I got away and ran across the street and he started firing at me and that's when the rider went down, and then all the others. I ran to the pool hall because Thurman keeps a gun behind the bar. The guy followed me down there and we exchanged fire and I killed him with Thurman's .38. That's about the size of it," he shrugged. "I'm sure Thurman told you how he saw it. I stand by whatever he says."

Muffin's eyes darted toward the box on her desk. "Thurman said when the shooting started, the place was full of Mexican workers. When I got there nobody was around but Thurman and two very scared drunks," she said. "Any idea what happened to the other witnesses?"

"Cops make them nervous," he said. "They have jobs to keep."

She blinked, her voice finding that metallic deadpan they'd taught her at the police academy in Casper. "Ever see the shooter before?"

"I've seen him hanging around the pool hall."

"That's it?"

"That's it."

"What do you suppose he was doing at Jake Pfeil's? He didn't murder the girl. Louvier's prelim says drug overdose."

"I have no idea, Sheriff," Kurt said. "Speculation is not my line of work anymore."

His remark annoyed her. "He didn't happen to be one of the

Mexicans who took you for a ride up Independence Pass, did he, Kurt?"

He could see where this was going. She thought he'd tracked down one of the assailants and decided to take him out.

"No, Muffin. I didn't set out to kill the guy. He was at Jake's place and he had a gun."

"Why were you going to see Jake Pfeil? You just said he wasn't your friend."

"A while back he left a hang-glider at my house. Lennon keeps bugging me to show him how to use it, and I don't want it around anymore. I've been trying to get Jake to come pick it up, but he never answers my phone calls."

She looked over at the box again, lost in some momentary rumination. "It's statistically amazing, Kurt," she said, "how much trouble you manage to walk into right out of the blue."

"I'm thinking about contacting the Guinness people," he said.

Her eyes remained diverted on the box. "Staggs came in this morning and I showed him the body," she said. "There's nothing I can do about him now, Kurt. I expect he'll send a couple of agents to pick you up."

Then her voice softened, losing its edge. "Don't worry about Lennon," she said. She was his old partner again, his friend. "I'll take good care of him till we can straighten this thing out."

"Staggs isn't going to arrest me."

She came closer and examined his face, holding his chin, moving his head from side to side. She seemed enthralled by the little cuts and bruises, the puffy ridge that would leave a permanent scar. He wondered if she wanted her turn to pluck out one of his stitches.

"I got a call from her husband," she said. "He'll be here tomorrow morning to claim the body."

He jerked his chin away.

"Do you want to talk to him?" she asked.

He imagined what the man looked like. Tall, dark haired, fastidious in a suit and tie, handsome. He imagined that they had met through their cause, their love of children. And now he would have to take his wife's mutilated body back home to her daughters.

"No." He shook his head.

"He'll want to know what happened."

"He can read the report."

She nodded, chewed at her lip. "Okay," she said. "I can't force you."

Kurt knew that Hans Gitter would tell the husband everything he needed to know.

"But there's something I want you to give him. I found this under the passenger seat in my Jeep." He opened the cardboard box and took out the handbag. "It's Graciela's. She stashed it there when we went to the Grottos."

"What's in it?" she asked, raising a suspicious eyebrow.

"I don't know. I didn't feel like going through it. Women's purses make me crazy."

Muffin smirked. She had never owned a purse in her life.

"Louvier's report says no bullet entry, no stab wounds, no blunt instruments, no drugs. But he can't rule out that somebody might've bashed her with a rock," she said, reaching for the bag. "Or pushed her off a cliff."

He saw her hesitate, her fingers feeling the intricate weave, the coarse threading. "Pretty," she said, probing at the unusual texture.

She slipped her fingers into the fold of cloth and spread open the drawstring. A hint of color rose in her cheeks. She slid her hands underneath the bag and lifted, measuring its heft and give.

"Did you notice the fragrance?" she asked.

The scent of her hair in the brush. "No," he said.

"It's amazing," she said. "You can actually smell the woman."

She dumped out the contents and spread the items across her desk. Room key, ballpoint pen, postcards. She opened the passport and studied the photograph.

Kurt didn't want to linger over Graciela's personal effects

again. "I'll leave my report of the shootout with Libbie," he said. "Right now I need to get back to Lennon. Mrs. O'Carroll says he's real nervous when I'm gone. I don't know how long it'll take him to get over last night. I'm going to check with a shrink."

"Hold on a sec," she said, her attention remote, distracted. "Something came for you."

She reached across the desk for a paper-wrapped rectangle secured with string. "About an hour ago a courier delivered this for you." She handed the package to him. "Expecting something special?"

Omar Quiroga's journal. Staggs's reminder of their unwritten agreement.

"It isn't ticking, is it?" he said, reading his name typed neatly on the address label.

Muffin noticed the wallet in the mess of Graciela's belongings and picked it up, ripping loose the Velcro strip. "Jesus," she said, thumbing through the stack of hundred-dollar bills. "There must be four or five thousand dollars here."

Kurt looked at Jake Pfeil's wallet. "Somebody should've told her about traveler's checks," he said.

He was satisfied that Muffin would turn over everything to Graciela's husband. The wallet, everything. Kurt knew that giving him Jake's money was little more than a facile attempt at absolving his own guilt, but it was the only thing he could do right now, and he needed to do something. Someday he would find another way to say he was sorry, but until then, a small gift for the children. Gitter would know what it was for.

Muffin tossed the wallet onto the pile. "Aren't you going to open that thing?" she pointed to the package.

"I know what it is," he said.

They stared at each other. They both knew he was going to lie.

"It's for Lennon," he said. "I'll let him open it at home."

He tucked the package into his parka and walked toward the

door. "I'd better make out that report and get going," he said. He couldn't risk Muffin getting her hands on the journal and finding out about Octavio Panzeca. That was the bargain he'd struck with Staggs: I keep Panzeca out of the press, you leave my mother alone and my brother's memory in peace.

"Kurt," she raised her voice, speaking his name with urgency.

He turned around.

"Not that you give a damn," she said, "but it's been hell around here trying to keep the department together in the middle of all this insanity. But I've always liked the work, and I think I'm handling the pressure pretty well so far. I guess it's because I had such a good teacher."

He tried to smile. She was the best cop he'd ever worked with.

"But I can't stay friends with somebody who doesn't respect me enough to cut me in."

He was sorry there were details about this business he had to withhold from her. She would end up hating him for it.

"When you fill out your report," she said, "do us both a favor, will you? Try to work out the thing that's bothering me about your story."

He looked at her, his eyes narrowing.

"Try to explain why the gunman in Jake's suite didn't just take your gun and walk away," she said. "Why he chased you down in front of a thousand witnesses instead of saying adios and driving off."

She was good. He wished he could take credit for some small measure of her intelligence.

"I don't like the idea that I can't tell a husband how his wife died," she said. "Or who killed their best friend and dumped him in the river."

Kurt expelled a lungful of breath that tasted dirty and old. "I don't like it, either, Muffin," he said.

She stared at him, her eyes cold and dark and hard. "Is this the part where you keep something for yourself, Kurt?" she asked.

He saw his mother leafing through the family album. Heard the doorbell ring.

"Or is there something you want to tell me?"

"Yeah, there is," he said. "I hope you find Jake before I do."

24

H E ARRANGED FOR LENNON TO SPEND THE NIGHT WITH Mrs. O'Carroll and then joined them for supper.

"Except there's one thing, Dad," Lennon said, one of his standard introductions.

"What thing is that?" Kurt smiled at him.

"Don't forget to pick me up tomorrow."

Kurt could see the worry in his son's eyes. "I won't forget, sweet pea," he said, softly raking the boy's cheek with a knuckle.

"I can only miss one more day of school," Lennon said, spooning mashed potatoes into his mouth, "or my friends will be very sad. I tell all the jokes."

Kurt left them playing dominoes at the kitchen table and drove into the clear starry nighttime toward Woody Creek. At the archway to John Romer's property he could make out the empty, floodlit corral and a scattering of illuminated tack sheds and outbuildings, but the flagstone fortress itself appeared dark and solemn, a shadowy presence lurking over the tidy structures of ranch life.

He got out of his Jeep and walked past their assortment of vehicles—camper truck, Suburban, Volvo, classic T-bird—and wondered if Romer was at home, if this would constitute an awkward situation. In the end he knew he didn't give a damn and crossed the cinder drive to a breezeway cluttered with stone frogs and flowering plants in large clay urns. On both sides of the door tall panels of smoked glass emitted anemic light from within. He banged the heavy brass knocker. After a few moments he banged again. Finally he tried the latch and discovered that the door was open.

"Hello!" he called out. "Hello! Is anybody home?"

He stood in the foyer by a huge gilt-edged mirror and gazed across the sunken living room. All was still, deserted, a formal space bathed in soft lighting. He could hear the laugh track of a television program somewhere upstairs.

"Maya!" he called. "Are you home?"

He walked up the stairway and followed the muted sounds down a long dim hall toward the gray incandescent light spilling from an open door. Inside the room Maya reclined on a canopied bed in a silky negligee. Waves of light from a large high-resolution TV flickered across her body like flames from a fireplace.

"Knock knock," he said in a quiet voice.

Her eyes opened. "John?" she said. She sat up and rubbed her face. "I've been waiting for you, baby."

"Maya," he said, "it's Kurt Muller. I've got to talk to you."

"Kurt?" she said in a sleepy groan. "Mmm, I thought you were John."

"I'm sorry if I startled you. We've got to talk."

She brought her feet to the floor and stood up, her legs unsteady. Hugging a bedpost for support, she reached down to search the nightstand for her tumbler. When she came toward him, weaving, her bare shoulders thrown back, she paused to take a long drink and stumbled a step, spilling the liquid down her chin. He could see her perfect white teeth through the glass.

"Excuse me, garçon, could you freshen my drink?" she said, rattling the ice.

Her floor-length negligee was little more than a gossamer drape. She had put on weight these past few years, the good life, but even in an inebriated state she still carried herself with the poise of a black-diamond skier. Her breasts were fuller now and bobbed slightly as she walked.

"Can I help you?" she said. "Or are you just browsing?"

She pressed her soft, sleep-warm body into his, the tumbler cold and wet against his shoulder blade. He felt himself becoming aroused and pulled back.

"Maya," he said, glancing around the bedroom, "can we go somewhere and talk?"

"What's wrong with here?" she said, pointing the glass toward the bed, sloshing drink. "You always did your best talking under the sheets."

She was slurring drunk. Her breath smelled of vodka.

"It's important," he said. "Let's go downstairs and get some coffee."

She gave him a haughty look, her eyes struggling to focus, her head floating. "You never turned me down in the old days, my dear," she said. "I still can't drive past Redstone without getting a little wet."

They once took a room in the Redstone Inn and bathed each other for an entire afternoon in an antique clawfoot tub, then ordered a candlelight dinner from room service.

"Maya," he said, removing her arm from his waist, "it's about Bert."

A lost memory passed over her face, erasing the dreamy smile. She turned to wobble off across the room. "I expect my husband home any minute," she said, weaving her way to the private bar. "He's been gone a fucking week doing the important work of the landed gentry. He won't be happy to see a man in his bedroom."

Kurt strode up behind her. "Maya," he said, taking her arm, "did you know about Bert? Did you know he was the one who killed Chad Erickson?"

She stopped and closed her drooping eyes. "Let go of my arm," she said. "I only take that from a man if he intends to bed me."

He grabbed her shoulders and turned her around. Her straps

fell and the negligee slid lower, catching on the soft swell of her breasts.

"Maya, goddammit," he said, shaking her, "why didn't you tell me? Why didn't somebody tell me?"

She lowered her eyes, her chin. "Let go of me, Kurt," she said. "I need a drink."

He let go of her and she tugged at her negligee, attempting to cover herself. She stepped to the bar and filled her glass with straight vodka from a bottle that had no cap.

"You could have told me after he died," he said. "Are you listening to me, Maya?" He pounded his fist on the bartop. "I can understand why you didn't tell me when I was investigating the thing, but you could have fucking told me after he died. It's been four years, Maya. It might've helped me understand."

She dropped an ice cube into her drink. "Understand what, Kurt?" she said in a husky voice. "Understand why he jumped off a mountain?"

She started to raise the glass but he caught her wrist and slammed it down, splashing cold vodka over their hands. "So now you're going to tell me everything," he said, the heat rising in his face. He held her wrist pinned to the bar. "You're going to tell me why my brother killed a man. And why you're so fucking sure he took his own life."

"You're hurting my wrist," she said. "Jesus, no wonder Meg left you, you son of a bitch."

He slapped the glass and ice splattered across the bar.

"If you're such an expert on marriage," he said, "why isn't your husband ever home? Do you spend every night like this, Maya? Just you and the bottle? I don't remember you being a lush."

He stepped back and looked around. The bedroom was the size of a schoolyard. Sofas, dressing tables, closets just for shoes. For purses. Doors leading to other doors.

"You're living like all the old broads in Aspen now," he said. "Locked up in a rich man's chateau. Pampered. I thought we promised each other, the four of us, we would always be different."

Tears streamed down her cheeks. "Oh, yeah, we promised a lot of things," she said. "We promised we would never hurt anybody, didn't we, Kurt?"

She was sobbing now, wiping at the tears. In spite of her denial yesterday, she was still bearing the wounds. They were as fresh as the day the Mountain Rescue men unzipped the body bag.

"Why did he do it?" Kurt asked in a quiet, angry voice.

She set out across the room, her hands groping in front of her for something to hold on to, and sat on the edge of the bed. Her chest was heaving; she struggled to control herself. "You think you know somebody," she said. "Sixteen, seventeen years together, you figure you know a man. Who says there aren't surprises? I'm still not sure I really believe it about him."

Kurt took the handkerchief from his pocket and walked over to her.

"I'm sorry I got her mixed up in it," she said, dabbing her wet eyes. "I'm sorry, Kurt."

"What are you talking about?"

"Meg," she said, raising her puffy eyes to him.

He stared at her, confused.

"Oh, Kurt," she said, the tears coming again, "you're such a poor stupid boy. Sheriff Kurt. Did you really think you could change the world by being a cop?"

"What the hell are you talking about?"

She pressed the handkerchief to her eyes and held it there. "I had to tell somebody," she said, catching her breath. "I found some old photographs in his army trunk. Horrible pictures from Vietnam. Dead people in cars. Souvenirs, I guess. Reminders of the person he had been. I was freaked by what I saw, but I couldn't bring myself to talk about it with him. And then," she said, fighting tears, "and then Chad was killed the same way."

"You told Meg?"

"I couldn't tell *you*. You were his brother, for god's sake. The fucking cop making a big deal out of the investigation. Meg was always there when I needed her."

"Maya," he said, closing his eyes.

"I'm so sorry, Kurt. I never should have told her."

He laid his hands gently on her shoulders.

"She was always such a missionary, bless her heart," she said. "She thought she could save him. She went to him and tried to be a friend. They got along so well. Meg wanted to help him find a way out of what he'd done."

"Did he threaten her?"

"No, no, of course not," she said. "He would never do something like that, Kurt. He loved her. He loved you. No, he denied it all. He had a good laugh that she would think he could kill somebody. He didn't know she'd seen the pictures."

She twisted the handkerchief. "But somehow Jake Pfeil found out she knew something," Maya said. "I guess Bert told him, I don't know. Meg thought she was being followed. There were anonymous phone calls. That's why she took Lennon and moved to Telluride. She figured if she left town, nobody would bother her. She was worried something might happen to your son."

Sweat broke out on Kurt's neck.

"Then one day Jake walked up to her in a shop in Telluride," she said. "He started showing up in her life like that. On the slopes, in a café. He didn't have to say anything—she got the message. That's when she decided to bring Lennon back to you and leave the state. She knew if the boy was with *you*, Jake wouldn't do anything to hurt him."

Kurt began to tremble with rage.

"Darling, darling," she said, grabbing his arms and pulling herself to her feet. She held him close, her warm tears wetting his shirt. "Every day without her son is a heartbreak."

He remembered how Meg had brought Lennon into the world. Twelve hours of hard labor, moving from bed to floor, struggling to avoid the cesarean. They had never done anything together with so much practiced understanding. Contractions, waves of pain, breathing in rhythm, the long slow drip of Pitocin into her veins. Kurt and the nurse-midwife held her upside down so the baby's crown would shift in her cervix. And in the end, at the last possible moment before exhaustion and the scalpel, their lovely boy pushed out into the light through one final scream of agony and relief. A child with wisps of red hair and sweet, full lips. A child as beautiful as his mother.

Kurt held Maya for a long time without speaking. "Just tell me one more thing," he said. "What makes you think my brother jumped?"

Her body sagged into his and he could feel the soft give of her breasts. "It was all falling in around him," she said. "The things he lived for weren't going to last. Our world was disappearing, Kurt."

She pulled back, her hands on his shoulders. Her face was swollen, her eyes a blur of tears. "He took a couple of wrong steps, my dear," she said in a hoarse voice. "I think he knew where they would take him."

He left Maya on the canopied bed in the dark stone fortress and drove back along Woody Creek Road toward Aspen. He knew Jake wasn't foolish enough to return to his suite in the Blake Building. He was probably in Mexico by now, or across an ocean. Kurt also knew that if by some small miracle the man was still in the Valley, there was only one way to find him. The conventional wisdom was 'follow the money.' In Jake's case it was 'follow the penis.' The one thing that had always got in his way.

He took the unmarked turn to Starwood, his headlights cleaving to the narrow winding road as it ascended the steep grade to the guardhouse. Harley Ferris was on duty. He stepped into the open doorway and leaned a large forearm against the frame.

"Evening, Harley," Kurt said, his motor idling.

"Evening, Kurt." Harley rested his other wrist on the ivory stock of the Colt in his holster.

"You going to let me in?"

Beneath a thick ridge of forehead Harley's small eyes narrowed. "Nope," he said.

"I'm sorry, man," Kurt said. "I didn't know it would turn out that way."

"The old dago wanted my ass. He tried to get me fired."

"I'm sorry, Harley. It's a nasty situation."

"Pussy always is."

Kurt glanced up the hillside at the mansions softly glimmering beneath the black tarp of stars. "Is she up there?" he asked.

Harley worked the bill of his blue cap up and down, an unconscious habit from the playing field. "Far as I know," he said. "The dago brought her home this morning. She looked like hell. Couple hours later Dwight dragged in her Miata. She musta got fucked up real bad."

Kurt knew that sooner or later Cecilia would run out of coke and have to come back down to score. And that meant going to her source.

"Take care now, Harley," he said, slipping the Jeep into reverse.

"You gonna be at the game on Tuesday?"

"If I'm not in jail."

Kurt drove down to the county road and parked in a stand of trees with a clear view of the Starwood turnoff. It was eleven o'clock. The Milky Way looked as vast and clear and awesome as he'd ever seen it. Crickets sang in the prairie stillness. He stretched his legs onto the passenger seat and began his long wait, listening to the rustle of small nocturnal animals in the brush. Every now and then a car would pass by, and once someone slowed for the exit to Starwood. The night grew colder and he took out the safety blanket and covered himself, settling in, fighting sleep. He remembered his first campout, seven years old, huddled inside a rain-battered tent with Bert and Jake, wind flapping the canvas, water soaking up through the ground sheet. The thunder and rain frightened him and Bert put his arm around his shoulders, telling him to hang tough, that everything would be all right. He remembered the flashlight beams dancing on the canvas and his father's voice in the storm, and Mr. Pfeil calling out their names. And later, the laughter in the house as everyone sat by the fire drinking Ovaltine and drying off under army blankets. Those last precious days of peace between the Mullers and the Pfeils.

He didn't realize he'd gone to sleep until the birds began their daybreak chatter. Smoky blue light surrounded him, the air crisp in his lungs. He sat up and worked his stiff neck, then got out of the Jeep to bend and crack his sore ski knees. It was cold enough to see his breath and he longed for a thermos of good strong coffee. He relieved himself against a cottonwood tree and jogged in place to stir up some body warmth. He dropped down and did his forty pushups. An hour later, sitting behind the wheel and watching the morning take shape around him, a doe nibbling near the trees, magpies hopping in the dirt across the road, he finally admitted to himself that this was a stupid idea. He was ready to crank the engine and leave when he heard the Miata buzzing down the mountain. She ignored the stop sign and screeched onto the county road, searching for the right gear, her motor revving obnoxiously in the dewy quiet.

He gave her a little road and followed her to Highway 82 and then northward toward Glenwood Springs. Traffic was already beginning to clog the other lane, backing up past the airport, the worker bees traveling to their service jobs in Aspen. There was no one going north except him and the sports car. In a few miles the valley floor dropped away and he could see the river glinting in the morning sunlight.

In the rearview mirror he noticed a car approaching quickly, someone in a hurry. The gray Mercedes pulled up close behind him and nudged out against the yellow stripe, then swerved back. The driver flashed his lights impatiently, nudged out again. It was an unsafe place to pass, the highway curving sharply along the terrace, a steep rock wall on the left, a dropoff on the right where Chip Bodine had tumbled to his death. Kurt realized that the crazy fool didn't know the road and refused to let him pass until they came to a pullout, then slowed and let the man go around him. The driver hunched over the wheel, his eyes focused straight ahead. *My god,* Kurt thought for an instant. *It's Panzeca.*

Near Snowmass the highway leveled out and he could see the sports car far ahead and the Mercedes between them, now maintaining a steady speed, keeping a measured distance from her.

If this is Panzeca, he thought, *he has the same idea.* Kurt reached over and popped open the glove compartment. The new .45 rested on a stack of repair receipts. He took it out and placed it on the seat beside him.

The road made a humpy descent from the high wall of the valley and flattened out alongside the river, following the shimmering course. In a few miles, to Kurt's surprise, the sports car turned off into the small town of Basalt. The streets were narrow and split into a maze of lanes. He lost her in the busy workday traffic leaving the big supermarket, then caught sight of the sleek shape jetting off down the main drag toward the east end of town. He hadn't seen the gray Mercedes since they'd left the highway.

At the far boundary of the business district, where the strip of Old West saloons ended abruptly and the road led onward toward the Fryingpan River, the Miata swerved around a tow truck at work and disappeared into the distance. By the time Kurt got there, the truck and its hitched-up Club Wagon were blocking the street. He didn't have to read the DWIGHT'S I TOW 'EM painted on the cab door to recognize Dwight's idiot brother Clifford fiddling with the hydraulic winch.

Kurt leapt from the Jeep. "Pull this goddamned thing out of the way, Clifford!" he shouted.

"You're gonna have to wait a few minutes," Clifford said, flashing his missing tooth, "till I git this rig straightened out."

Kurt grabbed him by his oily ears. "Back this thing up right now, hoss," he said, "or I'm gonna feed your ears to the pigeons."

Once the truck gave him room he floorboarded the Jeep down the two-lane county road, his worn tires squealing around rocky bends. Furious with himself, he pounded the steering wheel. The Miata was nowhere in sight.

A forest of spruce rose along the hills to the north. Off in the river, fishermen stood in hip boots, casting flies. He saw a mother and her son rummaging through their camper on the side of the road and stopped to ask if they'd seen a little green sports car.

"Yeah," the boy glowed. "Going thataway a hundred miles an hour!"

He drove on till he reached the promontory overlooking Ruedi Reservoir, a long finger lake where windsurfers skimmed across the blue water. He took out his binoculars and searched the campground at the shoreline. VW microbuses, Winnebagos, pickup trucks, Wagoneers, but no Miata. He scanned back across the picnic blankets and upward past a grassy meadow to where the county road trailed on, a ribbon of asphalt curling against the fir-shaded cliffs high above. Then he saw something. A flash of chrome and brake-lights, a puff of dust over someone's private drive. It had to be her.

Adjusting the binoculars' focus, he spotted an elegant gray car, perhaps a Mercedes, disappearing around a cliff. Kurt looked up, then back into the binoculars. Could it be?

He hopped in the Jeep, checked the clip on his .45, and sped off up the road, a tricky incline that hewed close to the mountain as it looped higher and higher above the reservoir. After three miles of grinding the old Jeep engine, the temperature needle hovering near the *H*, he discovered the turnoff. Tire tracks led the way down a soft dirt trail cut through Douglas firs, a rough passage between huge outcroppings of rock. He saw the house in a clearing ahead, a large new redwood A-frame, its triangle of glass glistening in the sun. Two vehicles were parked out front, the Miata and Jake Pfeil's four-wheel Suburban.

Kurt hid the Jeep in the trees and circled on foot through the woods until he reached the rear of the A-frame. Two umbrella tables and assorted lawn furniture were arranged on the sun deck. There were no sounds from the house, no signs of habitation.

The .45 held chest high, he raced across the stubbled clearing, twenty yards or so, and dropped down at the blind side of the structure, where the roof touched ground. He struggled to catch his breath, listening for voices. The silence was unnerving. He slipped under the wood railing and crawled along the deck till he came to the glass louvers. The back room was a plant-filled solarium with wicker chairs. Empty. He stood up and quietly slid open the glass door and made his way into the house.

He found them in a living room with a pyramidal ceiling and a magnificent glass view of the forest. Cecilia was on her knees in front of Jake, head down, thick dark hair obscuring her face. At first Kurt thought it was sex, then he noticed the rails of coke on the coffee table.

Jake looked up and saw Kurt approaching quietly with a gun in his hand. "Hello, little brother," he said, showing no surprise. "Did you come to join our going-away party?"

Kurt aimed the .45 at Jake's face. He held the gun with a cold unflinching rage, his finger poised on the trigger. He wondered if he was going to feel bad about this after it was over.

Cecilia raised her head. "I know this man," she said, pinching her nose. "Is he going to kill us, Jake?"

"It's okay, kitten," Jake said. "He's an old friend of mine. We go way back, don't we, little brother?"

Kurt thumbed back the hammer, a loud click. "Give me one good reason why I *shouldn't* kill you," he said.

Jake's eyes danced, his cheekbones grew hard. He studied Kurt's hand, the .45.

"You ruined my brother's life," Kurt said. "You chased my wife off from her son. Tell me one good reason why I shouldn't splatter your ugly face all over the paneling."

Jake crafted a careful smile. He seemed to admire Kurt for getting this far.

"Because if you don't put down that gun, little brother," he said calmly, "my friend Rusty is going to leave a big piece of lead in that thick skull of yours."

Kurt heard the step behind him. He turned slightly, angled his eyes, and felt the shadow of a man in the doorway.

"Don't be a hero," Jake said. "You don't want your little boy to wonder why his daddy never came home today."

The bodyguard named Rusty moved toward him with a

stealthy grace and in another second the gun was gone from Kurt's hand.

"Does this change our plans, Jake?" Cecilia asked.

"No, kitten, our ride will be here any minute," he said, taking her arm and helping her to her feet. "Come sit over here while I have a little tête-à-tête with my old buddy."

He escorted her to a cushioned chair near the picture window and then turned to peer out the bright panel of glass, looking upward for something in the sky.

"I don't know what I'm going to do with you, little brother," he said, his hands locked behind his back. "I really don't want to kill you. Do you need more money? Is that the problem here? As you've probably figured out by now, your investigative services are no longer required. My friend Cecilia has helped me understand who's been trashing me to the Feds. But if you and your son could use more cash," he said, "I'll see what I can do."

Kurt watched Cecilia light a cigarette. "Is that how you worked it with my brother?" he said. "Kept loaning him money till he owed you so big he had to do your killing for you?"

When Jake turned around, his eyes showed how truly used up he was.

"You shouldn't insult your brother like that," he said. "He wasn't for sale. You know that."

He sounded angered by his own explanation.

"Yeah, sure, he was on my payroll. Like I told you, he was tired of being poor. Tired of seeing the split-levels go up with somebody else's name on the mailbox. So I offered him an opportunity—strictly small-time transportation work—and he did a good job. I trusted him, little brother. I always trusted him."

Kurt began to understand something for the first time. He began to understand that Jake needed a brother as much as he did.

"So how did you get him to kill somebody for you, Jake?"

Jake regarded him for a long time. Sunlight reflected on his hair, revealing hidden strands of gray.

"I don't think you want to hear it," he said finally.

"Try me," Kurt said.

Jake waited. He seemed to be rehearsing sentences in his mind.

"He came to me with a personal problem," he said in a flat voice. "He thought his old lady was running around on him."

Kurt suddenly felt sick.

"I'm not sure how he knew. Little clues, the way you can always tell," he said, his hollow eyes fixed on Kurt. "He asked me to find out who she was sleeping with."

Cecilia shifted in the chair, crossed her bare legs. She blew smoke and watched Kurt without interest. This could have been the opera, as far as she was concerned.

"So I hired a private dick from L.A., a guy I use in real estate there. He produced some very entertaining photographs. Before I saw the pictures, I never realized what a sweet time a guy can have at the Redstone Inn."

Kurt closed his eyes. Jesus Christ.

"He wanted to know who was sleeping with his old lady, little brother, so I found out and I told him."

Kurt thought he could hear the distant thutter of a helicopter. In the end there would always be a helicopter. Rotor noise, cold wind, the smell of scorched oil. A body borne home.

"I told him it was Chad Erickson."

Kurt felt like somebody had taken him down at the knees.

"It was an easy make," Jake said. "Erickson had been around a long time, everybody's friend, their dime-bag connection. Mr. Boogie Down, the ladies' man. We all went to the same parties, right? The same tight crowd. It was an easy make, little brother."

"You son of a bitch," Kurt said.

"Erickson was an asshole. A mindless party boy," Jake said. "The Feds had his fingers jammed in a desk drawer and his only way out was to hand them my balls on a stick. I had no choice, Kurt. It was best for all of us."

For a brief moment Jake let go of that arrogance in his bearing that betrayed how soggy rotten his soul had become and he showed something of his old self, the simple small-town boy they all had been before the gradual corruptions. Kurt realized now that in spite of how sick and misguided Jake had become, he had tried to save Kurt from himself. The way Meg had tried to save Bert. They had all tried to hold on to the only thing that remained of their vanishing world. Each other.

"Staggs says the Feds were going to pull Bert in," Kurt said. "The day he died, they were coming after him. Did you know that, Jake?"

Jake looked puzzled.

"He thinks you might have taken Bert for a long walk up the Bells."

Jake's face ignited. "That lying bastard," he said.

Kurt knew Jake wouldn't do something like that to family. But he wanted to hear it from Jake's own lips. "Maya thinks he jumped," he said, his voice constricting.

"I'm sorry, Kurt," Jake said, his tall lean frame washed in magnified light. "I thought he could handle it. He'd done that business in Nam."

The sound of the helicopter drew closer. Jake turned again to look beyond the glass, moving his head from side to side, searching for the incoming flight.

Cecilia sat forward in the chair and gazed out the window. "Is it for us, Jake?" she asked.

"Yes, kitten, it's for us."

Kurt turned, too, but it wasn't a helicopter blade he saw glinting from the tower of boulders forty yards away. Sunlight flashed across a rifle scope.

"Get down, Jake!" he shouted, diving for the floor.

The bullet exploded against the glass and Cecilia screamed. The large triangle collapsed, jagged sheets dropping from high above like the thawing walls of an iceberg. Kurt covered his head with his arms and felt the glass hurl over him, a thousand needles pricking his back and legs. He thought the noise would never end. For a moment he lost consciousness, then startled when three pistol rounds went off by the window. He peered up to see Rusty kneeling at the shattered glass wall, firing three more rounds into the woods.

"Bastards!" he yelled. Blood was dripping onto the shoulders of his sport jacket from a nasty gash in his scalp.

Kurt rose to his knees, splinters of glass crinkling from his clothes like fine sand. He looked over at Jake. His old friend lay crumpled in a heap next to a knocked-over lamp.

"Boss, are you hit?" The bodyguard was shaking Jake's arm.

Jake flopped onto his back, moaned, and struggled to sit up. "It's gotta be the Feds," he said, broken glass tinkling all around him. "The fuckers missed me."

"Oh, my god," the bodyguard said. "Jesus."

Kurt saw her then, sprawled on the carpet. Blood gushed from a massive hole in her neck; pieces of glass punctured her body like darts. Her eyes were still open but she wasn't moving.

"Cecilia," Jake said, crawling toward her.

"Come on, boss!" Rusty begged, dragging him away from the body. "The chopper's on the ground out back. Let's get the fuck out of here!"

He stayed low, pulling Jake along. "Come on," he said, yanking him. "She's dead."

When they reached Kurt, Jake stopped to throw his arm around the bodyguard's bloody shoulder. "You all right?" he asked, his eyes wide with panic.

Kurt nodded. His shirt was wet with blood and his skin stung as though he'd backed into a hornets' nest. A long sliver of glass was lodged like an ice pick in his calf. He was fighting hard to stay conscious.

"Better come with us, little brother," Jake said. There was a deep cut under one eye and his face was smeared with blood. Glass glittered in his hair. "They're going to shoot this place to pieces."

But Kurt knew it wasn't the Feds.

"Jake," he said, "don't ever mess with my family again. Do you hear me?"

Jake could see that Kurt was having trouble holding focus. "Give him his gun," he told the bodyguard.

"Are you crazy, boss? Let's get out of here!"

"He's going to need a gun," Jake said. "Give it to him."

Reluctantly the bodyguard tossed the weapon onto the floor in front of Kurt.

"Do you hear me, Jake?" Kurt said, staring at the gun. "Stay away from my family or I'll kill you."

"I'm sorry, man," Jake said. He gave Kurt one final look of regret. "Take good care of your little boy."

The bodyguard hoisted Jake onto his back and trotted toward the rear of the house, to the solarium and deck and out to the rocky field where the helicopter had touched down, waiting, its engine roaring. Kurt knew he would never see Jake Pfeil again.

When he turned and looked out the broken picture window he saw a man emerging from the woods, approaching the house with a rifle tucked under one arm. Kurt picked up the .45, stuck it in the waist of his jeans, and crawled over to Cecilia Rostagno. She was dead all right. Blood soaked her dress, flowed from her long bare legs. When he looked out the window again he saw the man throw down the rifle and make his way slowly up the steps to the house. He was weeping, his face glazed with tears. Kurt glanced back at the body. He thought about closing her eyes but decided that the man should see her this way. Her eyes like milky white glass.

Kurt hobbled over to a chair next to the telephone. He used the nose of the gun to brush away pieces of glass and sat down. Sunburst stars swirled in his eyes and he felt woozy. He didn't know how much longer he could hold out. His calf was hurting bad but the sliver was stuck near a large blood vessel and he didn't want to remove it on his own. An inch one way or the other and he was in serious trouble.

Colonel Octavio Panzeca knelt down next to his stepdaughter and placed her bloody head in his lap. He spoke to her in Spanish, a gentle singsong that sounded like a nursery rhyme, and rocked her gently, his pants now streaked with her blood.

Kurt knew that because of this man Graciela Rojas had gone to her death in the river. He rested the .45 on the arm of the chair and watched the man grieve over the young woman he wanted so desperately to be his daughter, his flesh and blood. He loved her so much he was willing to do anything to keep her his own.

Kurt thought about killing him but knew that the man was already dead.

He picked up the telephone. Staggs could make everything right. His men would arrive in a hurry and remove the body to some remote rural morgue where no questions would be asked. The old colonel would get another home, another wife, in Tahoe or Winter Park. They would clean up the blood, sweep out the glass. And maybe this time they wouldn't leave a little piece of his treachery under the motor guard.

The telephone began to beep, startling him. He pressed down the tab and closed his eyes and tried to blot out the pain in his leg. He saw his mother painting landscape pictures in her backyard. And he saw Lennon, too, a wonderful boy who would have to live with the sins of his father. He thought about all the people he had loved and lost, and then he dialed the number. Fading in and out of consciousness, he told the voice on the other end very precisely where he was located and what kind of medical attention was necessary. Then he asked for the boss.

"I need your help," he said. "Please get here as fast as you can."

"Are you all right, Kurt? What the hell's going on?"

"You'll see when you get here," he said. "There's a lot we've got to talk about."

"Okay, hang in there, babe," she said. "I'm on my way."

"And Muffin," he said, rubbing his forehead, trying to rub out the awful hurting. "Bring Rollins, that young reporter from the *Daily News*. There's a story I want to tell him."

He hung up and sat there in a haze of pain, listening to a father sing nursery songs to a dead girl in his lap. For the rest of his life Kurt Muller would wonder which one the old man had been aiming at.

25

FOUR DAYS LATER KURT AND LENNON SAT IN THE PHOENIX airport, waiting for the flight to arrive. Lennon played with galactic creatures he carried in his backpack, and Kurt read the *New York Times* account of what had happened in Aspen. The article praised the Pitkin County Sheriff's Department for uncovering government misconduct while solving a pair of related homicides. County Commissioner Ben Smerlas was quoted as saying, 'Our sheriff and his staff are sometimes unorthodox in their procedures, but they always get the job done. They have the full support of the commission and the voters in this county.'

Un-hunh, Kurt thought. *Right.*

The loudspeaker announced the plane's arrival. Kurt folded the newspaper, stood up, and tested his leg. It was sore and stiff from sitting too long.

"Daddy, is this the one?" Lennon asked in an excited voice.

"Yes," Kurt smiled. "Better put your men in the backpack."

He thought about the offer Muffin had made the day before yesterday, when he went to see her at the courthouse.

'You're looking better,' she said, watching him hobble into the office.

'This ol' body's got more stitches than a baseball,' he laughed.

She opened the desk drawer. 'There's something I forgot to give you the other day when we were exchanging gifts,' she said. 'Libbie was supposed to type this up and get it over to Smerlas and the county commissioners, but you know her. I think the poor girl was having a protein attack that day. She sent the wrong one over.'

He looked at the resignation letter, his crabbed handwriting.

'The one she sent was the one where you ask for a three-month leave, personal time,' she said. 'I told Smerlas three months, six months, it doesn't matter to us. We'll hold off on all the office birthday parties till you feel like coming back.'

He smiled at her. 'I don't think so, Muffin,' he said quietly.

'You've got no choice. Nobody here can figure out your filing system.'

She was a good friend. He hoped the commissioners would give her a chance to prove herself in the sheriff's job.

'Kurt, you don't have to say yes or no right now. Take some time off. I checked your sheets and you've got about six years of overtime coming to you. Just don't drop out on us, okay? We need you at the wheel. Nobody else is ready yet.'

Deboarding passengers streamed through the gate. When he saw his mother in the crowd, Lennon dashed toward her, his backpack rattling as he weaved around the taller bodies in his way.

"Mommy!" he called out. "Are you all right? Hey, Mommy, it's me! Lennon Muller!"

Meg looked trim in her colorful cotton dress, an exotic import from India or some such place. Her auburn hair was shorter than Kurt's, ascetic in its severity. Tiny plastic clusters of fruit dangled from each ear.

"Mommy, you look beautiful," Lennon shouted. "Are you well enough to come home?"

She dropped to her knees and smothered him in her arms, kissing his cheeks. "Hello, sweetie," she said with tears in her eyes.

Kurt limped over and rested his hand on Lennon's hair. "Good to see you, Peaches," he said.

Watching them hold each other, Kurt realized how cheated these two had been. They could never get back those years apart.

Meg stood up. There was an awkward moment between them, then she leaned forward and gave him the expected hug. "Hello, Kurt," she said. "How's the leg?"

"Getting there," he said.

She pulled back and gazed at his face. "My goodness," she said. "I don't think I've ever seen you without a beard. You look a little . . . naked."

He blushed.

"Does your mother know I'm coming too?"

He nodded. "There's plenty of room," he said. "She'll be happy to see you."

He had forgotten that light trace of freckles across her nose. The same pattern on Lennon.

"Thanks for doing this, Meg. I need a little time with her alone."

He had made up his mind to tell his mother about Bert before someone else did.

"We'll find plenty to do together, won't we, kiddo?" Meg said, wrapping her arms around Lennon, smiling down at him. "We've got some catching up to do."

Lennon reached over and tugged at his father's pants. "Hey, you guys," he said. "Hey, let's all have a squishy hug."

The two grown-ups looked at each other. "A squishy hug?" Kurt said.

"Yeah, you know," Lennon said. "Like on television."

Meg dropped her eyes and smiled reluctantly. She didn't own a television and couldn't be blamed for this.

"You guys have to come down here," Lennon said, "and I'll show you."

Kurt knelt down, then Meg. They pressed Lennon's slender body between them and embraced. Kurt tried to remember the good days before the fighting and long silences and the final sad departure.

"Kowabunga!" Lennon said. "I can't breathe in here."

Meg laughed and kissed her son. "Let's give Daddy a hand," she said, seeing Kurt's difficulty with the leg.

Lennon seized his father's chest and grunted, struggling to lift him from his knees. Meg took Kurt's arm. With a little effort he was up and walking. They merged with the airport crowds herding toward the exits, Lennon between them, holding their hands. Up ahead an arrow pointed to Baggage Claim.

"Kurt," Meg said, glancing over their son's head. "I couldn't tell you about Bert. I just couldn't."

"It's okay, Peaches. Really."

Two nights ago they had talked about everything over the phone, a long, tearful conversation.

"It's all out now, I hope," she said. "No more secrets."

"And nothing to be afraid of anymore."

She looked wonderful today, walking with her son.

"I'm going to move back to Aspen," she said.

He smiled at her. Lennon's hand was warm and moist, a small beautiful part of them.

"Let me know how I can help," Kurt said.